Associate Professor Akira Takatsuki's Conjecture

2

The Supernatural Hides in the Cracks

Mikage Sawamura

YEN ON

NEW YORK

Associate Professor Akira Takatsuki's Conjecture

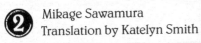

② Mikage Sawamura
Translation by Katelyn Smith

JUNKYOJU · TAKATSUKIAKIRA NO SUISATSU Vol. 2 KAII WA HAZAMA NI YADORU
©Mikage Sawamura 2019
First published in Japan in 2019 by KADOKAWA CORPORATION, Tokyo.
English translation rights arranged with KADOKAWA CORPORATION, Tokyo, through Tuttle-Mori Agency, Inc., Tokyo.

English translation © 2023 by Yen Press, LLC

Yen On
150 West 30th Street, 19th Floor
New York, NY 10001

Visit us at yenpress.com * facebook.com/yenpress * twitter.com/yenpress
yenpress.tumblr.com * instagram.com/yenpress

First Yen On Edition: September 2023
Edited by Yen On Editorial: Payton Campbell
Designed by Yen Press Design: Madelaine Norman

Yen On is an imprint of Yen Press, LLC.
The Yen On name and logo are trademarks of Yen Press, LLC.

Library of Congress Cataloging-in-Publication Data
Names: Sawamura, Mikage, author. | Smith, Katelyn, translator.
Title: Associate professor Akira Takatsuki's conjecture / Mikage Sawamura ;
    translated by Katelyn Smith.
Other titles: Junkyouju Takatsuki Akira no suisatsu. English
Description: First Yen On edition. | New York, NY : Yen On, 2023- |
    Contents: v. 1. Folklore studies —
Identifiers: LCCN 2022058928 | ISBN 9781975352974 (v. 1 ; trade paperback)
    | ISBN 9781975352998 (v. 2 ; trade paperback)
Subjects: CYAC: Ability—Fiction. | Teacher-student relationships—Fiction.
    | LCGFT: Light novels.
Classification: LCC PZ7.1.S284 As 2023 | DDC [Fic]—dc23
LC record available at https://lccn.loc.gov/2022058928

ISBNs: 978-1-9753-5299-8 (paperback)
       978-1-9753-5300-1 (ebook)

10 9 8 7 6 5 4 3 2 1

LSC-C

Printed in the United States of America

Contents

Chapter 1:
An Incident at School

"There is a fundamental difference between what you study in high school and what you learn in college."

Those were the words Naoya Fukamachi heard at his entrance ceremony to Seiwa University.

He had already forgotten whether the person who said them was the university president, the dean, or a guest speaker. But out of all the things said during the ceremony, for some reason, those words stuck with him.

"The education you've received thus far involved understanding what your teachers were saying in accordance with your textbooks, and then measuring the extent of your comprehension through testing. In short, you were 'memorizing how to solve the problems that would appear on the exam.' But now that you've overcome the major obstacle of the entrance exam, you will acquire a completely different method of learning in this place known as university. From now on, it won't be enough for you to simply solve assigned problems. You will have to find the problems, explore how they can be solved, and arrive at the solutions by yourselves. Starting now, you will be engaging in 'scholarship.'"

Scholarship.

Naoya honestly felt that the sentiment didn't quite hit home. He expected most of the incoming students felt the same.

Looking around at the students sat neatly in rows in the auditorium from their place onstage, the speaker continued in a calm voice.

"College is a place where you can learn naturally. So find something— even one thing—that interests you. Anything is fine. Look for something you're curious about, something you find intriguing. The subjects that capture your interest will surely lead you to the base of 'scholarship.' That base is extremely vast. You can learn freely and discover new horizons."

Naoya remembered thinking the speaker shouldn't exaggerate so much.

But he also thought it sounded kind of nice.

The days of learning through rote memorization of textbook and reference book contents were over. In college, he could study what he liked, as he liked. That thought made him a bit happy.

The question was whether he would actually be able to find such a subject.

Or rather, how much would he be at liberty to choose something? It was "scholarship," after all. The university wouldn't allow someone to study a subject if its contents weren't reasonably creditable. Properly speaking, it would have to be a subject that everyone recognized as truly academic.

...Or so Naoya thought.

"Now then, today's lecture is on 'bathroom ghost stories!'"

With an indescribable feeling brewing inside, Naoya gazed through his glasses at the man on the podium, who had started talking in a merry tone.

The man's name was Akira Takatsuki. He was an associate professor at Seiwa University.

He specialized in folklore studies. This lecture, Folklore Studies II, which took place on Wednesdays during third period, was a general education course in the Literature Department, but it was so popular that students from other departments also came to listen. Even in October, half a year since the course began in April, every seat in the spacious lecture hall was nearly full.

That was due in large part to Takatsuki's looks. He was an objectively attractive man. With his light brown hair shimmering in the window light, his kind, clean-cut features, and his tall, slender frame clad in a well-tailored three-piece suit, he looked like a model or an actor. He was young, too. He was in his mid-thirties but looked at least ten years younger, though it wasn't as if he had a baby face. Thanks to his looks, the seats in the front row were filled entirely with female students.

And yet, for some reason, that handsome man was talking about ghost stories that revolved around smelly places.

"Today's lecture will be the introduction, and next time we'll discuss. So today, I would like to introduce you to as many bathroom ghost stories as possible! There are quite a lot of them, actually. The well-known ones are 'Red *Hanten*,' 'Red Paper, Blue Paper,' 'The Hand Coming from the Toilet Bowl,' 'The Peering Face,' and 'Toilet-Bound Hanako-san.' I'm handing out some materials summarizing those examples, but I'm sure you're all familiar with many of them. Even modern flush toilets could not wash away the dark, smelly, dirty image of the era when outhouses were standard, which became a breeding ground for ghost stories. Not that I, myself, am particularly knowledgeable about that era, however. But even now, bathrooms are considered a common dwelling place for spirits."

As Takatsuki spoke, he gave a stack of handouts to a student sitting in the front row. Each student took a handout before passing the stack to the next person. As the materials made their way around, the students started to snicker and exchange glances with one another. The handouts had excerpts from ghost story collections and occult magazines on them—ones geared toward children.

That was the kind of content Takatsuki discussed in every Folklore Studies II lecture—*tsuchinoko*, the slit-mouthed woman, taxi-cab ghost stories, *kamikakushi*. Naoya thought that, since such topics were the subject of Takatsuki's study, the so-called base of scholarship must be quite vast, indeed. The words he had heard at the entrance ceremony were true.

Nonetheless, though the materials they covered were silly, the class itself was no joke. The object of the course was to "take a broad approach to the field of folklore studies" using "school ghost stories, urban legends, and so on." Modern folklore, one might say.

"Have the handouts made it all the way to the back? Then let's take a look at them in order—first, we have 'Red *Hanten*' and 'Red Paper, Blue Paper.' Their plot devices differ, but it can be said that these two ghost stories are quite similar. The first common feature: hearing disembodied voices after entering the bathroom. '*Shall I cover you in a red* hanten?' '*Would you like red paper, or perhaps blue?*' Common feature two: What happens next is dependent upon how those questions are answered. In the case of 'Red *Hanten*,' when someone answers, 'Put it on me, if you think you can,' they are killed, found covered in blood, and the blood spatter on the wall appears in the shape of a *hanten* jacket. In 'Red Paper, Blue Paper,' if you answer 'red,' you'll die covered in blood. If you say 'blue,' you'll be drained of blood or suffocated, turning a pale blue-ish color either way. Both stories have a lot of variants; sometimes instead of a red *hanten*, it's a vest or a cloak. Sometimes there are additional paper colors—white and yellow—and choosing one of the colors will allow you to survive. There's also a tale called 'Red Cloak, Blue Cloak,' which appears to be a combination of the other two stories. A version of 'Red Cloak, Blue Cloak' dates back as early as 1935, so it's possible that 'Red *Hanten*' and 'Red Paper, Blue Paper' were split and derived from this story."

Chalk in hand, Takatsuki scrawled the titles of the story variants across the blackboard as he said them aloud.

His voice was soft and pleasant to listen to even though he delivered his lecture with the aid of a microphone. His enthusiasm made his presentations a treat.

Nearly all of the students who struggled to stay awake or pay attention in other classes listened attentively to Takatsuki's lectures. It wasn't just the professor's looks or the comedic course content that made Folklore Studies II popular.

Takatsuki's lectures were—quite simply—fun to listen to.

"Incidentally, '*hanten*' is written in *hiragana* in the title of the story as a play on words, since both the type of jacket and the blood spatter can be pronounced that way. Often, the story starts with reports of ghostly activity in a school bathroom. Suspecting that the mysterious voice belongs to a deviant, the school calls in the police to investigate. Typically, it ends with a female police officer falling victim to the entity. Between the element of wordplay and the dash of realism added with the police being called, it makes for a well-crafted tale that is more than a mere ghost story. Personally, I think it's one of the best of its kind—stories about people being killed in bathrooms, that is. Stories should evolve over the course of their existence, after all."

Takatsuki drew a star on the board over the words "Red *Hanten*," dusted the chalk from his hands, then turned back around to face the class.

He pointed to the titles he had written.

"These stories have some other things in common, by the way. Does anyone know what they are?"

The students looked at the chalkboard. Some heads tilted in thought.

Red *hanten*. Red vest. Red paper, blue paper, white paper, yellow paper. Red cloak, blue cloak. Naoya had heard or read all of those words as story titles before. But when it came to another commonality between them—

Ah, Naoya thought.

Almost in unison, several of his classmates' hands shot into the air.

"Yes, you there. What is something these stories have in common?"

Takatsuki pointed to a girl sitting in the third row from the front.

"Um, is it…color? It's an important element in all of them…?"

Her tone was timid, perhaps from the anxiety of being called on.

Takatsuki smiled broadly at her and nodded.

"Yes, that's correct! Colors are key in each story. Red is the most common among them."

Truly, the color red made an appearance in every tale. Since it was the color associated with blood, perhaps that was apt for ghost stories.

"So common feature three: Color, particularly red, is a major device. There's actually a theory that the basis for these stories is girls experiencing their first menstruation. Red is the color of blood. And the setting of the stories? The bathroom. Starting one's period is a major event. Girls share these stories more often than boys, and we cannot ignore that factor when concluding why bathroom ghost stories are frequently very bloody. Now—has anyone noticed any other common features? Yes, you there."

Takatsuki pointed to a boy in the middle of the lecture hall who had his hand raised.

"Um, I could be wrong, but... Is it that they're school stories?"

The student didn't sound very confident in his answer.

Again, Takatsuki grinned.

"Exactly right. Well spotted! Yes, common feature four: The stories often circulate in schools. Especially elementary and middle school. School is also the setting for 'The Hand Coming from the Toilet Bowl,' 'The Peering Face,' and 'Toilet-Bound Hanako-san.' When studying these kinds of stories that spread through gossip—often categorized under the umbrella of 'anecdotes' by researchers—it's extremely important to think about what kinds of places they are shared in and by whom. The setting and the storyteller. These factors frequently have a great impact on the background of the story and the course of its evolution."

The class wrote down what Takatsuki said in their notebooks or the margins of the handouts.

Though it started with a list of children's ghost stories, the lecture had thus slid neatly into the field of "scholarship." Takatsuki had presented items for their attention and how the class should proceed with thinking about the topic.

"Schools, particularly elementary schools, regularly become the backdrop for ghost stories. I plan to focus on the theme of 'school ghost stories' in the future, but I think the reason bathroom ghost stories are so plentiful as a subset is because of the unusual nature of bathrooms. Schools are, essentially, places with a lot of people. You spend your time in classrooms with dozens of other students. But everyone is alone in the privacy of a bathroom stall. On top of that, bathrooms tend to be in the corners of school buildings, and the time you spend in them is minimal compared to other places."

Takatsuki continued.

"Mysteries are departures from everyday life. If the classroom is a *regular* place, then bathrooms are locations which deviate from that regularity. Therefore, bathrooms are places where mysteries are born and ghost stories dwell."

Takatsuki smiled again as he explained that was the kind of stuff he was researching. He looked genuinely happy.

It seemed that nothing Naoya had heard at the entrance ceremony was wrong.

Scholarship was freedom.

All it took was the drive to pursue one's passion.

At the end of Takatsuki's lecture, just as Naoya was about to leave his seat among the throng of his classmates, he felt his phone vibrate in his pocket.

He had a message from Takatsuki.

"Please come to my office to talk if you're free. It's about work."

Naoya looked over at the podium, where Takatsuki was erasing the chalkboard. The professor glanced at him and waved. His smile was especially wide. He seemed really excited about whatever the work matter was.

Naoya fired off a quick reply—*"I'll head there after I stop at the college co-op."*—before leaving the lecture hall. He made his way out of the school and headed for the building that housed the co-op.

The "work" Takatsuki mentioned was an occasional, part-time gig Naoya had been helping with since June. Naoya wasn't really sure if "work" was the right word for it.

Takatsuki had a website called "Neighborhood Stories." It was a collection of examples and categories of urban legends that Takatsuki had amassed to date, and he would often receive requests through the site from people who wanted him to solve the mysteries they had encountered.

Somehow, Naoya ended up becoming Takatsuki's assistant and

accompanying him when he went to investigate mysteries. Every disturbance they had investigated so far had turned out to be man-made, though.

Nevertheless, each time a request came in, Takatsuki leaped at the opportunity to check it out.

There was always a chance it would be the real deal, after all.

Takatsuki knew quite well that it was impossible to say with complete certainty that real monsters didn't exist in the world.

Naoya knew it, too.

The university co-op was fairly crowded. Providing them with a place to buy food, daily necessities, stationery, books, and so on at slightly cheaper prices than other stores, the co-op was a college student's best friend. Naoya grabbed a packet of loose-leaf paper and got in line at the register.

Just then, the student in line ahead of him took out his cell phone. He seemed to be getting a phone call.

"...Hey, Misa? ...Yeah. No, I'm sorry about last night... What, now? Oh... Uh, **I'm still at home.**"

Suddenly, the student's voice distorted.

"No, **I'm going to my part-time job soon...** Yeah. Um, **I'm kinda busy with work right now, so. We might not be able to meet up for a while. Sorry, I'll get ahold of you when I can.**"

His voice warped, the pitch vacillating wildly like some kind of filter was being applied to it. An unpleasant feeling like a chill ran down Naoya's spine, and he instinctively covered his ears, frowning.

Another nearby student looked at him curiously. Naoya retrieved his earphones from his bag, shoved them into both ears, and pressed PLAY on his MP3 player. The music flooding his ears drowned out the voice of the student in front of him, and Naoya finally let out a little sigh.

The boy in front of him was still on the phone. Every single thing he said to the person on the other end of the call—a lover he was thinking of breaking up with, perhaps—was a lie. Disgusted, Naoya looked away from him.

Naoya could tell when people were lying. Their voices always sounded distorted.

The ability was much more of a curse than a blessing. Humans lied a lot, unfortunately. Consequently, to Naoya's ears, the world was full of jarring, distorted voices. His portable MP3 player was essential. Listening to the distorted voices for any extended length of time truly made him feel ill. He paused the music just long enough to pay at the register, then left the co-op with music blaring in his ears again. He cut across the campus courtyard, making his way toward the faculty building.

The courtyard was crowded at this time of day. In addition to people just walking through, there were dance clubs practicing their routines and the drama club roping passersby into impromptu plays. Juggling balls thrown aloft by the street performance society flew through the air, and cherry blossom petals fell to the ground in a storm of colors. Every day was like a festival in the lively, bustling space.

But with his ears plugged up with his earphones, viewing the scene around him through the lenses of his glasses, Naoya felt like he was watching something projected onto a movie screen. Even though it was all real and right in front of him, Naoya felt like he was somehow removed from it all. Like there was a thin film wrapped around him alone as he slipped through the noisy crowd by himself.

"You will be lonely."

Those were the words Naoya was told when his hearing changed.

If you can hear lies, you'll be lonely.

Sure enough, Naoya went through life perpetually alone. Even when he entered college, he didn't join any clubs or make any new friends.

Although—ever since he'd met Takatsuki, things had begun to change.

Naoya arrived at Takatsuki's office.

It was on the third floor of the faculty building. Confirming he was at the right place via the doorplate—number 304, "Literature Department, Historical Literature Faculty, Folklore and Antiquities, Akira Takatsuki"—Naoya put his earphones away.

He knocked twice, and a voice from inside told him to come in.

Naoya opened the door.

"Welcome, Fukamachi. You'll have some coffee, right? Just a minute."

Takatsuki, who had been sitting at his open laptop at the large desk in the center of the room, stood up as he spoke. Naoya took a seat on a folding chair, feeling relieved at the oddly transparent nature of the professor's voice.

The office, three walls of which were lined with bookshelves, always smelled like a secondhand bookstore. With niche interest books on urban legends and monthly issues of the occult magazine MÜ mixed in between old-looking Japanese-style bound books and hefty research papers, the room felt very Takatsuki-like. Occasionally, one could find graduate students sleeping on the floor, but it seemed only Takatsuki was present today.

Takatsuki prepared their drinks on a small table in front of a window at the back of the room. Anyone was allowed to use the coffee maker and electric kettle on the table, but since Naoya wasn't one of Takatsuki's advisees, the professor always made coffee for him, treating him like a guest of sorts. Although recently, Naoya had started keeping his own cup for coffee in the office.

That was how much of a regular he had become to this room.

"So what kind of request is it this time?"

Naoya addressed the question to Takatsuki, who was returning to the table carrying a tray with two mugs on it.

Takatsuki smiled brightly as he placed the cup with the dog on it in front of Naoya.

"It's a really interesting one. And it happens to be similar to today's lecture."

"So it's a bathroom ghost story?"

"Not a bathroom, but a school. Fukamachi—do you remember Tomoki?"

"Tomoki?"

"Last month, we met with Miss Hana, right? The high school girl from Chofu whose friend disappeared? Remember the boy I talked to at the park then? The grade schooler? That's Tomoki Oogawara! He asked for my help!"

As Takatsuki spoke, the memory came back to Naoya.

Takatsuki usually liked to talk to the residents in the area around a place he was investigating. In Hana's case, he had asked people about the abandoned house her friend disappeared from. Naoya clearly remembered one of the locals being a young boy. He recalled the boy taking quite a liking to Takatsuki.

"The kid who seemed like he was the leader of the group, right? Didn't he tell you he was going to make you his disciple...? Don't tell me you went through with that."

"I didn't. But I did give him my business card back then and told him to contact me if he heard of any other mysterious or unusual happenings. And then yesterday, I got a phone call."

Takatsuki sat down in the chair next to Naoya's, bringing his own blue mug to his mouth.

Naoya was having coffee, but Takatsuki's mug was full of hot cocoa. Today he had even added adorable marshmallows in the shape of cats' paws to his drink. Naoya always wondered if it was a good idea for Takatsuki to drink nothing but sickly-sweet beverages, but according to Takatsuki, the brain needed glucose to function, so having sweets was important.

"It seems that a new ghost story has just been born at Chofu Municipal Fourth Elementary School, which Tomoki attends. They're calling it 'The Locker in Grade 5, Class 2.' Tomoki himself is in Grade 5, Class 3, so it sounds like this is the classroom next to his."

"Are we talking about a locker that you put things like cleaning supplies or school bags in?"

"Yes. Cleaning supplies, in this case."

The story, according to Tomoki, went like this:

"The locker in Grade 5, Class 2 is cursed.

After school, some girls in that class played Kokkuri-san. But Kokkuri-san wouldn't leave after the end of the game, and it started living in the locker.

Now the locker door sometimes opens on its own even when no one is touching it.

If you accidentally go near the locker when the door is open, you'll be dragged inside and transported to another world."

The children were so frightened by this story that, apparently, they sometimes wouldn't come to class. The situation had turned into a bit of a minor uproar, with some members of the PTA even suggesting that an exorcism was called for.

In the midst of that commotion, Tomoki had remembered Takatsuki. Apparently, he had shown the professor's business card to his homeroom teacher and said, "This person might be able to help."

"My business card has the URL for 'Neighborhood Stories' on it. The teachers looked at the website, and some of them looked into my background as well. I also received an email from the Grade 5, Class 2 teacher through the contact form on the site. It seems the school wants to make a formal request of me... Well, they probably just decided it would be less likely to prolong the fuss if they called in a university professor instead of performing an exorcism."

Takatsuki smiled wryly.

"Elementary schools are usually quite restrictive when it comes to allowing outsiders to enter. Even when it's for research, when we're talking about something that could have an impact on children, it's not uncommon to only be allowed to distribute questionnaires at most. But the school is making the request in this case. We'll be able to investigate freely. School ghost stories are the classic vehicle for anecdotal research, so this is an extremely valuable opportunity."

But that meant, in other words, that the school was in a rather difficult situation. Difficult enough that they had no choice but to allow outsiders to come investigate.

Naoya sipped his coffee and tilted his head to the side.

"But it's just a ghost story, right? Why did it become such a big deal?"

"Don't underestimate the effect scary stories can have on children, Fukamachi. Didn't you ever have that experience when you were little? Of hearing a scary story and being unable to sleep or go to the bathroom?"

"...Well, I mean."

Naoya's response was evasive. He remembered watching a horror movie called *A Nightmare on Elm Street* at a friend's house when he was young. It was a movie about people who were brutally murdered in their dreams by a monstrous figure with a scarred face and knives in his hands. For a while after that, Naoya was unbearably afraid to go to sleep at night. Thinking back on it now, it seemed silly, but at the time, he had seriously believed, at least partly, that he would be killed if he fell asleep.

"Even adults are afraid of scary stories. For elementary schoolers in particular, the line between reality and fiction is blurry. That enriches their imagination and sensitivity, so it's not an inherently bad thing... But fear is a particularly powerful emotion on the human spectrum of feelings. Extreme fear can cause hyperventilation and convulsions, and it can make the body freeze up. This story about the locker in Class 2 probably started with that *Kokkuri-san* game. Games like that have caused several incidents in the past. Some of them even made it into the papers."

Takatsuki licked lightly at the melting marshmallows, his eyelids drooping slightly in satisfaction.

Kokkuri-san. If Naoya was remembering correctly, the game had been popular with girls when he was in elementary school. Giggling to themselves in the classroom after school, bathed in the light of the setting sun, their fingers on a 10-yen coin, the girls had looked like they were performing some kind of secret ritual.

"I think I've read something about *Kokkuri-san* before. Basically, it's a kind of spiritualism, right? But because it summons low-level animal spirits, it's not very good?"

"Right. It's common to use the characters for 'fox,' 'dog,' and 'tanuki' when writing the name in *kanji*. And in the past, there were many theories that it summoned fox spirits. These days, it's not limited to just foxes, though."

Takatsuki wrote the *kanji* on the back of a paper that was sitting on the table. Naoya was starting to feel like he was attending a continuation of the lecture from earlier.

"*Kokkuri-san* is a form of divination that has existed since the Meiji period. It was probably based on Western practices like table-turning and using spirit boards. In table-turning, people gathered around a circular table and placed their hands on it. They called out to the spirit with a chant, and the number of times the legs of the table hit the floor as it tipped and swayed would be interpreted as the spirit communicating. In Japan, instead of a table, people would arrange three bamboo stalks in a tripod shape, place a tray on top, cover it with a cloth, and observe how the tray tilted. According to Inoue Enryō, the device got the name 'Kokkuri-san' because of the way it nodded up and down, and that spread throughout the country. The *kanji* used for the name came after the fact."

"In the version I know, you draw a Shinto *torii* gate, the syllabary, and other things on a piece of paper."

"That's the one that takes after spirit boards. That's what people tend to picture when you talk about *Kokkuri-san* these days. In the past, people used disposable chopsticks, but now, a 10-yen coin is more common. There are various similar games, like 'Dear Angel,' which were popular among elementary and middle school students all over the country in the early 1970s. Some were popular even when I was a child."

"Why was it so popular? I get why you would want to talk to ghosts or deities, but what's the point in listening to what a fox spirit has to say?"

"Probably because, to a child, it doesn't matter if it's a fox spirit or a god—it all falls under the umbrella of the incorporeal. I suspect everyone is a little afraid of spiritualism. Deep down they feel like it's something that shouldn't be done. But there's probably some thrill in violating that taboo. *Kokkuri-san* is a special game that combines innocent divination with the forbidden practice of spiritualism."

Thinking back, Naoya remembered that when the game was popular at his elementary school, there were some children who were extremely afraid of it. The school even banned the game because of that.

But there was still a group of girls who continued to play it for a while even after the fact.

To those girls, the mystique of *Kokkuri-san* must have been hard to resist. A mysterious spirit telling them who the boys they were crushing on had feelings for? There was probably no game more exciting than that to a child who was into divination.

"But ultimately, the game has become taboo as well."

Takatsuki explained:

"'There were kids who were traumatized by Kokkuri-san telling them they were going to die, and ones who were distressed when Kokkuri-san wouldn't leave after the game was done. There was a story in the paper in the 1980s about a girl who suddenly went limp in the middle of class. When the homeroom teacher picked her up, even though the rest of her body was listless, her right hand was stiff. She was taken to the school infirmary, laid down on a bed, and her hand was massaged, but she couldn't even speak. Apparently, all the other girls in her class said she was 'possessed by Sen-sama.' There was a game similar to *Kokkuri-san* at that school called *Sen-sama*. There were many other reports, in addition to this one, of being possessed by Kokkuri-san or the Angel."

"But isn't it just like you said before, Professor? Weren't those people just having convulsions and such? They were simply interpreting that as 'Kokkuri-san's doing' because it was popular at the time."

The unexplained was made up of "phenomenon" and "interpretation." Takatsuki said so himself, often.

People were afraid of what they didn't understand. It was scary to let an unfamiliar phenomenon go unexplained.

And so, people attached whatever explanations they could to those situations. They interpreted.

It certainly would be frightening to have a friend suddenly start acting strangely right in front of one's eyes. To cope with that fear, a reason for that phenomenon was crucial. "Sen-sama" was the reason for those kids. Their friend was like that because of Sen-sama—there was a legitimate reason for the unusual circumstance they were in. Even if their interpretation amounted to supernatural activity, it was better than having no explanation at all.

"Yes, that's probably true. And there's a possibility that whatever is happening at Tomoki's school right now will end up being just the same."

Takatsuki nodded and took another sip of cocoa. The sweet scent wafted gently toward the tip of Naoya's nose. Naoya lifted his coffee mug to his own mouth. The smells of coffee and cocoa melded together, mixing into the faint, lingering odor of old books in the room. To Naoya, this was the smell of Takatsuki's office. It was an oddly soothing scent.

"Putting aside what happened in Grade 5, Class 2 for now, I think Tomoki's school is probably in a state of mass hysteria at the moment. Fear is infectious, you know. In a contained space like a classroom, if some of the children start to panic, it's quite likely that panic will quickly spread to the other children. In no time at all, they won't even be able to have class," Takatsuki said.

"That's why I think it's a good idea to go investigate as soon as possible. The Class 2 homeroom teacher also asked me to come as soon as I could. Besides, there's a possibility that a real ghost is haunting the locker in that class, right? If that's the case, I definitely want to check it out immediately! And I absolutely want to open the locker door!"

"…Don't expect me to help if you get dragged to another world," said Naoya to Takatsuki, whose eyes shone with excitement. That's what the professor was thinking about, after everything they had just said?

Takatsuki always wanted the monsters to be real. So whenever he received a request to investigate a mysterious incident, he went in hoping it would be genuine.

"First off, I have to speak directly with the children who played *Kokkuri-san*! After all, with the information we have now, it's difficult to see how the game and the locker are related. I suspect the kids saw something strange happen with the locker while they were playing *Kokkuri-san*. Ah, how exciting! I wonder what's going on! I want to find out right away!"

At times like this, Takatsuki truly looked like he was enjoying himself. Even though he had been behaving like a teacher just a moment ago, now he looked like a dog faced with its favorite toy.

Naoya looked down at his own mug. It had a golden retriever pictured on it. He had bought the cup because it reminded him of Leo, his old family dog, but lately, there were many times when he looked at it and thought of Takatsuki. The way Leo had looked when he ran, barking up a storm, straight toward something he was interested in—Takatsuki was the spitting image of that.

* * *

The school wanted to schedule the visit on a Saturday, when there were no classes. After exchanging emails with the homeroom teacher for Grade 5, Class 2, Takatsuki and Naoya decided to go to the elementary school that very weekend, on Saturday afternoon.

Takatsuki's request to speak directly to the children who had participated in the *Kokkuri-san* game was initially met with reluctance, but when he asked again, saying it was necessary to "get an accurate understanding of what happened at the time," for some reason or another, the school agreed. They were told there were three girls involved.

They took the bus from Chofu Station—which they had been to for a prior case—and got off at the designated stop to find their destination mere steps away. A white, single-story schoolhouse situated beyond a schoolyard. A young woman and a boy were standing in front of the building's gate. Naoya recognized the boy. He had a cocky-looking face and a large frame—very much a "leader of the pack" sort of kid. Tomoki Oogawara. As soon as Tomoki saw Takatsuki getting off the bus, he started waving both hands and yelling.

"Heeey! Akiraaa!! You maaade it!!"

"Tomokiii! How are yoou?"

Takatsuki waved back at Tomoki. Naoya thought the boy should probably be addressing the professor with a little more respect, but Takatsuki didn't seem to mind. No wonder kids said things like "I'll make you my disciple" to him. When Takatsuki and Naoya made it to the school gate, the woman beside Tomoki bowed her head toward Takatsuki.

"Oh, um, my name is Marika Hirahara! I'm the homeroom teacher for Grade 5, Class 2, the one you were emailing with the other day! Thank you so much for coming today!"

She was a petite, pretty woman with a bob haircut, wearing a pinafore dress. She looked young enough to be mistaken for a student. She was so youthful that it wouldn't be a surprise if she hadn't been teaching for very long...

"I was worried about Miss Marika being alone, so I came too, even though I'm in a different class!"

As Tomoki stood haughtily with his arms crossed at her side, the woman he referred to as "Miss Marika" gave a wry smile. That was enough to give Naoya a general idea of her relationship with the students. Because she was young, there was probably a sense of her being more of a friend than a teacher, but it was clear that the students adored her.

"Hello, how do you do? I'm Takatsuki, from Seiwa University. I should be the one thanking you for today."

While Takatsuki was handing the teacher his business card, Tomoki looked up at Naoya with a dubious expression.

"Hey, hey, Akira! Who's this four-eyes? Your disciple?"

"Ah, Fukamachi is my assistant. He helps me with various things."

"Hmm... He looks kinda boring."

"T-Tomoki!"

Flustered, Miss Marika chided Tomoki for his casual assessment of Naoya. Used to being called a plain-looking four-eyes, Naoya gave a slight nod in her direction, not particularly bothered by it. They had met before, but if Tomoki didn't remember him at all, it was probably because Naoya's appearance was so forgettable that he had blended in with the scenery.

For the time being, the group decided to start by going to the staff room, so they headed toward the faculty and staff entrance. Takatsuki and Naoya put on visitors' slippers and went inside. Tomoki went around the building to the entrance where his own shoe locker was, changed into his indoor shoes, then rejoined the group.

Perhaps because it was a Saturday, there were few teachers in the staff room. When Miss Marika entered the room with Takatsuki and Naoya in tow, a middle-aged male teacher stood up. His graying hair, large, prominent nose, and deeply wrinkled brow gave him a vaguely gloomy air.

"Miss Hirahara. Is that the man you were speaking of...?"

"Yes, this is Professor Takatsuki!"

Miss Marika answered, standing up straighter like a student called on during class.

The man approached them with a look of exasperation, inclining his head toward Takatsuki.

"Hello, I'm Harada, the head teacher. Thank you for coming to help us at this time."

"I'm Takatsuki, an associate professor at Seiwa University. Thank you for having me."

Takatsuki gave his business card to Harada as well.

Harada looked between the card and Takatsuki's face, then glanced at his suit. Forcing a smile, he adjusted the sleeves of his own ill-fitting cardigan.

"I saw your face in photos online, but wow, you really are young... An associate professor at your age—you must be quite brilliant."

"Oh, no, I'm just someone who happened to have good luck in life."

Takatsuki beamed as he spoke, and Harada answered him with a stiff formality: "No need to be humble."

Despite the praise in his words, the way Harada was looking at Takatsuki had an air of suspicion. Perhaps he doubted whether calling in a university professor would be helpful. Well, it wasn't as if his feelings were incomprehensible, but nevertheless.

Harada let out a dramatic sigh.

"I'm really at a loss regarding this situation. I'm of the opinion that it'll sort itself out in time, but I can't just wait around and do nothing when even the PTA is in an uproar... Truly, Miss Hirahara, this is all your fault."

"I-I'm sorry."

Miss Marika shrunk back from Harada's scowl. Giving another affected sigh, Harada looked back at Takatsuki.

"I'm sure Miss Hirahara has already said as much to you, Professor, but I must ask you to keep this matter off the record. It's already having quite a large impact on the children as it is. If the media were to catch wind of the situation, it would cause even greater commotion."

"Yes, I understand."

Takatsuki continued with a pleasant smile.

"Rest assured, I will not discuss this matter with others. I might reference it as an example in my research, but if I do use it in a paper, the address and name of the school will be omitted, and the children's privacy will be prioritized."

Since Takatsuki's features and appearance were nice and tidy, all it took was him speaking in that elegant way for others to see him as a very gentlemanly, respectable person. In truth, he was the type of person kids wanted to make their subordinate.

It seemed that Harada had no intention of being present for the investigation. He returned to his seat after telling Miss Marika, "I'll leave the rest to you." When Harada's back was turned, Tomoki stuck his tongue out an obscene amount. Seeing that, Naoya remembered having teachers who were that unpleasant and scary when he was in elementary school. Apparently, Harada was just as unpopular as those teachers had been.

Takatsuki turned to Miss Marika, who was still standing with her shoulders hunched.

"Now then, I would like to speak to the children who participated in the *Kokkuri-san* game, if I could. I would also like to see the locker in question for myself."

"Ah, yes… The three of them are waiting in the classroom, so please follow me."

She guided them out of the staff room into the hallway. Grade 5, Class 2's room was on the third floor of the same building.

Tomoki, stepping ahead of the adults as if to lead the way, turned back to look at Takatsuki and started telling him about Chofu Municipal Fourth Elementary's very own Seven School Mysteries: "Akira! Right over there is the nurse's office I told you about! If you sleep in one of the beds, a burned soldier will appear!" and "In the science room on the second floor of that building over there, the skeleton model dances around at night!" Takatsuki had probably asked Tomoki about the Seven Mysteries before. The professor followed the boy's words happily.

Walking alongside Naoya, Miss Marika spoke in an admiring tone.

"Professor Takatsuki really does study ghost stories, doesn't he…? We were really lucky, finding an expert in the field."

"Yes, he certainly does conduct research on ghost stories. But he's not a psychic or anything like that, you know."

Miss Marika gave a small chuckle at Naoya's statement.

"There were parents who told me to call a psychic. But Tomoki was kind enough to introduce me to Professor Takatsuki, and I thought he looked reliable, so I asked him to come."

"I think you can count on him. It's just… Well, he's a pretty strange person. But more importantly—um, can I ask you something?"

"Yes, what is it?"

Miss Marika cocked her head to the side.

"Just now, the head teacher said something like 'this is your fault.' Is that because the ghost story originated in your classroom, Miss Hirahara?"

Naoya had been a bit bothered by the way Harada had looked at Miss Marika, like she was bad news.

Miss Marika's face fell.

"Ah, yes… That's right. Also—I think it's because I was with the children when they played *Kokkuri-san*."

"Huh? You were there?"

"Yes. They came to me, saying, 'We want to play *Kokkuri-san* after school, so you come too, Miss…' It was after school, and it would be bad if something happened, so I was there to supervise. I should have put a stop to it from the beginning, but I played the game myself when I was a child, and I was feeling quite nostalgic."

Her voice didn't distort at all as she spoke. She was telling the truth. Tomoki looked over his shoulder at them.

"Miss Marika plays with us a lot. I wish I was in Class 2… My teacher is a scary old geezer… If I can't be in her class, maybe you could be my teacher, Akira! I bet it would be fun! You're a teacher, right? Why not come to our school?"

"Hmm, unfortunately, I don't have my elementary school teacher's license."

Takatsuki smiled wryly as he answered.

"You don't have your license?! That's lame, Akira!"

"I'm sorry. Why don't you come to my university when you're grown up, instead? Hey, Tomoki... You've seen the locker in Class 2, haven't you? What did you think? Was it scary?"

In response to Takatsuki's question, Tomoki folded his arms like he was thinking.

"I dunno if it's really cursed or not. But I guess it's a little scary... **Just a little**, though!"

His tone was pompous, but Naoya could hear a slight warping in his voice when he insisted he was "just a little" scared. In actuality, Tomoki was frightened, but he was putting on a brave face.

Many of the other children were probably feeling the same.

In a group setting—like a school—the fears they were harboring would be amplified.

If the ghost story was based on the children's preconceptions, how did Takatsuki plan to solve the problem? Or, if the locker really was haunted—in that case, Naoya thought it likely that Takatsuki would take the locker home. He seemed the type to happily carry the thing home on his back, though Naoya hoped he wouldn't, since that would be embarrassing.

They arrived at the Grade 5, Class 2 room to find three nervous-looking girls gathered by the windows. One with a ponytail, one with a fishtail braid, and one whose hair was long and straight. As soon as they saw the door at the front of the classroom open and Miss Marika step inside, they started speaking all at once: "Miss!" "You're late, Miss Marika!" "We were getting tired of waiting!"

But as Takatsuki stepped into the room following their teacher, the girls fell silent for a moment.

They huddled together with their faces close, whispering back and forth—"Is that the college professor?" "Whoa, he's kinda hot?" "He looks like that one idol!"—in what was probably supposed to be a private exchange. Naoya could hear everything they were saying, though.

"Hello. You can call me Professor Akira! I was hoping to talk to you all for a little while. Is that okay?"

The girls responded positively to Takatsuki's cheery greeting, calling out "Yes!" as they approached. Takatsuki's face seemed to work well on elementary school students. Handsome guys really came in handy with their ability to get other people to let their guard down in an instant.

"Then could you start by telling me your names?"

"I'm Riho Kamikura."

"Akari Ishii."

"I'm Anna Mitsumura."

The girls scrambled to reply to Takatsuki's question. The one with the ponytail was Riho, the one with the braid was Akari, and the one with the long hair was Anna. Girls seemed to be quite precocious at this age. All three of them looked older, compared to Tomoki.

There was no one else in the classroom. Looking around gave Naoya an odd feeling of nostalgia, even though this wasn't his own school. Arranged in pairs, the chairs and desks looked surprisingly small and short from his current perspective as a college student. The graffiti etched into the surfaces of the desks told the story of their previous owners. In one corner of the blackboard were the names of the students presently on classroom cleanup duty. The word "aspiration," written out in every student's distinct handwriting, was hung all over the wall, accompanied by a large, pink sheet of paper with the monthly class goal on it: "Responding in a Loud, Clear Voice!" At the back of the room stood a shelf where students could store their bags and backpacks, with an unused corner section of the shelf reserved as a space for class library books.

And—next to the shelf, right beside the room's back door, there was an old, worn-out, steel locker. Its door was closed tight.

Takatsuki looked at it.

"Is that the locker in question?"

"No, the children were so afraid of the locker that I moved it to an empty classroom. That one is its replacement," Miss Marika answered.

Takatsuki nodded in understanding before turning back to the girls.

"Now then, I'd like you to tell me in detail about the circumstances of the day you played *Kokkuri-san*. Could you sit in the same seats you were in at the time?"

The girls moved to sit in chairs near the windows at Takatsuki's request.

Riho, in the seat next to the window, second row from the front. Akari, next to her. Anna, in the window seat behind Riho, in the third row. Riho and Akari sat sideways in their chairs so they could turn to look back at Anna.

"Those are the same seats? You're sure?"

"Yep, we're sure. We played the game right here. And..."

Anna looked at Miss Marika. The teacher nodded as if to say, "That's enough," then picked up the story where Anna had left off.

"*Kokkuri-san* wasn't particularly popular at our school. But it seems these girls heard about how the game is played from friends they made at cram school. They wanted to play it themselves, so that day, in those seats, they tried it out."

After the girls chanted "Kokkuri-san, Kokkuri-san, please come out and play" a few times, the 10-yen coin started moving.

They asked Kokkuri-san a handful of silly questions, such as which girls the boys in class had crushes on, and what the names of their future spouses would be. Each time the coin slid smoothly across the desk, they would stare in amazement and giggle softly at each other.

But eventually, they ran out of things to ask.

The girls decided it was about time to wrap up the game, so as a group, they chanted, "Kokkuri-san, Kokkuri-san, please go back to where you came from."

But the 10-yen coin simply moved around and around in circles without stopping.

Dismayed, the girls made their request again: "Please go back to where you came from." But the coin still did not stop.

And then, all at once, it slid over to the word "No."

The girls were shaken. Kokkuri-san wouldn't leave. It didn't want to.

They went back and forth—"Please go back." "No." "Please go back." "No."—several times, before, unable to stand it anymore, Riho had shouted, "Who do you think you are?! Get out!"

The coin moved then, toward the place where the syllabary was written out, and indicated three characters in order: "Chi." "Na." "Tsu."

Right then, something even stranger happened.

A small clattering noise came from the back of the room.

The girls and Miss Marika turned reflexively to look in that direction. It was the locker sitting in the corner of the classroom. As they watched, its door slowly started to open with a faint creaking sound.

"When they saw that, the girls all screamed...and ran from the room."

"Even though there's a rule that you can't stop or interrupt the game if Kokkuri-san hasn't left?"

Takatsuki looked at the girls with his head cocked, and the three of them cast their gazes down in embarrassment.

Anna opened her mouth to answer for the group.

"I mean... We were really scared. We weren't thinking about the rules."

"Well, it certainly would be frightening for the locker to open on its own. So what happened after that?"

"The girls were running down the hallway, so I rushed after them."

Miss Marika picked the story back up.

She caught up with the girls at the school entrance. All three of them were sitting in front of the shoe lockers crying loudly, and Miss Marika tried desperately to calm them down.

"Because of the commotion, other students and teachers who were still inside the school gathered around... They asked what was going on, and we ended up telling them about playing *Kokkuri-san* and the locker opening on its own. And I guess that spread around the school as a ghost story."

Miss Marika looked like she was at a total loss.

Lightly stroking his chin with one hand, Takatsuki asked, "And after that?"

"I asked another teacher to look after the girls, and I went back to my classroom."

"By yourself? That was quite brave of you, after such a frightening experience!"

"W-well, it was a little scary, but…I was too embarrassed to ask a colleague to come with me. And besides, the girls left their bags in the room. The paper they used for the game was still sitting on the desk too, and I couldn't leave it there…"

"How was the classroom when you returned?"

"It was more or less the same. The locker door was open, the *Kokkuri-san* paper was on the desk… I tried approaching the locker, but there didn't seem to be anything strange about it. Besides, the locker was quite old, and the fittings were loose, so it had opened on its own before. But I closed it, just to be safe, grabbed their bags, and left."

"What about the paper used for the game?"

"I grabbed that as well and threw it in the incinerator later. I remembered that when I played *Kokkuri-san* as a child, there was a rule that you had to burn the paper you used…"

"Ah, that's quite standard. So then—were there any other strange occurrences after that? Did anyone who played *Kokkuri-san* fall ill, anything like that?"

"No, not particularly… The girls calmed down after a while. There wasn't anything I would describe as strange."

As soon as those words left Miss Marika's mouth, the girls all started shaking their heads.

"That's not true! So many scary things happened!"

"The locker kept opening on its own!"

"During class and after school! And some kids heard a voice coming from inside the locker! They said it was Chinatsu's voice, for sure!"

Takatsuki leaned toward the girls.

"Chinatsu's voice? So you recognize the name Kokkuri-san spelled out?"

Suddenly, the girls faltered. They looked at one another guiltily, then hung their heads.

It was Miss Marika who spoke up in their place.

"Chinatsu—Chinatsu Mizunuma was a student in Class 2 until the summer."

She spoke of the girl in the past tense.

"Chinatsu was born with a weak heart, and she was hardly ever able to attend school. Even after making it into fifth grade, she was only able to make it to class twice. She had to be hospitalized at a facility far from here for surgery...so she moved away before summer vacation."

Miss Marika pointed to a chair in the very back of the room, just in front of the cleaning supplies locker, indicating where Chinatsu used to sit.

And then—

"—Splendid."

The word spilled from Takatsuki in a murmur.

Confused, Miss Marika looked at him.

Takatsuki held out his right hand as if asking for a handshake. With a somewhat bewildered expression, as if she was being lured, Miss Marika held out her own hand.

Takatsuki grasped it, and in one elegant movement pulled Miss Marika toward himself as if inviting her to dance. Miss Marika looked up at him, startled, her face close to his, and Takatsuki gazed back down at her.

"Truly splendid. It's perfect, Miss Marika."

"Huh? What? U-um...?"

Miss Marika's voice was bemused, but Takatsuki continued, beaming at her.

"It started with what should have been a silly game running amok, led to the strangeness with the locker, and now we have the death of a former classmate surfacing as support for the story! It's a flawless framework for a ghost story! Culminating in the idea that you'll be 'transported to another world' if you get close to the locker must be because the story originally had the shadow of death on it, right? I'm sure it's due to the awareness that 'another world' is synonymous with 'the afterlife.' Ah, this is really superb!"

This is bad, Naoya thought, drawing close to Takatsuki.

Though he had made an effort to behave rather like a gentleman so far, reaching this point, Takatsuki's logic had flown the coop. Mysteries were his favorite food, after all. When a ghost story he liked was served up in front of him, Takatsuki would naturally sink his teeth into it. He would keep going like this until someone stopped him. There was even a chance he would hold on tight to the person he was talking to, like a big dog jumping excitedly on a passerby during its walk.

Half the reason Takatsuki employed Naoya as an assistant was so Naoya could be the Sensible One and intervene when the professor's reason went missing. Putting a hand on Takatsuki's shoulder, Naoya began to admonish him in a calm voice.

"Professor Takatsuki. Why don't you calm down a little? Start by letting go of her hand, quickly now."

"What on earth are you saying, Fukamachi! You heard her too, didn't you? They basically said a dead classmate came back through spiritualism! Don't you think it's fascinating? There's no way someone could be calm about this!"

"And yet, the only one acting crazy is you!"

Naoya was at his wit's end, internally, thinking, *How did this man make it to thirty-four?* He genuinely wished he had a dog leash at times like these. Even at the best of times, Takatsuki had a habit of crowding into people's personal space. Naoya couldn't help but worry that sooner or later the professor was going to casually grab a woman's hand and lean in close to her face and be arrested for molestation or sexual harassment. Glancing around, he saw that Tomoki and the girls were all gaping at Takatsuki. At this rate, his job and reputation would be at stake.

"U-um..."

In that moment, pressed against Takatsuki, Miss Marika interjected in a voice that sounded like it was being wrung out of her.

"Sh-she's not dead! Chinatsu isn't dead!"

"...Pardon?"

"...What?"

Takatsuki, who was trying to pull Miss Marika into an even more passionate embrace, and Naoya, who was trying to stop him by pulling on his arm, both stopped moving at the same time.

All at once, Takatsuki stood up straight and let go of Miss Marika's hand in a hurry.

It seemed his reason had returned. He glanced nervously at Miss

Marika, whose cheeks were flushed bright red, and drew his shoulders in, embarrassed.

"I-I'm so sorry, truly... I was so excited about the story—I got so happy that I was about to hug you..."

"Ah, no, I don't really...mind..."

Face still red, Miss Marika fixed her slightly disheveled hair. The children were muttering—"She doesn't mind?" "She doesn't." "I guess not." "It's fine, isn't it?"—but Miss Marika pretended not to hear them, and it looked like she really was going to overlook the incident. Naoya couldn't help but think that it wasn't fine, but it would be bad if she decided to complain about it, so he figured it was best to let it go.

Miss Marika cleared her throat with a small *ahem*.

"A-anyway, Chinatsu isn't dead, she was hospitalized. The surgery was a success, and I heard she's in recovery now. So it's impossible that Kokkuri-san would have called her ghost out!"

"...But it could have been a living spirit, right?" Riho objected.

Akari and Anna nodded in agreement.

"I mean, if that's not what it is, then why would Kokkuri-san have spelled out Chinatsu's name? It's weird!"

"Yeah, it must be that just her soul came back to haunt the school!"

"I think so too! Otherwise, how do you explain it?!"

Seeing the girls in a panic, Miss Marika looked troubled again. It really must have become difficult for her to teach with the students like this.

It didn't matter to the children whether Chinatsu was alive or dead. Because Kokkuri-san had spelled out her name, Chinatsu's existence was at the heart of this ghost story.

Takatsuki leaned in close to Naoya and spoke in a low voice.

"Fukamachi—what do you think? Is anyone lying?"

"No. No one," Naoya answered, voice also lowered.

Since they arrived at the school, not one person whose voice they had heard had lied about the locker story. In other words, the game of *Kokkuri-san*, the 10-yen coin spelling out "Chinatsu," the locker door opening—it was all true.

Furthermore, there was a student named "Chinatsu" who had been in Class 2, and she wasn't dead.

Turning his gaze back to Miss Marika and the still-flustered girls, Takatsuki murmured, "I see... That's interesting."

The locker in question had been moved to an empty classroom on the second floor of the neighboring school building. It seemed it would still take some time for Miss Marika to calm down the anxious girls, so Takatsuki, Naoya, and Tomoki decided to go see it themselves.

But as they made their way down to the second floor and across the connecting corridor to the other building, Tomoki's behavior got stranger and stranger. He was oddly restless, unable to keep his composure, and kept fiddling with his hair and pockets.

Takatsuki spoke up.

"What's wrong, Tomoki?"

"No, uh... Um, it's just, I..."

Eventually, Tomoki stopped walking in the middle of the hallway and fumbled over his words.

"Tomoki... Could it be? Are you...scared?"

"A-as if!"

Tomoki's retort was intensely distorted.

Naoya covered his ears instinctively, and Takatsuki looked between him and Tomoki, smiling as his eyes narrowed.

"Oh? Then how come you've gotten all fidgety all of a sudden?"

"I... I have to go home soon! I have practice today! If I don't go soon, my mom will get mad at me!"

"I see. If you have practice, it can't be helped, then. What are you practicing?"

"Violin! So **even though I ain't scared at all**, I'm going home! See ya later, Akira!"

His declaration made, Tomoki turned on his heel and ran back down the corridor in a hurry.

Takatsuki watched him go with a small chuckle.

"...Tomoki was lying just now, wasn't he?"

Frowning, hands pressed over his ears, Naoya nodded.

"Yes. He lied about having lessons today. He's actually really afraid."

"Ah-hah-hah. He was acting tough earlier because Miss Marika and the girls were there. That's cute."

"But he really is learning to play violin."

"Oh? I definitely want to hear him play sometime. Now then—why don't you and I go see this locker for ourselves?"

The classroom they were looking for was at the very end of the hallway. Naoya walked alongside Takatsuki toward their destination. Their thin visitors' slippers slapped against the floor as they went. There seemed to be a collection of specific-use classrooms on this level of the building. There were science labs, computer labs, and audio-visual rooms.

The school was utterly deserted on a Saturday and terribly quiet. The hallway felt dark, somehow. Naoya remembered having to go back for something he'd forgotten when he was in elementary school. It had been in the evening, not on a day off, but with all the lights in the school building off except those around the staff rooms, the place had looked strangely empty. Even though Naoya knew the building well, it had felt unfamiliar, and oddly lonely.

"—You know, we talked a little about school ghost stories in our last lecture, didn't we?"

Takatsuki spoke as if he were reading Naoya's mind.

"Schools are interesting places, aren't they? Large groups of unrelated children in one place, forced to do the same things. There's a theory that ghost stories tend to develop in schools because children, whose spirits are suppressed in places like these, are able to experience some form of release through them. The idea being that the chaos of the mysterious counters the order imposed by the school... It's an interesting theory, but my own is a little different."

"What do you believe, Professor?"

"I think that, for children, schools are places where ordinary and extraordinary coexist, constantly, as two sides of the same coin."

"Ordinary and extraordinary, at the same time…?"

"Yes."

With a small snicker, Takatsuki looked at Naoya.

His normally dark brown eyes were suddenly tinged with blue. They were a deep, dark indigo, the same color as the night sky. Takatsuki's eyes changed color like this at times. While his smile shone as bright as the midday sun, the night stayed hidden in his eyes.

"I mentioned in class that mysteries are a departure from the ordinary, yes? 'Ordinary' is anything familiar, things we're used to, things we know and love. Things that, consequently, give us peace of mind. But in the crevices between ordinary things, where the extraordinary lies, that's where the mysterious lurks."

Those night-sky eyes focused on the placard of a room right beside Takatsuki.

The science lab. The place where, according to Tomoki, a skeleton model would dance around in the dark.

"Don't you think schools are built around various layers of the ordinary and extraordinary? For new first-years, they are entirely unfamiliar places. The students get used to them before long, and the spaces they frequent, like classrooms and shoe lockers, gradually become part of the 'ordinary.' Meanwhile, the ones they don't use as much, like science and music rooms, remain 'extraordinary.' That's why many schools have moving skeletons in science labs and portraits of Beethoven in music rooms whose eyes follow you around."

"So because the places are unfamiliar, we don't understand them?"

"Right. As I've said: People fear what they don't understand."

That was a common refrain for Takatsuki.

People fear what they don't understand. They don't like to leave things unexplained, so they create stories for the unknown. In doing so, they give names and concrete shapes to their fears and anxieties—and ghost stories are born.

"That's not the only way the ordinary and extraordinary are in conflict at school. I mentioned the relationship between classrooms and bathrooms in my lecture, but there's also the contrast between school hours and after-school hours."

The building they were in, usually noisy with the presence of many, was still—devoid of life. The afternoon sun streaming through the windows had disappeared, and all that remained was the red glow of the fire alarm lamps and the green light emanating from the emergency exit signs.

To elementary schooler Naoya, returning to retrieve his forgotten items, the empty school at night was just like another world. In that moment, the stories his classmates had told him about the Seven School Mysteries were entirely real. Without his noticing it, another step appeared in the staircase right as he approached it. A melancholy melody echoed from the music room, tapped out on the keys of the piano by blood dripping from the ceiling. A stark-white hand was snaking its way out of a toilet bowl in the bathroom. He was overwhelmed with those thoughts and fled the school building soon after.

The most extraordinary things the school harbored came out after school hours. That was probably why so many of the Seven School Mysteries happened at the end of the school day or at night.

"The girls in Grade 5, Class 2 who played *Kokkuri-san* did so after school. The perfect time for mysterious things to take place."

Takatsuki came to a stop as he spoke.

They had reached the corridor's end. In no time, they had arrived at the empty room where the problem locker was being kept. Nothing was written on the placard above the classroom door. That seemed to be another component of the extraordinary nature of this case.

Takatsuki reached for the door.

Then, just as he looked like he was going to open it, he paused.

"Come to think of it, schools on days off—and empty classrooms, too—are both extraordinary. The locker we're here to see is completely steeped in the unusual at the moment… Hey, Fukamachi."

Takatsuki stooped down slightly, peering into Naoya's face.

"Are you scared to go inside?"

When it came to extraordinary, Naoya thought this indigo-eyed version of Takatsuki fit the bill.

Seeing those eyes up close—midnight eyes that threatened to suck him up into their depths—nearly took his breath away, every time. The question that had plagued Naoya's mind since the day they met reared its head again.

What on earth is this man?

Takatsuki himself probably didn't know the answer. The professor didn't know how his eyes had gotten like this. He had no memory of when it happened. All he knew was that he had become this way after being caught up in a situation that could only be called bizarre.

It was why he was drawn to mysteries, why he sought them out.

Naoya's reply was awkward, arrested as he was in Takatsuki's gaze.

"Am I s-scared…? I mean, a little, but…"

"But?"

"…You're too close."

Naoya pushed Takatsuki away with a hand under his chin. He thought he heard a cracking sound from around the professor's neck but decided to pretend it was nothing.

"F-Fukamachi, um, I think my neck just—"

"You're imagining things. Open up the door already."

Putting a hand over his nape, Takatsuki looked at Naoya.

At some point in the last few moments, his eyes had gone back to being dark brown.

"It's scary because I don't understand it, right?" Naoya continued, returning Takatsuki's gaze. "So won't it stop being scary if I actually see it?"

"It might not be something that can be understood just by looking at it, you know. It could deepen the mystery."

"But at the very least, I'll know one more thing than I did before seeing it. That's better than continuing to be ignorant. I'm sure it is."

"…That's a wonderful way of thinking about it."

A grin pulled at the corners of Takatsuki's lips.

He reached his hand out again and opened the classroom door.

It opened silently, revealing a disused room that seemed to serve no purpose other than storage. No posters or bulletins hung on the walls, but thumbtack marks remained. There was no teacher's podium, and the desks and chairs were all piled up near the windows. The desks and chairs that had been in the Grade 5, Class 2 room were evidently the bigger kind meant for the older children. The ones here—used by lower grades—were surprisingly small.

And there, standing alone in front of the stacks of chairs and desks, was a single, gray, steel locker.

A locker which would normally have sat in the corner of a room being placed in the dead center of the class struck Naoya as so terribly incongruous that, somehow or other, it looked to him like a Western-style coffin standing there. The kind a vampire would come out of in an old horror movie.

The locker door was slightly ajar.

Naturally, it was impossible to see inside the locker through such a gap. An unknowable darkness appeared to be the only thing showing through the opening.

Once the ghost story about the locker had spread around the school, some of the children had surely come to this room to sneak a peek at the locker from the doorway. Then, trembling with fear, they must have run away. It wasn't hard to understand why Tomoki had wanted to flee.

Takatsuki walked over to the locker. He circled it once, looking at it carefully, and then—he put his hand on the door.

Unflinching, he opened it.

The locker was empty.

Not a single broom nor bucket to be found inside, and of course, no entrance to another world. All the locker from Grade 5, Class 2 contained was the faint, lingering smell of old cleaning rags.

Takatsuki, not yet ready to give up, stuck his hand in the locker and felt around the sides and the top of the interior. But there was no indication that he was about to be dragged to the afterlife.

Finally, the professor examined the door's metal fittings.

Just as Miss Marika had said, they had gotten quite loose and hardly caught the way they should have. It wasn't unthinkable that the door would open on its own, with the fittings like this.

"...Right. It's just a normal locker, after all."

Sounding bored, Takatsuki closed the door.

"Kokkuri-san isn't haunting it, and it isn't the door to another world. The ghost story was just born from the children's convictions, I suppose."

The likely truth was that the locker had just happened to pop open while the girls were playing the game. Because of the timing, they connected the door opening with Kokkuri-san.

"But then why did Kokkuri-san spell out 'Chinatsu'?"

"The principle behind things like *Kokkuri-san* still isn't thoroughly understood, but the general theory is that it works via the influence of the unconscious mind. One of the girls might have unintentionally called to mind their former classmate. Or..."

Takatsuki stopped talking for a moment and looked lost in thought. He went back to closely inspecting the locker, one hand lightly stroking his chin.

Even if the locker was nothing more than that, to the children, it was a source of fear, the place where Kokkuri-san was hiding. Judging from the earlier behavior of the girls and Tomoki, simply telling the students that there were no monsters inside wouldn't do the trick.

"So what are you going to do now, Professor?"

"...Hm. That might be it."

Takatsuki looked over his shoulder at Naoya.

"Hey, Fukamachi?" he said. "It might be unpleasant for you, but would be okay if I lied just a little?"

His smile was bright and wide.

Several days later, Takatsuki and Naoya paid another visit to Chofu Municipal Fourth Elementary.

It was a weekday. It was the same time of day during which the girls had played *Kokkuri-san*. Classes were over, and almost all the students had left. The school building was growing quiet.

They had asked Miss Marika in advance to keep all the students in Grade 5, Class 2 from going home.

At the moment, those students were lined up along the wall, watching Takatsuki and Naoya with frightened faces.

They weren't in Class 2—they were in the empty classroom.

In front of the locker that used to be in Class 2, they had set up one desk and two chairs.

On top of the desk was a piece of white paper. Written on the paper were the Japanese syllabary in *hiragana*, the numbers zero through nine, the words "yes," "no," "male," and "female," and a *torii* gate. It was Takatsuki's handmade *Kokkuri-san* paper.

The locker door, sure enough, was slightly open. Takatsuki walked over and closed it carefully. The metal fittings *clanged* shut.

Then Takatsuki looked around at the children who were cowering along the wall and greeted them.

"Hello. I'm sure you've heard from Miss Marika, but my name is Akira Takatsuki. I teach at Seiwa University. Call me Professor Akira, okay? Starting now, I'd like to exorcise the Grade 5, Class 2 locker that is haunted by Kokkuri-san."

The children looked at one another, then started talking noisily all at once, voicing their doubts about Takatsuki's capabilities: "Is he really going to do an exorcism?" "Can he do that?" "Won't he just get cursed instead?" One of the students said, "Okay, but why is a guy from Class 3 here?" And when Naoya looked in that direction, he saw that Tomoki had snuck his way in amidst the children from Class 2. Folding his arms over his chest snobbishly, Tomoki declared to the kids around him that "Akira is my disciple! I'm the one who brought him here!" In Tomoki's mind, it seemed, Takatsuki being his disciple was an established fact.

Bowing her head to Takatsuki, Miss Marika entreated the professor to do something.

Takatsuki gave her a reassuring nod, then looked back at the students.

"Now, with Fukamachi here, I'm going to call on the same Kokkuri-san who was summoned here before. And I'm going to persuade it to leave. So, everyone, please sit tight over there and watch."

Naoya sat in one of the chairs by the locker at Takatsuki's prompting. It was difficult to settle himself into a chair built for an elementary school student. It was probably harder for Takatsuki, who was even taller, but he managed to sit facing Naoya on the other side of the desk, with his long legs mostly hanging out.

Takatsuki took out a 10-yen coin and placed it on the *torii* gate in the center of the paper. He and Naoya each pressed down gently on the coin with their index fingers.

"Kokkuri-san, Kokkuri-san, please come out and play," Takatsuki chanted, his voice soft.

The coin didn't move. The children standing along the wall watched them with bated breath.

"Kokkuri-san, Kokkuri-san, please come out and play," Takatsuki chanted a second time.

Once again, the 10-yen coin stayed put.

"Kokkuri-san, Kokkuri-san, please come out and play."

Takatsuki chanted once more, and it happened.

The coin slid over the paper, circled the *torii* gate, then stopped.

The children yelped in surprise. Miss Marika craned forward to see.

"It really came…" someone murmured.

This game of *Kokkuri-san* was, of course, staged.

The other day, Takatsuki had proposed playing a fake game of *Kokkuri-san* to bring the commotion over the locker to an end.

Among the children, it was an indisputable fact that Kokkuri-san had summoned a spirit that was living in the locker. It would be hard to dispel that idea just by having an adult reason with the students.

"So it would be best to look at things from their point of view and solve the problem using their reasoning."

That had been Takatsuki's opinion.

The mystery that started with Kokkuri-san had to be finished with Kokkuri-san.

"That said, I made a promise not to tell a lie in front of you. So I won't lie with my voice. If I spell things out through the 10-yen coin, it won't hurt you, right?" Takatsuki had said.

It was a matter of semantics, but Naoya also couldn't think of any other way to calm the children down.

"Kokkuri-san, Kokkuri-san, where do you usually stay?"

At Takatsuki's question, the coin slid over to the syllabary. The professor was the one moving it. Naoya had been told to put his finger on the coin and pretend to concentrate.

Dashing over to the desk, Tomoki followed the coin's movement with his eyes, reading the characters it indicated aloud.

"F-A-R!"

Far.

Kokkuri-san's answer was a lie, but it was Tomoki giving it a voice. Naoya only heard lies as distorted when they were being spoken by their originator. Simply reading someone else's words from the side, Tomoki's voice didn't warp at all.

"Kokkuri-san, Kokkuri-san, please go back."

The coin slid back to the *torii* gate. It seemed to be necessary to have Kokkuri-san return to the gate temporarily after each question asked. Naoya thought that, perhaps, the purpose of that kind of tedious procedure was to add to the very ceremonial atmosphere.

"Did you come to this school several days ago?"

Yes.

"Did you come when Miss Kamikura and the others played *Kokkuri-san*?"

Yes.

Takatsuki kept asking questions. At first, the only one standing nearby and reading the coin's answers was Tomoki, but after a while, other children approached, and eventually everyone was gathered around the desk.

"Is your name 'Chinatsu'?"

Yes.

As soon as the 10-yen coin gave that reply, a strong shudder ran through the children. "I knew it," Naoya could hear them whispering.

"Why did you come to this school?"

I wanted to see them.

"Who did you want to see?"

Everyone from class.

"Is there anything you want to say to the class?"

I didn't mean to scare you.

"Anything else?"

I wish we could have played together more.

As a group, the children read Kokkuri-san's response out loud.

In that way, the words they spoke would become a kind of suggestion. They would become a charm, certain to shatter the fear of ghost stories that had taken root in the children's hearts.

And—their impression of Chinatsu as a terrifying spirit would be rewritten to that of a former classmate who felt lonely.

At that moment, there was a small *clang.*

The children gasped. Some of the girls let out small screams.

Naoya's eyes looked toward the source of the sound.

The door to the locker, which Takatsuki had shut earlier, was slightly ajar.

With a faint *creeeak,* the door gradually opened wider.

Naoya looked at Takatsuki reflexively, but the other man didn't seem perturbed at all. He simply glanced at the locker before returning his gaze to the 10-yen coin and continuing his line of questioning.

"Did you enjoy the time you spent with everyone in Grade 5, Class 2?"

It was fun.

"Do you like the children in Grade 5, Class 2?"

I like them.

Oh, Naoya thought. *That's right.* This ghost story was made up of two components: Kokkuri-san and the locker. It wouldn't be enough to just deal with Kokkuri-san. It would be meaningless if they didn't also exorcize the ghost that was haunting the locker. Takatsuki had probably tampered with the locker beforehand—perhaps even when he had gone to close it—so that it would open again at the right time.

Beneath their index fingers, the coin was moving.

I want to play together again.

"We get it! We understand, Chinatsu!"

It was Riho who spoke.

"I'm sorry! I'm sorry I was afraid of you! Even though we were class-mates, you were lonely because you hardly ever got to hang out with us, right? Please come back to our class when you're all better!"

"Yeah, we'll be waiting for you! All of us! So get well soon, okay?"

"We'll hang out again! I like you too, Chinatsu!"

"We won't be scared anymore, because you're our friend!"

Akari, Anna, and the other children as well—one by one they called out.

We did it, Naoya thought, inwardly celebrating. Success. The children's impressions of Chinatsu and the locker were probably changed now.

They wouldn't be afraid of either of them anymore.

"Kokkuri-san, Kokkuri-san, please go back to where you came from."

At Takatsuki's request, the 10-yen coin slid back to the *torii* gate.

The creaking locker had stopped moving.

Holding their breath, the students stared at the coin.

"Thank you very much," Takatsuki said.

The magic words to bring the game to an end.

Just as Takatsuki and Naoya removed their fingers from the utterly still coin, the locker door, which had opened nearly a full quarter of the way, quietly closed once more.

"I truly can't thank you enough."

After all the children had gone home, Miss Marika accompanied Takatsuki and Naoya to the school entrance to see them off. She bowed her head deeply toward them.

"Thanks to you, Professor, the children seem to have calmed down. I think it'll be all right now. Their expressions had all clearly changed from how they were before the 'exorcism.'"

"I'm just happy to have been able to help. This case was also extremely useful for my research."

Miss Marika had been informed ahead of time that the game of *Kokkuri-san* was going to be staged. She agreed with what Takatsuki was hoping to do and had allowed the whole thing to happen.

"Chinatsu won't be an object of fear for the children in Grade 5, Class 2 anymore. That's good news, isn't it, Miss Marika? You must be relieved."

"Yes, I am, really…"

"Of course you are. After all, you're the one who spelled out Chinatsu's name that first time, aren't you?"

Miss Marika's face suddenly stiffened at Takatsuki's words.

Surprised, Naoya looked back and forth between the two of them.

Takatsuki was smiling as he always did.

Her features hardened—Miss Marika returned his gaze.

"It hit me the other day, when I asked the girls to describe the circumstances of their game. With the seats arranged like this, I thought, there would be another person sitting here," Takatsuki said.

"And when she was sitting in the seat she played *Kokkuri-san* in, Miss Mitsumura looked back at you and started to say something. But you interrupted her and started talking yourself. It sounded a little forced to me. I think, at that time, what Anna was trying to say was, 'And Miss Marika was sitting next to me.'"

"Wh… What are you talking about?"

The smile Miss Marika showed him was wooden, forced.

"I mean, that is—**I didn't participate in the *Kokkuri-san* game.**"

Her voice distorted. Naoya pressed a hand over one ear.

Placing a hand on Naoya's shoulder, Takatsuki shook his head at Miss Marika.

"It's wrong to lie, Miss Marika."

With those words stated so plainly to her face, Miss Marika looked like she would burst into tears at any moment.

Takatsuki took a step toward her. Miss Marika shivered as if frightened of him.

Ignoring that, Takatsuki stooped down so he could look into her face.

"I don't mean to blame you or anything. I expect you had your reasons.

I'm simply interested in what those reasons were. Because it was your actions that resulted in the creation of this ghost story."

Takatsuki spoke with a smile on his model-like face and a melodic voice. Just as he said, his tone didn't sound like one of condemnation.

He only wanted to know the truth.

The reason why this single ghost story was created. The context.

"Please, Miss Marika, tell me. Why did you bring Chinatsu's name into this?"

Miss Marika looked down to escape Takatsuki's gaze.

Her shoulders trembled, and a moment later a faint voice spilled from her lips.

"It's…because…the kids…"

Her voice shook as much as her frame, but it didn't warp at all.

In that quaking voice, fumbling over her words as they caught in her throat, Miss Marika finally spoke the truth.

"I did it because, those children, they—they forgot about Chinatsu."

"Forgot about her?"

Takatsuki tilted his head to the side.

Miss Marika slowly lifted her head.

She looked up at Takatsuki's far-too-near face, and her eyes were filled with tears.

"…Chinatsu was only able…to attend class…twice."

Takatsuki waited quietly for the stuttering tale to continue.

"She didn't even get to go on field trips, or educational outings. Her seat was always empty, and before I knew it, she was relegated to the corner in the back of the room. She couldn't…attend her own good-bye party…either…"

Miss Marika's voice faltered, and her eyes returned to the floor. Tears streamed down her cheeks and off her chin, pattering onto the ground by her feet.

And yet, when she raised her head again, Miss Marika looked like she was angry.

"…But! But Chinatsu was still a member of Class 2!"

With the back of her hand, she wiped roughly at the wetness on her face, then glared up at Takatsuki.

"A little while after summer vacation, I made a suggestion to the class. 'Why don't we write letters to Chinatsu?' It would be wrong to force them, so I decided it would be fine if it was only the ones who wanted to participate. I told them to bring the letters to me once they were done and I would put them in the mail all together..."

When she continued, Miss Marika's voice was just slightly hoarse.

"...but not a single child turned in a letter."

"Well, that was inevitable. The children didn't have enough time to become friends with Chinatsu," Takatsuki replied.

Miss Marika clasped her hands together.

"I know... I know I shouldn't have been upset with them. I'm the one at fault. I mean, when I heard Chinatsu was going to be in my class, I decided then and there—she might not be able to attend school very much, but we should still treat her like a valuable member of the class, and I would guide the other children in doing so... It was totally hopeless. But I even made whoever was on class duty take extra notes during lessons for Chinatsu's sake."

Even with Chinatsu gone, Grade 5, Class 2 carried on as usual. It made sense, because she was practically a nonentity in the class to begin with, at least as far as the other children were concerned.

But to Miss Marika, it was unbelievably sad.

"I went to Chinatsu's house to speak with her before she moved away. She told me, 'Even though I hardly got to go, school was fun. Everyone was so nice. I really liked them.' Doesn't that break your heart? It made me think... Do the other kids even care about Chinatsu?"

"That's why you brought up her name when playing *Kokkuri-san*. You wanted everyone to remember her."

"But... I never thought it would cause such a panic..."

All at once, the fire left Miss Marika's eyes. She shrunk in on herself, as if overwhelmed by the weight of her surging regret. Tears started to rain down around her feet again.

She had probably only meant to play a small prank—nothing serious. She had just wanted to make the children remember Chinatsu, even a little.

Instead, Miss Marika's attempt at mischief had effectively killed Chinatsu.

The girl became an object of fear for her former classmates, a ghost summoned by Kokkuri-san. And that fear spread like wildfire, beyond the walls of Grade 5, Class 2 and throughout the school.

Miss Marika really must have been at a loss when confronted with the magnitude of her own mistake—and with the reality that she had caused her students to be afraid of Chinatsu.

"Miss Marika, thank you for telling me," Takatsuki said. "I fully understand."

He looked down at the crying woman, his face a bit awkward.

"I apologize. I had no intention of making you cry... I really do lack the sense for these kinds of things, and I was thoughtless. But, ah—it's okay, Miss Marika."

Peering into her face again, Takatsuki spoke kindly.

"It's true that Chinatsu became a terrifying specter for a while, but that's not the case now. At least, not in the hearts of your students, hm?"

The children had called Chinatsu their friend, earlier. "*We like you,*" they had said. "*Let's play together again.*"

Of course, their words hadn't been directed at the real Chinatsu. Hardly any of them had ever had the chance to actually play with her. There were probably students in the class who had never even exchanged a single word with her. By that measure, Chinatsu's link to Grade 5, Class 2 was still tenuous.

However, through this incident, the children were able to see Chinatsu's existence in a new light. First as an evil spirit, and ultimately as a classmate. There was no denying that.

"If an evil spirit is appeased, it becomes a guardian deity. That's a part of our country's culture. We've protected our communities this way since long ago."

"Professor Takatsuki..."

Miss Marika looked at Takatsuki, tears spilling over her pale cheeks.

The professor took out his handkerchief and dabbed gently at her wet face.

"But you know, Miss Marika, all I did was a quick fix with that exorcism. From here on out, it'll be up to the leader of this community—you, their teacher, that is—to give more meticulous care to the students. It'll be fine; you can do it. If you can care that much about one child, I have no doubt you'll manage."

Takatsuki pressed the handkerchief into Miss Marika's hand and smiled.

By the time they left the school, the sun was starting to set.

It got dark early at that time of year. The school gate was directly west of the visitor's entrance. Looking across the schoolyard toward the gate, Naoya had to squint at the red glow on the horizon.

The students must have all left already; Naoya couldn't see them anywhere, and everything was quiet. The wind blew through the empty grounds, and the meager playground equipment in the corner looked abandoned with no one playing on it.

"Will the 'Locker of Grade 5, Class 2' ghost story really fade out of the school now, do you think?"

Naoya posed the question as they set out toward the gate. Takatsuki smiled.

"A story that's spread around that much won't disappear so easily. The 'exorcism' I did was only for Class 2. I think the story will continue to be shared at Chofu Municipal Fourth Elementary."

"...Is that okay?"

The school had asked Takatsuki to put an end to the uproar caused by the ghost story. If the story persisted even now, wouldn't that be cause for more chaos in the future?

But Takatsuki looked at Naoya and replied, "It's fine."

The professor looked over his shoulder at the school building and spoke in a contented voice.

"Ghost stories are an unavoidable part of school, perhaps because the children themselves seek the stories out. School life is, essentially, an endlessly repeating routine. A little bit of the extraordinary is necessary to spice up the mundane. As long as the class at the center of the ruckus calms down, the rest of the classes will follow suit."

After Takatsuki's game of *Kokkuri-san* earlier, a discussion was held among the children, and it was decided that the locker in question would be returned to Grade 5, Class 2. The decision was proof that the kids weren't afraid of the locker anymore. There might be some children who were still a bit trepidatious, but Miss Marika would handle things from now on.

How the students from other classes would interpret the locker's return was another matter entirely.

They hadn't been present for the "exorcism." Perhaps the locker's ghost story would enter a new era, its development spurred on by the children's rich imaginations making up for any missing context.

"Ooh, maybe they'll add a part to the story about a cool college professor being called in to break the curse!"

"What are you doing inserting yourself as a character into the story? Besides, don't you think it's a bit shameless to call yourself 'cool'?"

"I make a point to take the public's appraisal of me seriously. Oh, right—Fukamachi, take this."

Takatsuki pressed something into Naoya's hand.

A 10-yen coin.

"…Professor, is this from earlier…?"

"Yep. The one we used for the game. According to the rules of the game, it has to be spent within three days, so I'll leave it to you, okay?"

"Leave it to me? That game of *Kokkuri-san* was fake from the start, though."

"Well, about that… When we were playing, did you move the coin by yourself at all, Fukamachi?"

"Pardon?"

Naoya tilted his head in confusion at Takatsuki's question.

Takatsuki had been the one in charge of moving the coin, he thought. Naoya was just supposed to look serious and put a finger on it, that was all.

Taking out the paper they had used for *Kokkuri-san*, Takatsuki stared at it intently while he spoke.

"That last thing the coin spelled out, 'I want to play together again.' That...wasn't me."

"—What?!"

Naoya stared up at Takatsuki in shock.

"Huh? But then... Then why did the coin move?"

"You and I were the only ones touching it at the time. If it wasn't me, and it wasn't you...then who on earth was it?"

As usual, Takatsuki's soft, clear voice was completely undistorted.

He wasn't lying.

He really hadn't moved the 10-yen coin.

"While we're on the subject—the locker door. When it opened, the timing was almost too good, wasn't it?"

"Wait, what? ...That wasn't some trick of yours or something?!"

"No, I didn't have the time. Besides, some kind of opening mechanism wouldn't be impossible, but it would be surprisingly difficult to make it close on its own."

"Huh...?"

Instinctively, Naoya looked back at the school.

From the schoolyard gate, the building sat full east. Sunlight still lingered in the western sky, but on the eastern horizon, night was already falling. A few twinkling stars had appeared, and the looming clouds were quickly turning indigo. The school was on the verge of being blanketed in darkness.

A school building at night was the epitome of "extraordinary." It was the place where every ghost story could become real.

"For the time being, I'll have to keep in touch with Tomoki and keep investigating whether anything strange is happening at this school."

Takatsuki grinned. His eyes were the same color as the night sky.

Clutched in Naoya's hand, the 10-yen coin suddenly seemed a little heavier.

Chapter 2:
Studio Ghost

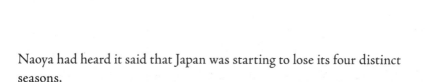

Naoya had heard it said that Japan was starting to lose its four distinct seasons.

He thought it might be true. Autumn, especially, seemed to be less clearly definable. Whether global warming or something else was to blame, he didn't know, but the summer heat lingered on, and even in October, Naoya found himself wearing summer clothes. And then, all of a sudden—even though he had barely had a need to wear any of his fall clothing—it was getting colder, and he was forced to drag all of his winter jackets and coats out of storage.

There were probably all sorts of ways this change impacted the world—such as the autumn leaves not changing color as beautifully, or the fall clothing market suffering—but this year, at least, there was only one effect it had on Naoya.

"...*Achoo!*"

"Hey, Fukamachi. You sick?"

It was the first Monday in November.

Naoya's third period course, Introduction to Modern Japanese History, had just finished. But right as he was about to stand up, Naoya let out a violent sneeze, and a nearby brown-haired student called out to him.

Youichi Nanba. He was a fellow Literature Department first-year, and in the same language class as Naoya. He was friendly, always starting conversations with Naoya whenever they crossed paths.

Sniffling, Naoya adjusted his slightly misaligned glasses.

"Ugh… I messed up a little. I couldn't be bothered to get out my blankets last night, so I slept with just a thin sheet, but it ended up being cold."

"For real? Do you need a tissue?"

"It's okay, I have some…"

Taking out a pocket pack of tissues he had been given in front of the train station, Naoya blew his nose.

"You might as well take these anyway," Nanba said, pressing three more packs of tissues into Naoya's hands. They were all kinds Naoya had seen before being distributed outside of the station.

"Ah… I got these ones, too. The same ads. Contact lenses, pachinko, a real estate agent…"

"Yeah. For college students living on our own, roadside tissues are a fundamental handout."

"You're right. Because we don't have to buy boxes of tissues as much."

Naoya left class with Nanba and started walking around campus. Until just a few days prior, he had been fine not wearing a jacket during the day, but now it was so cold it almost felt like winter. Naoya did up the front of the navy-blue duffle coat he had owned since high school. He had pulled it out of storage in a rush that very morning.

Nanba was wearing a leather jacket that looked like it was from a second-hand store. Like Naoya's, his shoulders were shrugged up against the icy wind. Perhaps, Naoya thought, it was time to take his scarf out of storage as well.

"Oh, right. Fukamachi, what are you doing for SeiwaFest? Or I guess I should ask, you're coming to SeiwaFest, right?"

"SeiwaFest…?"

"The school festival. Come on, it's next weekend."

"Right…"

Naoya nodded. He felt a little empty-headed, maybe because his nose was so stuffed up.

Seiwa University's school festival, SeiwaFest, was a big event spanning three days that was held every year around this time. All the various student organizations and clubs and such set up food stalls or put
on elaborate performances in the courtyard. There were also celebrity
guest appearances and concerts, and the number of attendees recorded
every year was quite high. That's what Naoya had heard anyway—it
basically didn't concern him, since he wasn't a part of any clubs or student groups. All he knew was that there were no classes during the festival, so he didn't have to go to school for those few days.

"I'll be running a crepe stand with my club, so make sure you come get
one. Then go vote for us in the Courtyard Food Contest, okay? I guess
we came in third last year, so we're all fired up to get first this time."

"Crepes...? What club are you in again, Nanba?"

"Tennis."

"...What do crepes and tennis have to do with each other?"

"Don't worry about that. For whatever reason, the tennis club does
a crepe stand every year, apparently. A lot of the sports clubs have food
stands. I've heard there's a ton of pretty good ones, and if you win first
place in the contest, you get a cash prize."

"I see, so all this ruckus that's been going on is because of the festival?"

Naoya looked around. All over campus, students could be seen craft-
ing things out of plywood and cardboard. They were probably making
signs and decorations for their stalls.

"I went to SeiwaFest once when I was in high school, and man, the difference in scale between a college festival and a high school one is massive.
There were international students with food stalls for their home country's
cuisine, the pro wrestling society had set up a ring and was holding matches
with people who just walked up and decided to try it, the Noh club put on a
performance, and right after that they had celebs doing a panel. It made me
wish I was old enough to go to college right then and there..."

"And now that you are a college student, you're going to be rolling up
your sleeves and selling crepes at the crepe stand, huh?"

"...Well, I have to, don't I? Clubs work on seniority, so the first-years have to pick up a lot of shifts... We cover shifts for the upperclass-men, too... I'll be cooking and handing out fliers and restocking ingredients..."

"That's rough. Well, I don't mind coming to buy one if there's a savory option."

"You don't like sweets, Fukamachi? Got it! I'll make you our club's secret recipe—a walleye *okonomiyaki* crepe with extra seaweed, so make sure you come!"

"How on earth is that a crepe... *Achoo!*"

Naoya turned to the side to sneeze, while Nanba asked concernedly if he was all right.

"Fukamachi, you definitely have a cold. Why don't you go home and sleep? Do you have classes after this?"

"...I have a free period, and then Western Art History I."

"Skip it, it's not compulsory."

"But it's a pretty interesting subject..."

"Geez, you're studious. I have a class now, so I gotta go, but don't push yourself too hard!"

Nanba shoved another package of tissues into Naoya's hand, then turned and headed inside the nearest school building. *Why did he have so many tissues on him?* Naoya wondered, but he stashed the pack inside his bag, grateful to have it.

Another gust of wind blew through, making him shiver. He decided to kill time reading in the well-heated library until his next class.

But as soon as books came to mind, Naoya remembered something else.

He had been thinking of going to Takatsuki's office today to return a book.

Takatsuki had several books he himself had authored sitting on the shelves in his office. One of them overlapped nicely with the topics they were currently discussing in Folklore Studies II, so Naoya had bor-rowed it as a reference. It contained more terminology than Takatsuki typically used in his lectures, but it had still been accessible to a layman, and Naoya had just finished reading it the night before.

The book was hardcover and added a moderate amount of weight to his bag, so Naoya decided to return it first. He changed course from the library, heading toward the staff offices building.

As he walked along the path that hugged the school building, he saw what he now knew to be students preparing for SeiwaFest. Some painted signs, and others unfurled lengths of cloth that looked like they were going to be made into banners. The group hammering away at big, thick planks of wood was probably the drama club's prop department. Everyone looked like they were in a hurry, but they also seemed to be having fun.

"Hey, is it really okay for me to paint this lantern? It's not someone's personal property, is it?"

"Ah, it's fine! One of the upperclassmen gave it to us. She said she bought it on a whim during a school trip, but it's just been taking up space at home, so we might as well use it to decorate our food stall."

"Gotcha! What color should we use? Red, since it's a paper lantern? Or maybe something like light blue would look cute?"

Several girls stood talking around a small, round paper lantern that had the name of a city printed on it.

Naoya averted his eyes from the lantern instinctively. He pushed up his glasses and looked down. He took his earphones out of his bag and put them in his ears, shoving the world just a little bit further away.

He wasn't suited for things like this.

Doing things in groups, being in noisy, excited crowds.

The atmosphere settling over campus at that moment made Naoya somewhat uncomfortable. It reminded him of the periods leading up to middle- and high-school cultural festivals. When it came to events where the main purpose was for everyone to work together as a team, Naoya was hopeless.

Working together with everyone was, after all, about being on good terms with everybody in the group. You put in the effort to accomplish something together, made some shared memories, and grew closer as people.

But that was entirely at odds with the self-imposed rules Naoya lived his life by.

He had drawn a line—a line between himself and the rest of the world.

He didn't get too involved with anyone. He didn't get closer to others more than was necessary.

Because if he did get close to someone, Naoya would inevitably know when they told a lie.

People didn't like to be caught lying. They didn't expect their falsehoods to be exposed so casually, and they got uncomfortable when someone pointed out what they had done.

And even more importantly, most people couldn't help but be creeped out by Naoya's ability to detect lies just by listening to people talk.

So, with those circumstances in mind, if someone like Naoya wanted to live peacefully in the world, some rules were necessary.

Naoya was careful to be as unassuming as possible, so that his power wouldn't be found out.

He would talk to anyone who talked to him, and he was friendly with people like Nanba for a short time. But he didn't hang out with others a lot. Naoya conducted himself well so he wouldn't be isolated or ostracized, but he made sure not to let anyone become more than an acquaintance.

He drew that invisible line around himself so that even if he had to participate in things now and then, he wouldn't get more involved than was required, and he could successfully keep his distance from others.

That way, even if someone told a lie, he wouldn't get hurt every single time.

Naoya had decided on his rules upon entering middle school. Even though those around him got fed up and called him cold-hearted, he had no other means of protecting himself.

And so, whenever there was a big event at school, Naoya always got the urge to run and hide.

Field day. The cultural festival. The more enthusiastically his classmates united, the more Naoya thought of himself as a fundamentally different creature, the more he felt like all he did was stick out like a sore thumb. He would even start to worry—*is it okay for me to be here?*

Or—*maybe I really am something different.*

That feeling... It never went away.

Takatsuki had told him once, citing a story from the *Kojiki*, that going to another community and eating its food meant becoming part of that community.

One summer night when he was ten, Naoya had been forced to eat a lollipop at a festival where the people who gathered there all hid their faces behind masks. His ears had been like this since that night. Takatsuki had speculated that it might have been a festival for the dead, and Naoya agreed. His deceased grandfather had been there, after all.

The underworld. The afterlife. Whatever you wanted to call it, wherever that festival had been, it had seemed so otherworldly.

If that was the case, then Naoya, who had been made to consume some of their food in their world, probably already belonged to that realm.

The price he had paid that night—being "lonely..." Wasn't that what it meant?

As he walked, Naoya looked down at his own hands.

According to the story in the *Kojiki*, because Izanami ate food in the underworld, she could never return to the world of the living. But here Naoya was. He had returned to and was living in this world. Blood flowed as it should through his hands, his fingers, his body. He looked like a living person. Other than his ears, he was no different than other human beings.

In the end, that was it. Just his ears.

Naoya's ears alone separated him from the world of the living.

He reached up to touch them; his earphones were still in place.

If it was only his ears—wouldn't it be better if he just destroyed them?

Could he become someone who belonged with other people?

"...Achoo."

Sneezing again, Naoya snapped out of his daze.

He felt like his thoughts had strayed into bad territory. Maybe he really was ill. He needed to go home and sleep as soon as his classes were over.

Escaping from the cold, Naoya went into the faculty building and headed for the third floor.

When he got to Takatsuki's office, he took his earphones out and knocked on the door.

Multiple female voices answered—"Yes?" "Come in!"—catching Naoya off guard.

For a moment he thought he was at the wrong room, but Takatsuki's name was on the door. The voices probably belonged to other professors, or possibly graduate students.

After a moment's hesitation, Naoya finally opened the door.

"Um, excuse me…"

Speaking in a low voice, Naoya entered the room and looked around. Takatsuki wasn't there. Instead, there were two female students sitting in folding chairs at the big table in the center of the office.

He recognized one of them. Ruiko Ubukata—a first-year doctoral student and one of Takatsuki's advisees. She was quite pretty, with her long, silky black hair flowing down her back and her red-framed glasses. Her appearance was composed now, but sometimes she slept on the floor of the office in a messy, disheveled heap.

Naoya hadn't seen the other girl before. She had a light complexion and her hair pulled into a neat bun on top of her head. Her simple, charming features somehow resembled those of the handcrafted folk-art dolls sold at souvenir shops.

Ruiko flapped her hand at Naoya, beckoning him over.

"Ah, Fukamachi, long time no see! How have you been?"

"Fine, I guess… You seem to be doing well, Miss Ruiko."

Naoya gave a small nod of his head in Ruiko's direction, and the girl sitting next to her stared at him with big, round eyes.

Then she turned to Ruiko and said, "Ruiko! Don't tell me this is 'Dog Boy'?!"

"Yeah, isn't he cute?"

"Wow, he really is! This is my first time seeing him. So *you're* Dog Boy! Wow, it's nice to meet you!"

The girl seemed happy to meet Naoya, for some reason. But wait—
what the hell was she calling him?

Seeing Naoya's bewilderment, Ruiko laughed and explained.

"Ah, sorry, sorry! It's because of the personal mug you brought here. It's
got a dog on it, right? So the graduate students who haven't met you were
like, 'There's been a new mug with a cute picture on the rack recently,'
'Let's call him Dog Boy for now.' They decided to just go ahead and give
their mysterious junior a nickname. We don't mean any offense, really!"

"...Well, I mean, it's fine, I guess..."

"Speaking of, before you brought your own cup, they were like, 'The
Great Buddha guest mug is getting a lot of use lately,' 'Let's call the new
guest Great Buddha,' and they were referring to you as 'Buddha Boy.'"

"...I'm really glad I brought my own mug in, then."

For some reason, the cup reserved for guests in Takatsuki's office was
one with a multicolored picture of the Great Buddha on its entire surface. Until recently, Naoya had been using it, because he had no other
option.

The girl with the bun spoke up again.

"I'm Yui Machimura! I'm a second-year in the master's program! You
can call me Yui!"

Yui smiled so brightly her eyes crinkled up a bit. Like that, she really
did look like a folk doll. Naoya felt the strange urge to display her on a
shelf.

"If you're looking for Professor Akira," Ruiko said, standing, "he got
called to the registrar's office for a bit. He shouldn't be gone long, so why
don't you have a seat here and wait? I'll make you some coffee."

"Oh, no, I don't need to talk to Professor Takatsuki or anything. I just
came to return a book."

"Oh, really? Do you have a lecture after this?"

"I have a free period, and then one more class after that."

Naoya replaced the book in its spot on the bookcase. Ruiko chuckled
a bit at his reply and took his mug down from the rack.

"Then you might as well spend your free period here. Come on, sit, sit."

Overpowered by Ruiko's smile, Naoya took a seat in one of the folding chairs.

Yui took a number of snacks out of a plastic college co-op bag that was next to her.

"Here, eat whatever you'd like! Juniors are allowed to mooch off their upperclassmen, you know!"

"Right, thank you very much..."

With her urging him so enthusiastically, Naoya pulled an individual-sized bag of peanuts and rice crackers toward himself for the time being. As soon as he did, Yui started piling other sweets up in front of him as if telling him not to be shy. Not that he could eat all those snacks even if they were right there.

Naoya realized this was his first time visiting Takatsuki's office at this time of day. The reason he had yet to meet any graduate students besides Ruiko was probably a simple matter of timing. That's why he hadn't known about the "Dog Boy" nickname.

Just then, the office door opened, and Takatsuki walked in.

"I'm back— Oh, Fukamachi is here. At this hour? That's rare. Is everything all right?"

"Ah, I just came to return your book... I mean, that's what I had planned on, at least."

"Are you okay? You look like you're on the verge of running away from your doting older sisters."

Noticing Naoya's discomfort, Takatsuki smiled wryly.

"Miss Ruiko, Miss Yui, you shouldn't tease Fukamachi too much. He's not even affiliated with our seminar yet, you know. Also, Fukamachi doesn't eat sweets."

"Whaaat? But you're going to end up in Professor Akira's seminar anyway, right?"

Hearing about his aversion to sweets, Yui withdrew the chocolate truffles she had been holding out and replaced them with veggie crackers instead. It seemed the only thing in that co-op bag was snack food.

"No, I haven't decided yet..."

Naoya declined the crackers as he answered, and Yui blinked at him in surprise.

"Huh? But you brought your own personal mug here!"

"...That's because I'm here often for part-time work."

"But since you're helping Professor Akira, that must mean you're into folklore! Come on, you should join his seminar! It's fun!"

Undergraduate students chose their majors in their second year and joined research seminars in their fourth. Naoya, who had chosen the Literature Department—not because he particularly wanted to study it, but because he thought it would be the best fit—had yet to decide on a major. Although, of all the courses he had taken so far, Takatsuki's was definitely the one he found most interesting.

Watching Yui shove more snacks at Naoya and pester him to join the seminar, Takatsuki grinned again.

"Sorry, Fukamachi. Most of my advisees are girls, and it's like they're all starving to fuss over younger guys."

"Why would they be starving for tha... *Achoo!*"

Naoya sneezed again.

Yui promptly took out a pocket pack of tissues and handed it to Naoya. It was one of the ones left at the entrance of the college co-op, containing a leaflet for a local certification school.

"Dog Boy, do you have a cold? Take these. Use them, okay?"

"...Thank you... But please stop calling me 'Dog Boy'..."

Naoya wondered how many tissues he was going to be given that day, but he decided he might as well accept what he was offered. He was grateful, since he was going through tissues quite quickly at the moment.

Ruiko looked over her shoulder at Takatsuki while she prepared Naoya's coffee.

"Professor Akira, do you want some cocoa? I'll make it for you."

"Thank you, Miss Ruiko. Some marshmallows would be lovely, too!"

"Of course, gotcha! Seriously, how can he drink stuff like this and still look like that...?"

Muttering to herself, Ruiko grabbed the bag of Van Houten cocoa.

Yui turned her attention to the document in Takatsuki's hand.

"Oh? Professor Akira, is that a flier for SeiwaFest?"

"Ah, yep. The official design hasn't been finalized yet, but the registrar's office gave it to me to review. Apparently, it's been decided all of a sudden that I'm going to participate in a panel during the festival."

"Whoa, for real?"

Taking the seat across from Naoya, Takatsuki placed the flier on the table.

There was an event schedule printed on it. There were times and places listed for the live panel and radio recordings the celebrity guests would be attending.

"This is the one I'll be in."

Takatsuki pointed to an event that was scheduled to take place in the afternoon on the second day of the festival, at a special stage set up in the courtyard. The name of the event was "A Panel with Popular Actress and Seiwa Alumna, Sarasa Fujitani." Sarasa Fujitani appeared in TV dramas and movies a lot. She was beautiful, with striking, slightly upturned eyes, and although she hadn't been cast as lead actress very much recently, her roles had still been quite significant.

Eyes alight, Yui leaned over the table.

"Wow, Sarasa Fujitani! I like her a lot. You get to see her up close, Professor, I'm so jealous. But wait—don't panels like this usually get a broadcaster or a member of the steering committee to be the moderator? Why you?"

"Someone else is moderating. I'm there to be Miss Fujitani's guest. I was told her office called out of the blue yesterday. I guess she saw the appearance I made on television before and asked for me. We're close in age, as well."

"Huh, I thought she was still in her twenties... Oh, you're right. It says here she's thirty-one. Whoa, and she made her debut when she was still attending Seiwa."

Having pulled up Sarasa Fujitani's Wikipedia page on her phone, Yui announced those facts about her to the room.

Ruiko returned to the table, coffee and cocoa in hand, and peered at Yui's phone from beside her.

"Ah, yeah, that's right. She auditioned alongside five thousand other people and was suddenly picked for the lead role. It was that movie *What Sleeps in the Forest*. I liked that one."

"Oh, I saw that movie, too! Didn't she have a non-speaking role?"

"Yep! She was amazing, acting just through her body language with no lines. She hasn't been as lucky with roles lately, though... Also. She's a bit of a character these days, isn't she?"

Ruiko grinned, but Yui just blinked at her, confused.

"Huh? Did she say or do something weird?"

"Well, I mean, I guess I wouldn't go that far, but... You didn't hear? She was a guest on a variety show a little while ago and out of nowhere she said, 'I've got ESP,' and everyone else made fun of her. Since then, every time she's on a variety show, it's like they always end up talking about that, and now she's being called the 'Psychic Actress' or something. Her asking for Professor Akira—isn't it because he studies ghost stories and stuff?"

"Well, who knows? It seems all her office communicated to us was that Miss Fujitani had requested me."

Takatsuki took his mug of cocoa from Ruiko.

"Anyway, there's nothing wrong with an actress having an interest in ghosts, and if she's fine with me being her guest, I'm happy to do it. I really liked her debut film, too... Hm? What's wrong, Fukamachi? Do you not like Sarasa Fujitani?"

Takatsuki was looking at Naoya with his head cocked to the side. He seemed to have noticed Naoya's slight frown. As ever, he was very observant.

Looking down at the coffee cup he was holding, Naoya answered.

"I don't dislike her or anything. I just find the ESP thing a little odd."

"Did you see that program as well?"

"No, I didn't... I don't like variety shows."

He couldn't handle programs where groups of entertainers bantered noisily back and forth. Most of the time on those shows was spent exaggerating and making up stories for laughs. They were probably just trying to make the program interesting, but still. That didn't change the fact that they were lying.

So, to Naoya, those were the types of shows he avoided. All that laughing mixed with the wildly distorted voices made him feel ill, and he usually just ended up changing the channel.

He had a feeling that Sarasa Fujitani's claim about extrasensory perception was just one of those things entertainers made up for ratings. Though he couldn't be totally certain, since he hadn't heard her voice when she said it.

"I feel like, when people say stuff like that on TV, it seems like they're lying... I mean, if she really does have ESP, would she have announced it so publicly like that?"

Naoya sipped at his bitter coffee after making that statement.

If it were him, he would definitely hide something like that. Having an ability that other people didn't have was not something Naoya would want others to know about. Just like his ears, he thought he would do whatever was necessary to keep that ability a secret.

Yui, however, seemed to feel exactly the opposite.

"You think so? If it was me, I'd probably tell people. I mean, it's kind of amazing to have a special power like ESP. I wish I had a power like that!"

"Same here," Ruiko chimed in, nodding. "If ghosts really exist, I'd like to see them at least once. I don't have the least bit of supernatural ability. I'm kind of jealous of people who can see ghosts."

"So you both think it would be nice to have a sixth sense or something?"

"Well, I don't think I would like it if I could see ghosts all the time. But don't you think it would be interesting? Ghost story research done by people who can actually see ghosts? Though I guess it would be tough to prove the 'can actually see them' part, even if you published papers on it."

Naoya's had asked the question without thinking, but Ruiko answered him with a casual smile. Since she planned on becoming a researcher like Takatsuki one day, maybe the question of ESP's existence was just one of the things she thought about.

Takatsuki laughed and shrugged his shoulders a little.

"In short, the difference is whether you consider having special powers a positive thing or a negative one. Well, all the students who end up in my seminar love scary stories. They're all the type who would want to see ghosts if they could."

"...Speaking of, you said you'd like to see them too, didn't you, Professor?"

"Yep. Because I don't have extrasensory perception or anything like that. You're in the opposite camp, right, Fukamachi?"

"I'd avoid it at all costs..."

Just then, Naoya felt a chill down his spine.

Was it a ghost? No—it couldn't be. Naoya didn't have ESP either.

"...*Achoo!* '*Choo...* Ugh, e-excuse me..."

Naoya sneezed twice in a row. He took out one of the tissues Yui gave him before and blew his nose.

"Fukamachi, are you sure you don't have a cold? Your face is a little flushed."

Takatsuki reached out his hand as if to check for fever.

Gathering up his things, Naoya stood to avoid that hand.

"Um, I don't want to get anyone else sick, so I'll go now. Thank you for the coffee."

As Naoya was about to head for the door, Takatsuki called after him.

"Don't push yourself. Go home early if you aren't feeling well. Ah—wait a moment, Fukamachi."

Naoya stopped and turned toward the professor, who had stood up and was holding something.

"Here. Take these."

He handed Naoya a packet of tissues.

At Takatsuki's side, Ruiko and Yui each handed him another.

Naoya shoved the three new packs into his already tissue-filled bag. He staggered out of Takatsuki's office, everyone's calls of "Take care of yourself" and "Go get warmed up and go to bed early" following him out the door.

*   *   *

That evening, as directed, Naoya went home and curled up in bed early.

But when he woke up the next morning, the runny nose and sneezing hadn't gone away. He felt like he had a slight fever but realized he didn't have a thermometer in his apartment. Or any kind of cold medicine, for that matter. This was the first time he had gotten sick since he moved into his own place in the spring.

Naoya's first-period class that day was his compulsory language course, so he decided to attend that at least, and made his way to school after buying a face mask at the convenience store. Voluntarily choosing to forego the rest of his Tuesday classes, he went back home and collapsed into bed. That night, when he woke up with a dry throat, he finally thought, *Ah, this might be bad.*

He felt like his fever had worsened, and he had horrible chills. Since he had gone straight home to sleep after his language class, he had forgotten to pick up a thermometer and medicine at the store.

He wasn't sneezing anymore, but Naoya was badly congested. When he tried to blow his nose, he felt a tremendous pressure in his ears. *This is really bad,* he thought again, taking a drink of water and grabbing his phone to look up the nearest clinic. He found the address of one by the train station, vowed to go there when he got up, and climbed back into bed.

Then—the next morning.

The renewed dryness in Naoya's throat woke him long before his alarm clock. When he sat up, a terrible flash of pain shot through his head. But the pain in his ears was even worse. They were both throbbing so fiercely that Naoya was sure, if he were a character in a manga, he would have sound effects in huge, bold letters floating around him to show how much his ears hurt.

What is this? he wondered, swinging his legs out of bed and standing up.

He stumbled immediately. Naoya felt totally sapped of strength, so much so that even he was surprised. His studio apartment seemed to be spinning. His entire body felt hot.

"Ugh... This isn't good... What do I do...?"

Muttering to himself, he managed to make it to the kitchen sink and drink some water. The pain in his ears was so intense that Naoya instinctively curled in on himself. He had never gotten ear pain from a cold before.

Naoya knew he should go to the doctor, but he had no confidence in his ability to leave his apartment and walk to the place by the station. The lack of energy might be due to his not having eaten much since the day before, but he didn't have an appetite, either. Still, figuring he should have something in his stomach, Naoya rummaged around the refrigerator but couldn't find anything he would be able to prepare, feeling as he did. He managed to find a tomato, rinsed it, ate it whole, then tottered back into his bed.

Staring up at the ceiling from under the covers, Naoya suddenly realized that this was what it meant to be alone.

Ever since Naoya had gained the ability to hear lies, his relationship with his parents had been strained. Nevertheless, when he had lived with his parents, they would still bring him to the doctor and take care of him when he was sick.

But Naoya didn't have anyone to look after him now.

His mother would probably come if he called, he thought. It wasn't like there was a huge distance between Yokohama and Tokyo. He couldn't bring himself to contact her, though. When he made the decision to live on his own, he also chose not to rely on his parents if he could help it.

But at a time like this, he didn't have anyone else to call.

"…So this is…how people end up…dying…without anyone noticing…"

The unfunny joke came tumbling out, unbidden. Naoya had also developed a habit of talking to himself sometimes, ever since he moved into his own place.

Well, he thought, *a cold isn't going to kill me.* It would be fine—he'd feel a little better after some more rest. Clinging to that optimistic thought, Naoya curled up under the blankets and covered his ears.

He was awoken by his phone ringing at his bedside.

A phone call. Takatsuki's name displayed on the screen.

Naoya realized he had Folklore Studies II that day. He checked the time—the lecture would just have ended. It was his first time missing the class. He stared blankly at the name on the screen. What on earth could Takatsuki be calling about?

Finally tapping the button on the screen, Naoya picked up the call.

"...Hello?"

"Ah, Fukamachi! Sorry to bother you."

Takatsuki's voice sounded the same as ever.

Naoya's ear throbbed and he held his phone a little further away.

"Fukamachi? Fukamachi—are you there? Hey, are you okay?!"

"...Sorry, I'm...not feeling well... It seems like a cold...after all..."

Knowing his voice sounded hoarse, Naoya wondered if Takatsuki would be able to hear him. He put the phone back to his ear.

"Um, so... If you're calling...about work...I won't be able to...come in...for a bit..."

"What are you talking about?! No! This isn't about work. I'm calling because I was worried!"

The voice on the other end of the line sounded a little angry, and Naoya was confused.

"You weren't in class today, but your attendance has been perfect otherwise. You didn't seem well on Monday at my office, and I was wondering how you were. Then I searched my memories of yesterday and today and didn't remember seeing you even once on campus. You have classes into the afternoon on Tuesdays, and you're usually at school by morning on Wednesdays, so I definitely should have seen you around! Then I realized you must not have come to school!"

Naoya remembered, his head fuzzy with fever, as Takatsuki spoke, *Right. This guy has an insanely good memory.*

Takatsuki's memory was abnormally good. In addition, his eyesight was excellent, and he could recall everything he saw as a clear image in his mind. He could also review his memories as he pleased far after the fact, and apparently even had the ability to zoom in on details.

What a waste, Naoya thought. *Using a superpower like that to check in on someone like me.*

"I only went in for first period on Tuesday," he told Takatsuki. "But...I went home right after... I've been sleeping a lot, but I keep getting worse... My ears...hurt..."

"Your ears? Right—you live alone, don't you? Have you been to the doctor? Are you running a fever?"

"I meant to go to the clinic...but I didn't have the energy... I didn't take my temperature. I don't...have a thermometer... I forgot to buy medicine, too..."

"It's like you're trying to parody someone who is no good at living alone." Takatsuki sighed into the phone. Naoya had thought the same thing. After a pause, Takatsuki spoke up again.

"Okay. I'll leave now. What's your address?"

"...Pardon?"

"I'm asking you to tell me where you live. I'll grab some things at a nearby drugstore and then head your way."

"Huh... You don't have to, really, I'm fine."

"You clearly aren't fine in the slightest! Fukamachi, listen to me. Do you have any idea how awful you sound right now?"

Naoya reluctantly gave up the address of his apartment building in response to being scolded. After reiterating that he would be over soon, Takatsuki hung up.

The professor seemed determined to come over, even though Naoya was sure Takatsuki didn't have that kind of free time on his hands.

He stared at the darkened phone screen, then buried his face back into his pillow.

"...I *am* fine, though..."

Whispering to himself, Naoya rolled over just as his ears throbbed viciously again. He scrunched his body up tight and squeezed his eyes shut. His head swam. He felt like there were small fires burning throughout his body.

Since when had his fever gotten this bad?

Naoya didn't get sick often, but once he fell ill, his condition tended to deteriorate pretty badly.

It was just like back then.

The summer he was ten years old.

He had been staying at his grandmother's house in Nagano. He had caught a summer cold, spiked a huge fever that lasted several days, and wasn't able to attend the festival he had been looking forward to for ages.

And then, in the middle of the night, he had heard the sound of drums.

He thought the festival must still be going on and snuck out of his grandmother's house by himself. The banging of the drums was calling him: *boom, boom, buh-boom*.

Feverish, eyes closed, Naoya remembered that night.

The scene from that night spread out vividly behind Naoya's eyelids.

A myriad of blue paper lanterns, like will-o'-the-wisps floating in the dark. A tall wooden stage erected in the middle of the square. Two to three rings of people circling the stage, all swaying as they performed the festival dance. Every one of them wearing a mask, so there was no way to know who anyone was. Foxes, cats, old men, *tengu*—the various masks hid the dancers' faces from view, because the faces of the dead should never be seen.

Ah, I better put on a mask too, quick.

It would be bad if any of the dead saw his face. They would definitely lure him away.

Naoya knew that, but the mask he was sure he had worn that night was nowhere to be found. It was a *Super Sentai* mask that his cousin had bought for him. He knew now. That mask had been his protection that night. It had prevented the strange, dead dancers from sensing his true form.

But now, Naoya had nothing to hide his face behind.

Without his realizing it, the festival dance circle had broken up.

The masked people approached Naoya, surrounding him.

A man in a monkey mask and a *yukata* silently reached for Naoya. Panicked, Naoya dodged the man's grasp, but another hand clamped down on his shoulder from behind. He turned to see a woman wearing a kimono and a horned, grinning demon mask. The thin fingers digging into his shoulder were pallid and cold and hard as steel.

Somehow shaking the hand off, Naoya scanned the crowd for the silhouette of his grandfather. The grandfather who had helped him escape from the festival that night instead of being made to pay the price. But he couldn't find his grandfather's form and fire-breathing jester mask anywhere in the advancing group. Countless hands were reaching out for Naoya now.

Inevitably, they caught him, grabbing at his body all over and knocking him to the ground. Naoya struggled. *Stop it. I'm scared.* He wanted to scream, but his voice wouldn't come out. The dead were leaning over him, on top of him, peering down at his face. Old crone masks. Dog masks. Round-faced woman masks. And behind them, an expanse of dark, deep, indigo night sky, and rows and rows of blue lanterns emitting their cold light. *Boom, boom, buh-boom.* The banging of the drums resounded in his ears. *Boom, boom, buh-boom. Boom, boom, buh-boom—*

"—Fukamachi!"

Suddenly, he heard Takatsuki's voice.

His eyes opened in surprise, and he saw the ceiling of his own apartment. He must have fallen asleep at some point. Deeply relieved, Naoya realized he must have been dreaming.

But then he heard it again—*boom, boom, buh-boom*—and flinched in alarm.

The drums. He could still hear the drums from his dream.

Wait—no.

The booming noise wasn't drumming—it was someone banging on Naoya's apartment door.

"Fukamachi! Fukamachi! Are you okay?!"

Not just someone, it was Takatsuki.

Naoya scrambled out of bed. His knees buckled immediately, and he struggled toward the door. Even though the apartment had an intercom, Takatsuki was still pounding on his door.

"Fukamachi?! Fukamachi! Fuka—"

"—Professor, you're being a nuisance to the neighbors."

Finally reaching the door, Naoya opened it to find a frantic Takatsuki standing on the other side. He was wrapped in a gray coat and blue scarf and was carrying a large drugstore bag.

Takatsuki took one look at Naoya and said, "Oh, Fukamachi, thank goodness, you're alive! You weren't answering at all, so I was about to kick down your door!"

I'd rather you didn't say something that violent while looking so relieved, Naoya thought. Takatsuki really could have kicked his door in, which was troubling. Even though the professor looked like a refined gentleman on the outside, he was surprisingly good in a fight.

"Don't exaggerate... Ow..."

"Fukamachi?!"

Clutching at his ears, Naoya sunk to the floor. Takatsuki hurried to prop him back up and put a hand to his forehead.

"I knew it, you're burning up! I bought a thermometer, so let's take your temperature right away!"

Takatsuki helped guide Naoya back into bed with an arm around his shoulders.

Bundled up beneath the futon, Naoya was handed a thermometer and obediently tucked it under his armpit. He looked up at Takatsuki hazily.

Naoya wasn't wearing his glasses, since all he had been doing was sleeping. But his eyesight wasn't really that bad anyway, and he could see the professor's face clearly.

Why does he look so worried? Naoya spoke.

"...You're not wearing a mask. I don't know if I'm contagious."

"It's all right. I made sure to buy one."

Takatsuki took a face mask out of the drugstore bag and put it on. It was meaningless if he didn't put it on before entering the apartment, though.

Suddenly, in the middle of taking off his coat, Takatsuki frowned as if he was remembering something.

"...Um, Fukamachi, I'm sorry."

"Huh...?"

"I said I would be here right away. I'm sorry I took so long. I was so worried. What would I have done if you died while waiting for me?"

"I told you not to exaggerate..."

Naoya noticed it had gotten a bit dark outside as he replied.

He glanced at the clock and saw that about an hour and a half had passed since Takatsuki's phone call. Naoya's apartment was only one train stop from the university, and the walk from the station took ten minutes. It really had taken Takatsuki a while.

"...Professor, aren't you really busy? You didn't have to go out of your way to come here... Oh! You didn't come across any birds on the way here and collapse, did you?! There are quite a few crows and pigeons in front of my train stop."

Thinking the odds of that happening were quite high, Naoya started to sit up without thinking.

Takatsuki was afraid of birds. Sometimes, when he encountered one, he would faint.

But Takatsuki pushed Naoya back into bed with his hands on his shoulders and answered in an ashamed tone.

"No, that's not it. I was late because... Well, I'm not familiar with the area..."

"...Oh."

Naoya had forgotten.

Takatsuki couldn't read maps. He always got lost when he went somewhere for the first time.

It seemed to be a negative side effect of his perfect memory. He couldn't match up the overly detailed visual information in his head with the simplified layout of the map. Walking around by himself with nothing but the address to go on, there was no way Takatsuki would have made it to Naoya's apartment without issue.

Feeling more and more helpless, Naoya buried his face in his pillow.

"...That's why I told you there was no need to come..."

"As if I had a choice."

"I mean, it's not like university professors usually trouble themselves to check in on their sick students at their homes... Why did you come here, seriously?"

Something started beeping. Takatsuki reached out and pulled the thermometer from Naoya's armpit himself. He frowned at the display.

"Thirty-eight point eight degrees Celsius. You don't seem to have a cough, so I don't think it's pneumonia. It could be the flu—but you said your ears hurt. Does my voice sound normal to you?"

"...Now that you mention it, I think my hearing is off. I don't think my right ear is picking up much...and it really, really hurts."

"I see. There's an ear, nose, and throat specialist near the university who accepts patients until seven o'clock, so let's go there."

"An ENT...? For a cold...?"

"Your cold probably turned into an ear infection. That's why your temperature is so high."

"Huh..."

Naoya had gotten ear infections as a child, but he didn't remember having such a high fever.

Takatsuki reached into the drugstore bag again, his expression serious.

"Ear infections are dangerous when you're an adult. I've dealt with them before. I got a horrible fever, I was exhausted, and when I could talk the only thing that would come out was 'my ears hurt.' Also, I'm just saying, but people *can* die from colds, you know?"

Taking out a fever-reducing patch, Takatsuki applied it to Naoya's forehead as he went on speaking.

"KenKen came to help me out when I was sick. But you don't have a KenKen, so here I am."

Takatsuki's tone sounded like he thought what he was saying was a matter of course.

Naoya touched a finger to the cooling patch. Perhaps due to the fever, the scene in front of him seemed unreal. He couldn't get used to seeing his apartment—where he was always by himself—with Takatsuki inside it. But, as if to prove that he wasn't still dreaming, the patch stuck to his burning forehead and felt cool and soothing, and Naoya turned his vacant gaze back to Takatsuki.

"…Hey, Professor. Earlier…"

"Hm? What is it?"

"Earlier…why were you knocking directly on the door? I have an intercom."

"Because no matter how many times I rang the intercom, you didn't answer."

"Oh… I was sleeping, so I must not have heard it… But still, you didn't have to bang on the door like that… For a second…I thought I was hearing drums."

"Drums?"

Takatsuki sounded puzzled.

Realizing the other man wouldn't understand if Naoya just blurted something random out like that, he explained.

"Um, I… Before you got here…I think I was dreaming…"

"I see. What kind of dream was it?"

"I dreamt about that night… About that festival…"

Takatsuki was quiet.

He knew about Naoya's past. Just by mentioning "that festival," Takatsuki would understand.

"Unlike that night, the people wearing masks came after me. There were so many of them, but none of them said a word… They were silent… All I could hear was the drums. But it turns out that drumming sound was you, at the door…"

He had been dreaming before, but this was reality.

Wanting to be sure of that, Naoya kept talking, enduring the endless throbbing in his ears.

"I was so relieved when I woke up and realized it wasn't real. Because I wasn't a child in the dream. I was me, now… I thought I had wandered into that festival again… And I thought, *oh, this time for sure, they're going to take me away*, and I was so… I was so…scared…"

That night when he was ten—he had a high fever then, too.

If that festival really was a festival for the dead, maybe the reason he had been called there that night—maybe it was because he had been close to death.

Thinking about the dream now made so much fear well up in Naoya's chest that his hands shook. It had felt so strangely real. He could clearly remember the feeling of a hand digging into his shoulder.

Maybe the dead were still waiting for him under that dark sky. Perhaps they were always swaying, dancing, calling out to him. Telling Naoya they wouldn't let him escape next time.

"I see. That really is a frightening dream," Takatsuki said. "But you're all right. It was just a dream. I have nightmares, too, sometimes."

"You do…?"

"Yeah. Although they might be a bit different from yours, since yours are based on things you actually witnessed. Mine are all from my imagination— they really are just dreams."

"…Is it okay if I ask what you dream about?"

Naoya was still gazing up at Takatsuki, his mind fuzzy.

With a wryness that showed only in his eyes, Takatsuki answered, unreserved.

"Let's see. There are a few things—I dream about my back being torn up quite a lot."

"Your back…?"

"Yep. It doesn't hurt since it happens in the dream. My skin splits open, and there's blood and flesh everywhere… And then there's this great cracking, breaking sound, and black wings emerge from the gashes on my back."

Naoya had heard that Takatsuki had some old scars on his back.

When the professor was a child, he had been spirited away.

After a month-long disappearance, he was found lying in the street. Though he had no life-threatening injuries, the skin spanning from both of his shoulder blades to his hips had been torn away.

The marks made it look like Takatsuki had had wings ripped from his back, and since the place he was discovered was close to Kurama in

Kyoto, his mother became convinced that he had been carried off by *tengu*.

She said they had kidnapped him, and just as Takatsuki was on the verge of becoming a *tengu* himself, they cut his wings off and returned him to civilization.

The way his eyes changed color, his unusually good memory—those things started after his disappearance.

"I'm—I'm crouching in a pool of my own blood. I shouldn't really be able to see what's happening on my own back, but it's a dream, you know? And also, there's a big, huge, wing-shaped shadow falling over me, so I can tell. I don't know what to do. I think, oh, I really have become something inhuman, I won't be able to be with everyone anymore... I get sad, and so scared."

Takatsuki laughs, saying how troublesome it is to be having nightmares as a man in his mid-thirties.

He was a prisoner of his own past—just like Naoya.

But unlike Naoya, Takatsuki didn't remember the events of his own past. Perhaps he had no choice but to experience it through the various nightmares his imagination concocted.

"...What do you do...when you have a dream like that?"

"Well, first I take a shower to clear my head. Then I think about what kind of delicious things I'm going to eat that day."

"...So simple."

Takatsuki replied, "If you can eat something you think is delicious, it's a blessing, you know?"

He's so resilient, Naoya thought.

He had lived longer than Naoya—was it because he was an adult?

Or was it because Takatsuki had had no choice but to be strong?

"Oh, when you're feeling better, let's go out to eat. We can get anything you'd like. Come to think of it, I haven't asked what your favorite food is, have I? What do you like to eat, Fukamachi?"

Takatsuki's voice was soft and pleasant.

Naoya answered straightforwardly.

"…Edosei's…barbecue pork buns…"

"Edosei?"

"It's a meat bun shop in Chinatown. Their buns have more flavor than regular ones, and they're filled with big pieces of barbecue pork… The dough is different than the ones you get at convenience stores, too. It's so tasty…"

"Chinatown? Ah, right, you're from Yokohama. Good, then let's go together next time. But before that…Fukamachi, are you hungry? You probably haven't eaten much, right? If you think you could get something down before going to the doctor, it would be better to have some food in your stomach."

"Yeah… My appetite came back a little…from talking about pork buns… I think I could have something small…"

"Got it. Then I'm going to use your kitchen. I bought ready-made porridge and soup, but since I'm here, I might as well make you some porridge myself. After you eat some, even if it's only a little, we'll go to the doctor."

Takatsuki started walking away from the bed.

Naoya watched him.

"Professor."

"Hm?"

"…Um…I'm sorry. For causing you trouble."

Naoya, half shrouded in blankets, murmured those words, and Takatsuki laughed.

"You know, Fukamachi, you should learn to rely on others a little more."

He returned to Naoya's bedside just to gently pat Naoya's head with one of his large hands.

"No one actually survives on their own. It's okay to ask for help when you need it. Don't forget that—understood?"

"…"

Takatsuki sounded like he was admonishing a small child. Naoya instinctively withdrew further into the blankets, away from that hand. He could tell Takatsuki was smiling on the other side.

Even though Takatsuki was usually so childish, even though he had been just like a little lost boy himself only a short while ago, he sometimes treated Naoya like he was a kid.

For some reason, that annoyed him, and Naoya burrowed deeper under the covers.

The floorboards creaked, signaling that Takatsuki was walking away from the bed again. Peeking out from under the blanket oh-so-secretly, Naoya saw the professor standing in the kitchen in front of the open refrigerator. He grabbed an egg, found some cooked, frozen rice in the freezer, and nodded.

For some reason, Naoya kept watching Takatsuki as he filled a small pot with water and put it on to boil.

Other than the movers, Takatsuki was the first person Naoya had had in his apartment.

It's okay to ask for help when you need it, Takatsuki had said.

Even though Naoya had thought no one else would worry about him anymore.

…Even though he had thought he was alone.

Naoya could hear the soft bubbling of boiling water and smell the scent of hot food. Someone else was making food for him. That fact made him oddly happy—he felt so taken care of that he wanted to cry. Maybe this was a dream after all.

Takatsuki glanced over his shoulder. Surprise colored his face.

"Fukamachi…? Do your ears hurt that much?"

It was only then that Naoya realized he was actually crying, and he quickly hid back under the blankets… He wished he was dreaming.

Naoya remembered being told that Takatsuki didn't cook much, but the porridge he made actually tasted just fine.

Even so, he wasn't able to eat much of it. Takatsuki told him the leftovers would be fine to reheat later and quickly shepherded Naoya into a taxi that took them to the clinic.

The influenza test came back negative. After that, Naoya was called into the examination room and greeted by a wizened old doctor with white hair. He diagnosed Naoya with an infection in both ears and said, "I'm just going to make a small incision in your ear drums." There was no use arguing over it, so Naoya found himself urged into the examination chair, and in no time at all, both of his ears had been incised and stuffed with cotton. He was told that pus would drain from his ears for a while, and he needed to change the gauze frequently. He was surprised to learn that having holes in his eardrums did not mean he was completely unable to hear.

Once Takatsuki accompanied him back home, Naoya took his prescribed medication and went to sleep.

He woke up in the night, and Takatsuki was gone. A note, written in the professor's tidy handwriting, had been left by his bed. It read: "I'll come back tomorrow to check on you. I'm leaving the key in the mailbox." There were also some sports drinks and a drinking glass.

In the end, it took about three more days for Naoya's fever to subside entirely. Takatsuki came to check on him the first two days, but on the third, Naoya told him not to. No matter how much Takatsuki said he should rely on others, it wouldn't do to get too dependent.

By the start of the next week, he felt well enough to go to school. At his one-week follow-up appointment, the doctor confirmed that he was recovering well and simply said, "Your eardrums won't close up completely for a little while longer, so be careful not to get water in your ears."

Then, starting that Friday, it was SeiwaFest.

Naoya spent the first day of the festival relaxing in his apartment, grateful not to have classes.

But the next morning, he remembered his promise to go buy a crepe from Nanba's club's stall. He was pretty sure Nanba had mentioned his shift being on the afternoon of the second day.

Naoya had promised, so he had no choice but to go. He wrapped a wool scarf over the top of his duffle coat and headed toward the university on still somewhat unsteady legs.

When he made it to campus, he was overwhelmed at the sheer number of people there.

Judging from all the high school uniforms and the people who looked like working adults, there were quite a lot of outside attendees. Music was blaring, and a constant stream of announcements informed the crowd of the event schedule. Stalls were lined up from the school gate to the courtyard, and a tremendous number of students stood by them trying to entice customers their way.

"How about some pad thai? Currently offering super-sized portions! Just say 'mega meal' when you order!"

"Come to our maid and butler café in building two, room 201! We've swapped the roles for today only, so our hunky maids and beautiful lady-butlers are waiting for you! Welcome home, master!"

"We've got super-spicy brothless dandan noodles made by Chinese exchange students here! They're absolutely delicious! If you buy them now, you get a free palm reading while you eat! Would you like a palm reading, sir? You're looking awfully unlucky!"

Leaflets were being handed to him from all sides; hawkers buffeted him from every direction. *So this is a college festival*, Naoya thought. Just as Nanba had said, the scale was unlike any school festival he had experienced before.

Naoya put his hands over his ears. He hadn't put any gauze in them because they weren't draining fluid anymore, but he still couldn't hear well. Everything sounded muffled.

The doctor had told him not to use earphones for the time being, so he had left his faithful MP3 player at home. But he didn't feel comfortable walking around a place this crowded with his head between his hands.

Stepping off the path to avoid the thrum of people, Naoya opened up the festival pamphlet he had received at the gate, searching for Nanba's stall. There seemed to be various shops and programs happening inside the school buildings as well, but Naoya's current plan was to eat a crepe and go straight home. He turned the page of the pamphlet.

Then—

"Hey."

A deep voice called out to him just as a big hand landed with a *thwap* on top of his head.

Startled, Naoya swung around to see a massive, frightening-looking man standing there.

He had distinct, straight eyebrows, piercing almond-shaped eyes, a prominent nose, and dignified features, on the whole. The dignity was overpowered, though, by the lasting impression his fierce gaze made. The man was well-built in addition to being even taller than Takatsuki, so that Naoya—who was not quite five foot eight—had to look up at him. Dressed in a lot of black and looking like he did, it was hard not to assume his day job was something unsavory. But this man was a detective with the Tokyo Metropolitan Police Department.

Kenji Sasakura—a childhood friend of Takatsuki's who Naoya had met a handful of times. The person Takatsuki often referred to as "KenKen."

"What are you doing here?"

"...Would you mind not asking me like you're conducting an interrogation? What's wrong with going to my own college's festival? I should be the one asking you that, Mr. Sasakura. Are you off duty?"

"Yeah. The food at this festival is great. And Akira is doing that panel with Sarasa Fujitani today."

"Huh. Are you a fan of hers, perhaps?"

"Not really. I've just watched a few of her movies before."

Sasakura was staring at Naoya with a face that was scary in the best of times.

"So, Fukamachi, why do you look so haggard?"

"Well, just last week, I got a cold that turned into an ear infection."

"Fragile, aren't you? How much weight did you lose?"

"I don't have a scale at home, so I'm not sure, but...I had to tighten my belt by a couple notches, so..."

"You're too skinny, you idiot. You need to eat something. My treat."

"...It's fine, you don't have to force me..."

Grabbing Naoya's arm in a vise-grip, Sasakura headed for the rows of food stalls. From an outsider's perspective, it probably looked like Naoya was being abducted. Several people turned to look at them in concern, but Sasakura dragged him along, completely unbothered.

And—there was Nanba, standing behind a stall just a short distance away. Nanba looked up and saw Naoya.

"Hey, Fukamachi! You came after all...! Uh, wait, hold on, are you being kidnapped right now? Who's this old— Er. Uh, this older guy?"

"An acquaintance."

Sasakura, hand still around Naoya's arm, answered Nanba's stiff question in a threatening tone.

Nanba looked up at Sasakura's fierce expression, swallowed hard, then turned his attention to Naoya. His eyes were searching for confirmation that nothing fishy was going on, so Naoya waved a hand to indicate everything was fine. He didn't blame Nanba for the misconception. That was just how intimidating Sasakura looked, though he wasn't at all a bad person at heart. He was actually quite caring and kind.

Nanba looked between the other two men a bit more, then seemed to decide there was nothing he needed to worry about, in any case. His face was still a little stiff, but he plastered on his best customer service smile.

"G-gotcha! How nice of you to show your acquaintance around the festival, Fukamachi! Anyway, you should have one of our crepes! I'll take care of you, whaddya say?"

"...Oh, yeah. That's why I'm here."

"No kidding! Then just wait here, we'll have it right out for you! You're having the one I mentioned before, right? The *yakisoba*-stuffed walleye *okonomiyaki* crepe with extra seaweed? And, um, for you Mr. Scary Guy?"

"You didn't have to call me that... Fine, I'll have this one."

"One chocolate banana special, coming up! Thank you for your business!"

"Thank you for your business!"

The other club members at the stall called out cheerfully with Nanba in unison as he took their order. It was as if they were running an *izakaya* rather than a crepe stand.

What Naoya received was an even more leveled-up crepe than he had originally been told about. It was, to put it another way, a

Hiroshima-style *okonomiyaki* with walleye in it, wrapped into a cone shape like a crepe. Naoya left the crepe stand, wondering if such a thing could really be called a crepe, while Nanba waved him off.

"Your friend is pretty spirited."

Sasakura pushed his way through the crowd with his huge frame as he spoke. The crepe he was holding was pretty amazing in its own right. It was really more of a parfait. Stuffed with custard and an entire banana, the crepe was topped with whipped cream, vanilla ice cream, and sliced banana pieces sprinkled over it like flower petals. The whole thing had been drizzled with chocolate sauce.

Naoya watched as Sasakura skillfully plucked a banana slice off the crepe with his mouth mid-stride.

"You like that kind of stuff, too, Mr. Sasakura? I thought Professor Takatsuki was the only one with that level of sweet tooth."

"If you hang around Akira, you develop a taste for sweets. Every year, that club's stall has a ridiculously good deal, stuffing this much into a crepe for that price. It's nothing to sneeze at."

"Wow, you know even more about the festival than I do..."

Naoya took a bite of his own crepe. It was about ninety percent *okonomiyaki*, but the faint sweetness from the surrounding crepe went surprisingly well with the sauce and the seaweed. He had thought it would be an acquired taste, but it really wasn't bad.

"Mr. Sasakura, when you fill out the ballot for the food contest in your pamphlet, please vote for the crepe stand. It seems they're really eager to win this year."

"Huh? You shouldn't just vote for your friend. It's supposed to be fair."

"I mean, it's not that serious..."

Right then, there was a sudden eruption of activity at the special events stage.

Music started blaring from the speakers and the massive screen on the stage lit up. The crowd in the courtyard all turned to look in that direction. It seemed that a panel was starting.

A moment later, a woman holding a microphone walked onstage. She looked familiar; she was probably a TV announcer of some sort. She started speaking with a bright smile.

"Thank you for waiting, everyone! It's time for Sarasa Fujitani's panel! Please put your hands together for Seiwa University's very own star, Sarasa Fujitani!"

The music swelled.

The person who appeared next on stage wasn't Sarasa Fujitani—it was Takatsuki. As always, he was dressed in an elegant suit and smiled as he held his hand out toward the wing of the stage.

A delicate hand reached out to take Takatsuki's.

Sarasa Fujitani stepped out to a sudden cheer from the crowd.

She was wearing a black and white houndstooth coat that fit so snugly it was practically a minidress, and black tights that made her legs look slender and shapely. She had a small, high waist, long black hair that flowed down her back, and a surprisingly narrow head. She was, in a word, doll-like. She was even prettier than she appeared on television, with a flashiness that caught the eye, and she didn't look at all like she was in her thirties.

Takatsuki escorted Sarasa—who smiled bashfully and waved at the audience—across the stage toward her chair with an easy gait. Even walking arm in arm with a celebrity, the professor managed not to be outshone. A high school girl standing near Naoya whispered, "Who is that guy? An actor?" Naoya understood how she felt.

As Takatsuki and Sarasa took their seats, the announcer started talking again.

"Now then, allow me to make the formal introductions. This is Sarasa Fujitani, an actress. And Ms. Fujitani's lovely escort, Associate Professor of Historical Literature at Seiwa University, Akira Takatsuki. Pleasure to have you both here! Professor Takatsuki—how are you feeling? What's your impression of Ms. Fujitani, seeing her from up close? You looked totally composed leading her across the stage just now, but you just met for the first time today, right?"

"Yes, that's right."

Takatsuki took the microphone in hand to answer the announcer's question.

"Well, an actress is on an entirely different level than a normal person, don't you think?"

"A different level? And by that you mean...?"

"Her looks and her presence, you see. The genuine article is much more beautiful than what you see on TV and in movies. Don't you agree, everyone?"

Takatsuki addressed the people packed into the courtyard.

Sarasa grabbed the mic for herself with an "Oh, you!"

She spoke in a slightly idiosyncratic alto.

"You're one to talk, Professor, with your showbiz face and style! Really, what are you doing teaching at a university? Should I introduce you to an agency?"

"The thing is, I'm better suited to researching things like *Kokkuri-san* and the slit-mouthed woman than delivering lines in front of a camera."

Takatsuki smiled brightly as the audience burst into laughter. He didn't look nervous in the slightest, probably because he was used to lecturing into a microphone in front large groups of students.

As the announcer started to list off Sarasa's filmography and representative works, Naoya thought about when he should leave. He planned to stay at least until he was done eating his crepe, but at some point, Sarasa was probably going to start talking about ESP and whatnot. She was bound to start lying, and hearing a warped voice in his current condition would be rough.

But the crepe Nanba made specially for him was no joke. Sarasa's introduction was finished before Naoya had polished off the crepe, and the panel began in earnest.

"So, regarding today's panel, Ms. Fujitani requested Professor Takatsuki as her guest, is that right? Ms. Fujitani, why did you choose Professor Takatsuki?"

"Because he's so cool and handsome, of course!" Sarasa answered, and the crowd laughed again.

"That's part of it, but also, I have a personal interest in Professor Takatsuki's research. You specialize in urban legends and ghost stories, right?"

"Yes, that's exactly right!"

Takatsuki nodded, his golden retriever smile coming to the fore.

Sarasa leaned in toward Takatsuki a little.

"I'm dying to know, Professor, do you think ghosts really exist? Either your professional opinion as a researcher or your personal thoughts would be fine."

"Unfortunately, I've never seen a ghost of any kind, so I cannot say with certainty that they exist."

Takatsuki's face was projected large onto the screen behind him as he answered.

"It's difficult to define what 'ghost' means in the first place. There's a lot of debate in the folklore world over what the difference is between an apparition and a ghost. Folklorist Kunio Yanagita wrote that apparitions are tied to places, while ghosts are not. He also said that apparitions will appear to anyone, and usually show up around dusk or twilight, but ghosts tend to show themselves to particular targets in the middle of the night. However, these definitions are already outdated. At least insofar as those that appear in ghost stories are concerned, neither seem to be limited by place, time, or target. So what *is* the difference between a ghost and an apparition? I think it probably boils down to the fact that ghosts are dead things which appear in the form they occupied while they were alive."

Takatsuki's gentle, beautiful voice flowed confidently just as it did during class. This was his wheelhouse. The panel was supposed to be Sarasa Fujitani's, but it had become the Akira Takatsuki show.

"Actually, this is still insufficient as a definition. Reason being, there are things which are not easily labeled as either ghost or apparition. A well-known example would be the *youkai* called Ubume. In the late Heian period anthology *Tales from Times Past*, volume twenty-seven, chapter forty-three, 'Taira no Suetake, Morimitsu's Vassal, Encounters an Ubume,' we have what is said to be the first mention of this *youkai*. Ubume approaches people trying to cross rivers and urges them to hold her baby. Some people claim Ubume is a fox spirit in disguise, while others prefer to wrap the story up neatly by saying she's the soul of a woman who died in childbirth. If she's a fox spirit, it's safe to say she's an apparition. But if she's the soul of a dead woman, that makes her a ghost."

"So are you saying it's impossible to distinguish between apparitions and ghosts?"

"Not impossible so much as dependent on the viewer," Takatsuki said in response to Sarasa's question.

"For example, let's say there's something standing there that looks just like a ghost at first glance."

Takatsuki gestured toward the announcer, who was startled.

She pointed at her own face as if to ask, 'Who, me?'

Smiling, Takatsuki assured her, "Just for example's sake," then turned to Sarasa.

"If that were the case, what would you think it is, Ms. Fujitani?"

"Huh? Um... Well, if it looks just like a ghost, then I guess I would think it was a ghost."

"And yet, in the past, especially in the case of people living in the countryside rather than in urban areas, they would have thought, 'Ah, another fox spirit in disguise,' or, 'A *tanuki*, at it again.' Because to them, the average mystery was the work of a fox or a *tanuki*. Even if they accepted the existence of ghosts, when they encountered one, they believed it was a fox or a *tanuki* in disguise. That may seem a bit strange from a modern point of view. But how a given mystery is perceived is dependent upon the viewer and the cultural context to which they belong. Ah, my apologies—you don't have to play the role of a ghost anymore."

Takatsuki thanked the announcer, who had been standing stiffly with her arms dangling out in front, resembling a ghost. Looking relieved, the announcer dropped her hands while the crowd chuckled.

At Naoya's side, Sasakura muttered, "Hey, isn't this supposed to be Sarasa Fujitani's panel? Is it all right for Akira to do all the talking?"

"...I mean, it was Ms. Fujitani who brought up the subject. He seems to be well-received anyway."

As the two people who usually acted as Takatsuki's common sense exchanged subtle looks, the professor continued chatting away happily onstage.

"However, if you look at the ghost stories told in modern times, you can see how conditions have changed since previous eras. You almost never hear a modern story about a fox or a *tanuki* being the cause of the mystery, but there are plenty which plainly state the involvement of ghosts. This is probably due to shifts in society and to urbanization distancing foxes and *tanuki* and the like from places where humans live. We are no longer in the era of those kinds of animals playing tricks on people. Consequently, when someone sees a mysterious specter, they are most likely to interpret it as a ghost. So, when it comes down to it, it may in fact be adequate to say in modern times that a ghost is a dead thing appearing in the form it took while it was alive."

"Then, um, circling back around, do you think ghosts exist, after all?"

Takatsuki seemed like he could keep talking endlessly. Sarasa forcibly returned the conversation to its starting point.

Rather than looking discouraged, Takatsuki's eyes lit up.

"Of course, both now and in the past, there are cases where, as the proverb goes, 'the ghost, when examined closely, is nothing more than withered grass.' But personally, I think it's reasonable to assume ghosts genuinely exist, given the sheer number of people in modern times who talk about having seen them. I am actually dying to meet a real ghost, myself!"

"Right... That's true. It's not strange to believe in ghosts, is it? I mean... I think they're real."

Sarasa Fujitani started speaking, her expression serious, following Takatsuki's statement.

Here it comes, Naoya thought, instinctively bracing himself. Sarasa was sure to say "I can see ghosts" if the conversation kept going in this direction. Naoya didn't want to hear the lie.

"Um, Mr. Sasakura, I think I'm going to go—"

Naoya had somehow managed to finish his crepe. After a quick heads-up to Sasakura, he was planning to leave.

But—

He could hear Sarasa Fujitani as she continued to speak onstage.

"Professor, just now, you said that there are a lot of people who claim to have seen a ghost, right? Actually...I have, too, several times. The first time was when I was a child, at my grandmother's funeral—"

Confused, Naoya reflexively looked back at the panel.

Sasakura stared down at him.

"What, do you have an errand to run or...? Fukamachi? Hey, what's wrong?"

His tone was worried, but Naoya just put a hand to his ear, unable to reply. On the stage, Sarasa was still talking.

"—and when I turned around, my grandmother was standing right there. Even though her body was right in front of me."

Her voice when she talked about seeing the ghost—it didn't sound distorted in the slightest.

Sarasa's voice *was* all muffled, but everyone sounded like that to Naoya at the moment.

But did this mean that her story about having ESP wasn't a lie?

Right then, a single thought struck Naoya's mind like a bolt of lightning.

Without thinking, he looked around at his surroundings. The panel was in full swing, but there were tons of people talking otherwise. Someone taking a phone call. Vendors speaking with customers. People chatting with friends.

Countless words overlapped; dozens of voices reached Naoya's ears.

But, for the first time, Naoya realized that not a single one of them sounded distorted.

It can't be, he thought.

"...Mr. Sasakura."

"What is it? Your ears still hurt?"

"They're fine. I'm fine, but, um... Could you tell me a lie?"

"The hell?"

"Please, just do it."

Sasakura's expression made it clear he thought this was nonsense, but at Naoya's pleading, he said, "It's pouring rain today."

The weather that day was bright and sunny.

Naoya's eyes opened wide. That settled it.

When did it happen? he wondered. He wasn't sure. The past few days, he hadn't spent a lot of time talking to people. At the very least, he knew it hadn't been before the ear infection. Maybe that was the cause, or perhaps it was due to the incisions in his eardrums?

Whatever the reason, at present, Naoya could no longer hear when someone was lying.

A single *hah* escaped his lips.

Naoya was torn between elation that it was real and disbelief that it had occurred this way. He never thought it would be so simple. How many times had he thought that if he just destroyed his ears, he could return to normal? He had always been too afraid to follow through, in the end. If this was all it took to make him a regular person again, he should have done it ages ago. Even with holes in his eardrums, it wasn't like he had lost his hearing entirely.

Regardless, Naoya's days of being scared of everyone lying to him were over.

Just then, he caught sight of Takatsuki onstage.

In an instant, the joy swelling in Naoya's chest was punctured.

For a moment, he couldn't breathe. He could feel the smile that had bloomed on his face contort unnaturally.

Staring dazedly at Takatsuki's face, made large on the screen, Naoya let the hand at his ear drop.

What if, he thought.

If his ears had become just like anyone else's…

…then that person—Takatsuki…

How would he react? What would he say?

"Fukamachi. Hey, are you sure you're feeling okay?" Sasakura asked him.

Naoya stood there, frozen, unable to give him an answer.

* * *

Ultimately, Naoya ended up staying in the courtyard with Sasakura until the panel ended.

Even after Takatsuki and Sarasa had left the stage, Naoya remained there, stock-still. Sasakura took hold of his arm again.

"Hey. We're going to Akira's office."

"Huh…"

"You're gonna rest a bit. Your face is really pale."

"…No, um, I'll go home. I can rest at home… Please, let me go."

"Don't be stupid. You look like you could collapse at any second."

Paying Naoya's resistance no mind, Sasakura grabbed him by the nape of the neck with the hand that wasn't already holding his arm. Then he set off toward the faculty offices building, escorting Naoya along like a detainee.

Though other school buildings were being used for the festival, the faculty building was not. It was fairly deserted; the distant hustle and bustle of the courtyard was all Naoya could hear through the walls.

When they arrived at Takatsuki's office, Sasakura opened the door without knocking.

"Akira. Let this kid rest here for a—"

His voice, which had been directed into the room, cut off abruptly.

Maybe Takatsuki wasn't in. That would be preferable, Naoya thought, looking around the office.

No such luck.

Takatsuki was standing inside the room.

But he wasn't alone. There were two more people standing there as well. One was a plump, middle-aged woman, and the other—a beautiful woman in a black and white houndstooth coat.

Sarasa Fujitani.

"—Sorry. We'll come back later."

"KenKen, Fukamachi, it's fine. Come in."

Sasakura had been about to turn right back around and close the door, steering Naoya by the neck the whole time. Takatsuki's voice stopped him.

The middle-aged woman frowned.

"This won't do. We would like what we came here to discuss to be kept in confidence."

"It's all right. That big guy there is a detective, and he can keep a secret. The student with him is my assistant, so he'll be accompanying me if I decide to take your case."

Quieting the woman with his cheerful smile and words, Takatsuki opened up the office door that Sasakura had been in the process of closing. He put a hand on Naoya's shoulder as if to take over for Sasakura.

"Are you okay? You look a little tired; sit over there. You too, KenKen."

Takatsuki made Naoya and Sasakura sit in adjacent folding chairs on one side of the table, then addressed the two women standing opposite.

"Please have a seat. I'll hear you out. Before that, would you like something to drink?"

"No, that's fine. We won't be here long."

The middle-aged woman's reply was curt. She pulled out the closest folding chair for Sarasa, then took the one beside her for herself. It seemed the two of them had only just arrived in Takatsuki's office.

The woman took a business card out of her shoulder bag and handed it to Takatsuki as he sat down across from them.

"I'm Sarasa Fujitani's manager, Miyahara… Ordinarily, this kind of thing would be out of the question for an agency, but Fujitani insisted. I worried we would be bothering you, but…"

"I apologize for my selfishness, truly."

Sarasa bowed her head over the table as she apologized.

As soon as she opened her mouth, Naoya's gaze fell to it involuntarily. It was strange to hear a voice in person that he had only heard on TV before, especially up close like this. He was struck by the odd reminder that celebrities were in fact real people. Sarasa's presence alone made the familiar office feel like a movie set.

She continued talking.

"I just really thought this would be the perfect opportunity. It's not like I get a lot of chances to speak with university professors. Especially ones who specialize in ghosts and apparitions and even investigate strange incidents! I mean, I really think it must be fate, somehow... The truth is, Professor Takatsuki, I have a request to make of you."

"Yes, what is it?" Takatsuki responded with a smile.

Sarasa looked at Miyahara. The other woman nodded reluctantly and reached into her bag again, this time taking out something that looked like a booklet.

"This is the movie Fujitani is currently shooting. It's called *The Manor*, and the screenplay is an original work. The genre is suspense leaning toward horror... It's about a woman who marries a wealthy man and sees ghosts in his old, Western-style home. Fujitani will, of course, be playing the female protagonist."

"Well, spoilers, but it turns out that what the protagonist thinks is a ghost is actually her husband's mother, who has a rare blood type and needs an organ donation. The husband married the protagonist to get her organs. As you might be able to guess, it ends with the manor going up in flames."

Unconcernedly giving away the movie's plot, Sarasa continued.

"From the plot alone, you might think it sounds like a B-tier movie, but I think it could be plenty interesting. The director isn't very well-known yet, but he has a lot of novel filming approaches. Plus, the other interesting thing is that you get the feeling not all the ghosts in the movie are actually humans. Our plan is to make people think later, after watching the reveal, 'Wait, the thing I saw in that one scene, maybe it was actually a ghost.' So I've got a lot of hope for this project, but—it's just, weird things keep happening at the studio."

"Strange occurrences at the studio? It's like *Don't Look Up*, isn't it! So what's been happening, exactly?"

Takatsuki leaned forward, clearly excited.

"At first," Sarasa answered, "we had some sound trouble."

She explained that filming was currently taking place on sets built at the studio. Actual buildings in the countryside were being used for exterior shots of the Western-style mansion that was the film's backdrop, so outdoor scenes were being shot on location, but all the indoor scenes were being filmed in studio sets.

It started during the filming of a living room scene. The main character, having just moved into the manor after marrying her husband, would be reading a book by lamplight at night when the sound of a music box would start coming from somewhere she couldn't identify.

The music box sound effect was meant to be recorded separately and matched up with the video in post. Sarasa was only supposed to act like she had heard a sound.

But she said that when they were filming, the sound of a music box could actually be heard on set.

"At first, we all thought it was someone's cell phone going off, but... That didn't seem to be it. Even though we all said it was creepy, we carried on filming."

"And everyone who was present at the time heard the music box?" Takatsuki asked.

Sarasa nodded. At her side, Miyahara chimed in.

"I was there, too, I heard it. No doubt about it."

"What song was it?"

"I only heard it for two, maybe three seconds, so I'm not sure. But the song they planned to use in the movie is 'When You Wish Upon a Star,' I believe."

Miyahara's tone was businesslike.

Sarasa continued her story.

"Similar things happened a few times after that. We'd be filming and suddenly the sound person would say 'there's a weird noise,' so we'd pause, but—when they checked the footage, there was nothing. The sound person said he had heard something like a woman sobbing..."

Then, the strangeness started to escalate.

Several crew members started saying they had seen a long-haired woman in white clothes. Some of the crewmembers were women, but they all had short hair, so it probably hadn't been a case of misidentification. The mysterious audio issues continued, and even people apart from the sound team said they heard a woman sobbing. Before long, rumors of the movie being cursed began to circulate among the crew. They weren't sure who had done it, but one day they found salt left here and there around the studio as if for protection.

"But as soon as we noticed it, it was like someone went around and dissolved all the salt with water... It seriously creeped me out. And then, finally, during filming one day, I saw it... The ghost everyone was talking about."

It was during a bedroom scene. The protagonist, nodding off in bed while waiting for her husband to come home, would be awoken by something ripping the covers off of her and throwing them to the floor. Sarasa was lying in the bed, and the crew member whose job it was to pull the covers off of her was waiting at the foot of the bed, outside the camera's view.

When the director called "Action!" and she felt the cue of the blankets being pulled, Sarasa opened her eyes—and happened to glance at the studio ceiling.

The bedroom set only had about half a ceiling, as only enough of the framework had been built so that the film equipment could still move around in the set.

Sarasa saw someone standing on that framework.

There was no reason for a crew member to be standing there. It would be a dangerous place to stand, to begin with. Sarasa intended to keep the scene rolling, thinking how unsafe it was, but then—she made eye contact with the person.

Breaking character entirely, she immediately let out a gasp.

The figure standing there was the woman in white, her long hair hanging down over her face.

Without thinking, Sarasa shouted, "Who's there?!" bringing the scene to a halt. But when she looked back up at the frame, there was no one.

"The director was angry, the crew was all flustered, it was so awful... Somehow, I managed to keep filming after that, but now I'm kind of scared to go to the studio."

"...Scared?"

In response to Sarasa's last few words, which were said in a groan as she covered her face with her hands, Takatsuki looked puzzled.

"You said you have ESP. That wasn't your first time seeing a ghost, right? And yet, seeing them still frightens you?"

"Of course it frightens me!"

Sarasa removed her hand from over her face.

"Isn't that obvious? No matter how many times you see one, you don't get used to it. How could you not be afraid, knowing there's a dead person there?"

"I see. I apologize, that was rude of me. I personally wish I could see ghosts every day, so I'm not confident that seeing one would be frightening for me."

Takatsuki smiled, not looking the least bit remorseful. For a moment, doubt over her decision to consult with the professor flashed across Sarasa's face. Miyahara, at her side, continued to look sour.

As outside observers, Naoya and Sasakura simply sat and listened to the story without interrupting for the time being. Sasakura appeared to be readying himself to intervene in case Takatsuki went into his usual "senselessness mode," but at that moment, Takatsuki was calm. He wasn't showing any signs of becoming a large, overexcited dog, as he often did.

Which had to mean—he didn't believe the story Sarasa just told.

Whenever Takatsuki wasn't champing at the bit over a case, it meant he had surmised from the beginning that it wasn't actually supernatural. He wasn't interested in falsified ghost stories. He was looking for the real deal.

Still, Naoya thought, concentrating desperately on Sarasa's voice.

As expected, he couldn't hear any distortion in her tone.

That could have been due to Naoya's ears losing their ability—but he also couldn't rule out the possibility that Sarasa Fujitani was telling the truth.

He could usually tell whether someone was lying in an instant, but right then, Naoya had no clue. He hadn't thought that would irritate him so much.

Sarasa gazed at Takatsuki with big, cat-like eyes.

"So, um… Professor, I was really hoping you would be willing to visit the studio."

"I wouldn't mind. But I'm not a medium, so I wouldn't be able to do an exorcism or purification, you know?"

"I know. I just thought we might be able to learn something by looking at the situation from your perspective… There are quite a few crew members who are scared, too. If a college professor comes to investigate, some of them might be able to relax a bit, I think."

"On the contrary, I have a feeling it could cause unnecessary panic. There may be people who think 'A university professor has come to investigate, so there *must* be something supernatural going on!' But…"

Right then, Takatsuki's gaze swept over Naoya.

Trying to escape from those questioning eyes, Naoya instinctively looked down at the table.

Takatsuki's eyes opened a little wider as he stroked his chin with one hand. He was quiet for a short while, as if in thought. He had to be wondering why Naoya, who usually covered his ears automatically when someone told a lie, hadn't done that at all while Sarasa spoke.

Once more, Takatsuki looked at Naoya, then returned his gaze to Sarasa.

"Right. Okay, I'll come by the studio. Perhaps I could be of some help."

"Really?!"

Sarasa's eyes lit up at Takatsuki when he accepted her request. Next to her, Miyahara only frowned harder, but Sarasa paid her no mind.

"Then, Professor, I know it's last-minute, but could you come tomorrow? I think it would be best if you visited as soon as possible… Shooting starts again tomorrow."

"Tomorrow? That's fine. I don't have anything scheduled… Fukamachi, would that work for you? If you aren't feeling well, you don't have to come."

"…No, it's fine."

Even Naoya didn't understand why he answered that way.

He should have refused. He should have come up with some excuse, anything, said he was ill.

Instead, what he said was:

"I'm fine. I'll go."

"Really? Well then—Ms. Fujitani, please tell us the studio address and what time we should be there."

With a small sigh, Miyahara handed Takatsuki a note with the address written on it.

And so, case accepted, the plan was made for Naoya to call on the studio along with Takatsuki.

The studio was situated beside the Tama River. It was only a few minutes' walking distance from the train station, but as expected, the moment Takatsuki was allowed to take the lead, he started walking in the completely wrong direction.

"I'm sorry. I really would have gotten lost and been late without you here, Fukamachi…"

"…I don't mind."

The guard at the gate had been told ahead of time about their visit by Sarasa, but they were made to wait at the gate until Miyahara came to collect them.

Casually, Naoya put a hand to his ear.

He suspected their condition was unchanged.

After getting home the day before, Naoya had turned on the TV and spent hours watching variety shows and talk shows. He didn't hear anyone's voice distort.

It should have been cause for celebration. The ability he had always hated was gone.

Instead, far from being happy, Naoya found that he was frustrated.

Takatsuki looked down at Naoya in concern.

"Fukamachi. Are you really feeling okay? Also, today is the last day of the festival. Are you okay with not going?"

"I'm fine… I'm not really interested in the school festival anyway."

Naoya tried to bury his chin in his scarf as he replied.

"Really? It's just that you've seemed out of it again since yesterday, so

I'm a bit worried. I know I asked before, but—yesterday, you didn't hear Ms. Fujitani's or Ms. Miyahara's voices warping, did you?"

"...No."

Naoya gave a small nod at Takatsuki's question.

Takatsuki had made the same inquiry the day prior, after the two women had left.

Naoya's answer had been the same then. He hadn't been able to hear their voices distorting at all, so it would have been a lie to say otherwise.

But what he should have said to Takatsuki at the time was something else entirely.

He should have told the professor honestly: *Right now, I can't hear lies.*

Naoya hadn't been able to get the words out.

Takatsuki was looking around restlessly, his shoulders slightly bunched up against the cold. Naoya watched him surreptitiously. It was the professor's first time at a movie studio, apparently. Although, from the outside, the studio just looked like a row of large buildings.

If he knew Naoya's ears had become the same as a normal person's—what would Takatsuki think?

Takatsuki's interest in Naoya came from Naoya's past encounter with something undeniably strange.

And from the ability Naoya had gained from that encounter, which set him apart from regular humans.

The reason the professor continued to bother with him, Naoya thought, was because, in a sense, their situations were similar. That was probably why Takatsuki had gone out of his way to take care of Naoya at his apartment, as well.

But if that's true—

Naoya couldn't help but think that if he lost his power, if he became the same as everyone else—

He would no longer be within the realm of Takatsuki's interest.

I don't want to stop working with you. I want you to continue being my assistant.

That's what Takatsuki had said to him once, but the reason he always brought Naoya along on investigations like this was likely because Naoya's ability was somewhat useful to him. If all he needed was someone who was in charge of directions and common sense, it didn't have to be Naoya in particular. Anyone would be fine.

What should I do? He had to tell Takatsuki the truth. Naoya not refuting anything Sarasa said the day before was probably why Takatsuki had accepted this case in the first place. Even though there was a possibility the entire thing was made up.

"Sorry to keep you waiting. Please follow me."

Miyahara finally came to get them.

As she led them toward one of the buildings, Miyahara spoke in a low voice.

"I would like to ask you a favor before we enter the studio. I didn't tell the director or the staff the reason for your visit today. The director is already quite on edge what with the issues that have occurred every day. If any further nuisances come along, it could interfere with filming. Therefore, I'd like you to behave as if you're just personal guests of Fujitani, only here to observe the shoot. What do you say?"

"I have no issue with that... However, I was hoping to speak directly with the studio staff about the goings-on. Is that all right?"

"I don't mind if you're honest about your job. It shouldn't be a problem if you're just a professor taking a personal interest in the studio's strange phenomena for the sake of your own research. Just please keep the fact that it was Fujitani's request a secret."

Miyahara's expression was, as ever, quite stony.

"There are so many moving parts in filming a movie. If even one thing is thrown off track, it could throw the whole production into disarray. The current atmosphere is by no means a good one. I would like to avoid introducing any additional stress to the environment."

Her tone was businesslike and could even be taken as cold. In fact, this whole thing was probably nothing but a nuisance to Miyahara. After all, her work was being hampered by a commotion over a ghost, of all things.

"Are you not afraid of ghosts?" Takatsuki asked her.

"You learn quickly in this industry that it's humans you need to be afraid of, not ghosts."

Miyahara snorted and then laughed.

"It's eat or be eaten in the entertainment industry. I've been Fujitani's manager since her debut. This is a critical time for her, professionally and age-wise. If she can't survive this, the number of roles she'll get will steadily decrease. That's why she needs this movie to succeed, truly. It's her first leading role in ages."

Miyahara stopped walking as they reached the doors of one of the studio buildings. She turned to look up at Takatsuki, bit her lip for a moment, then spoke again.

"I thought it would be fine to let Fujitani do as she pleased. I allowed her to invite you here, and even kept things quiet with the agency. So, Professor Takatsuki, I'm begging you. Please, don't do anything unnecessary."

Naoya couldn't help but fidget uncomfortably at the barefaced wording of Miyahara's statement.

Takatsuki returned her gaze, eyes slightly narrowed.

"What do you mean by that?"

"Isn't it obvious? I mean that outsiders should be quiet and behave themselves. There's no need to work too hard to figure out what's causing the disturbances. Just the fact that you came here should be enough to satisfy Fujitani."

Miyahara turned back toward the studio building, her tone dismissive.

She opened the heavy-looking door and showed Takatsuki and Naoya inside. The interior resembled a large warehouse. The ceiling was startlingly high. Several sets had been assembled in the space: a bedroom, a living room, and an entrance hall with a large staircase leading to the second floor. The set walls were properly wallpapered, the flooring was elegantly laid, and the rooms were furnished. Nevertheless, with ceilings that only covered part of each set, they definitely had the feeling of stage backdrops. Their artificial nature was obvious in person, but the sets would probably look real once they were color-corrected and such on film.

There were crew members everywhere inside the building—people making lighting adjustments, carrying equipment, checking cameras, walking around with clipboards in hand. Naoya's eyes were wandering around the room when he felt Takatsuki nudge him gently. Turning around in confusion, Naoya saw the professor silently point toward a spot next to the entrance. Someone had put salt there. They had been told the salt had been dissolved once, but it seemed somebody had replaced it.

"Oh, Professor Takatsuki! You came!"

Sarasa, who was sitting in a chair in the corner of the set reading a script, waved a hand in their direction. Heading off somewhere else, Miyahara said, "Well then, I'll leave you to it."

Putting her script down, Sarasa came trotting over to Takatsuki. She was wearing an eye-catching blue dress and had her hair tied up elegantly. She looked slightly older and completely different than how she had at the school festival. The look was well suited to her role in the movie as a "woman who marries a rich man."

"It looks like they're still doing checks, so I'll show you around set a little bit... I think my manager told you, but I guess you're supposed to be a 'professor friend' of mine who is 'just here to observe,' so I won't be able to introduce you to the director. Sorry."

"I don't mind. Instead, afterward, I'd like to hear what the crew has to say."

"Sure thing. Well, let's start over here."

Sarasa led them over to the bedroom set.

A thick, slightly timeworn carpet was laid over the set's wooden floor, and a large bed acted as the focal point. The side tables and lamps looked antique, giving the feeling of a bedroom in an actual mansion. The blue wallpaper with a navy-and-purple flower pattern over it, which would have been a rare find in the average house, made the set appear dim and closed off.

"I wear a white nightgown in this scene, which really sets the wallpaper off nicely. And that bed, when I was looking up from it... That's where it happened."

"I see. Did anyone besides you see it at the time?"

"No... It was just me, then. It disappeared so quickly, even I only saw it for a second."

"About where was it?"

"Just there, where the ceiling opens up—above the joists. Huh, hold on, Professor Takatsuki?!"

Sarasa stared in surprise as Takatsuki toed off his shoes and climbed onto the bed without permission.

But Takatsuki just stretched out on his back and looked up at the spot Sarasa had indicated.

"Ah, yes. If you look up from this position, that area comes into view first."

"Pr-Professor! You're going to get in trouble! Please get off of there right away."

Naoya rushed over to the bed to pull Takatsuki out of it.

But as soon as he did, Takatsuki walked over to stand directly beneath the joist in question.

"Hmm, it would be difficult to stand up there without a ladder or something. I mean, is it even possible to stand on that? I'd like to try. Ms. Fujitani, could I borrow a stepladder or something?"

"Professor, please stop. You'll be in trouble if you mess up and break the set."

Naoya tried desperately to discourage Takatsuki, who was attempting to move about as he pleased. If he couldn't fulfill his role as lie detector, Naoya at least wanted to perform his duties as the Sensible One.

Just then, a short, young, female member of the crew came over to them.

"Ah, there you are, Ms. Fujitani! The director is asking for you!"

"Wha? Oh no, already? Umm, I'm sorry, Professor Takatsuki. I have to go, so would you mind not getting into anything for now? Jun—sorry, this is an acquaintance of mine. He's a university professor. He's here to observe filming today, so could you stay with him for a bit? It would be great if you could show him around set a little."

"Sure, no problem!"

The girl Sarasa referred to as "Jun" nodded. Sarasa hurried off toward the entrance hall set.

When she was gone, Jun looked up at Takatsuki, her expression a little puzzled.

"Umm… So, you're a college professor? You know Ms. Fujitani?"

"My name is Takatsuki. I teach at Seiwa University. I met her yesterday when we did a panel together at the school festival."

"A panel? Wow, I don't really get it, but that's cool!" Jun replied, clapping lightly.

She had short hair and was wearing a crew member jacket and black jeans. She told them her role in the studio was as a production assistant, then laughed and added, "It's pretty much no different from being a part-timer."

As they moved from the bedroom set to the living room, they could see Sarasa near the entrance hall, apparently having a briefing with a bearded man in a black cap. A number of other actors and crew members were also standing around them.

"Is that the director?" Takatsuki asked.

"Yep, that's Director Sayama. He's worked on a lot of music videos and commercials, and this movie is his first feature film."

"Is that so? He must be looking forward to completing it, then."

"Yeah, Ms. Sarasa is also pretty excited! She's really nice to the crew, too. She's super kind, and sometimes she even arranges for us to get super fancy catering at her expense. I really want this movie to be a hit! Although…I mean, it might be a little difficult, since it's a horror…"

Jun's smile was a tad wry.

It certainly wasn't common for horror movies to become wildly popular. Plenty of people didn't like scary movies, and a lot of horror films had a less-than-top-tier feel to them, at any rate.

"I quite like horror movies. Oh, right—I heard scary things sometimes happen on the sets of horror movies. Is that true? I'm actually researching scary stories at the university. If you know of any, not just ones limited to this place, I would love to hear them. Aren't film studios often said to be haunted?"

Takatsuki segued naturally into gathering information.

"Whoa, that's so cool! There are academics who research stuff like that? You have perfect timing—did Ms. Sarasa not tell you? There's an apparition here."

Lowering her voice, Jun sidled up close to Takatsuki, who stooped down to match her height.

"Did you see it, too? The apparition. What did it look like?"

"I didn't see it, but I heard it's a woman with long hair and white clothes who stares down at people with a vengeful look on her face! Ms. Sarasa said she saw it during filming! There was also a sudden music box sound, and the sound of a woman crying!"

"I see. Did you happen to experience any of those things yourself?"

"I heard the music box! But everything else I just heard from other people."

"Who did you hear about them from?"

"Umm, Mr. Hamamura, the sound mixer, and the prop master, Mr. Wada, I think? Did you want to talk to them? I'll introduce you."

"Oh, please do, that would be so helpful."

Takatsuki nodded, and Jun started by taking them to meet the prop master, Wada. He was a short, slender man in his twenties.

Wada was in a corner of the studio, painting lampshades with a paintbrush. He seemed to be applying a thin layer of color to them to make them appear antique.

"Huh? You're a college professor? I see... Yeah, I saw the ghost."

The man readily admitted to having seen the specter.

He told them that he had been preparing props on the second floor of the set when, by chance, he turned around and saw a woman in white with long hair. Since there were no such women among the cast or crew, he thought some random person had walked on set without permission. But when he called out to her, she seemed to disappear.

"Well," Wada said. "A failing actress committed suicide in this studio before, so I don't think it's out of left field for the place to be haunted."

Takatsuki nodded interestedly while, at his side, Naoya strained desperately to listen to Wada's voice. He still couldn't tell whether there was any distortion.

"I have to get back to work," Wada told them, standing up with a cardboard box full of equipment in hand. He went up the wooden staircase built behind the set to the second floor.

Next, they spoke to Hamamura, the sound mixer, a solidly built middle-aged man with a shaved head.

"…Right, the issue with the audio."

Hamamura's expression was slightly troubled. He rubbed his smooth-shaven head with one hand, answering in an indistinct tone.

"Uh, yeah. It was like, uh, a woman sobbing. It came over the mic a few times… It didn't show up in the audio, though… That, I think, maybe I could have misheard it… Stuff like that happens sometimes. At my old studio, things would get picked up in recording, and I'd have to go back later and fix them."

"Oh, even at another studio? If you don't mind my asking, could you tell me about that?"

"Um, sure, that's fine. I can't tell you the specifics of the movie, though. Is that okay?"

"Yes, absolutely!"

"It happened during filming on location for a previous film, at a mountain in the countryside. The shooting equipment was acting strange from the start—"

As Takatsuki took the opportunity to collect other ghost stories, at his side, Naoya gradually grew less and less sure of what to do with himself.

He couldn't tell when people were lying, he couldn't actually be of use, so what on earth was he doing here?

Both Sarasa and Wada claimed to have seen a ghost. Hamamura was saying he heard one's voice.

But all of them could be lying.

What do I do? Naoya didn't know. Who was lying, and who was telling the truth? He was only just realizing, now that his power was gone, how much he had relied on it. Hopeless impatience and frustration burned in his chest. Who was telling a lie? Who was the liar? Who was it—

"..."

All at once, Naoya felt like his heart was being crushed in his chest.

He realized—he was no different.

He was essentially lying to Takatsuki right now.

He was still pretending to have his power. He was pulling the wool over Takatsuki's eyes.

How was that any different from being a liar?

Naoya's legs shook. Startled, Takatsuki propped him up by the shoulder.

"—machi? Are you okay?"

"Professor... Um, I—"

Just as Naoya was about to speak, the studio erupted in a flurry of activity. It seemed filming was about to begin. People were gathering around the entrance hall set. With a murmured "*Crap,*" Hamamura ran off in that direction.

Grabbing Takatsuki and Naoya by their arms, Jun led them into a darker area slightly away from the set.

"You can watch from here! Please make sure to stay quiet, okay?"

Leaving Takatsuki and Naoya behind, Jun hurried to join the rest of the crew. With the mood shifting to one that clearly prohibited talking, Naoya shut his mouth and looked toward the set.

Sarasa and an actress who appeared to be playing the role of a servant were standing in the entrance hall. With the lighting in place, the artificial set took on a whole new character. Naoya could see Miyahara standing amidst the crowd of crew members surrounding the set. Silence fell over the studio, and the director's voice called, "Aaand, *action!*"

In her blue dress and high heels, Sarasa started walking slowly toward the back of the set, where the grand staircase led up to the second floor, as if she had just entered through a front door. The entrance hall wallpaper was a deep moss green, and the floor was made of dark brown wood. Just like the bedroom set, this one was dominated by a dark color palette and a sense of entrapment. But walking through that, her body language radiating vitality, was Sarasa. With her eyes wide and her face filled with emotion, she looked like she had yet to notice the oppressive atmosphere encompassing the mansion.

"What an incredible estate... I can hardly believe it. Me, the lady of this house."

Sarasa shrugged her shoulders with a small chuckle.

Apparently, this scene took place immediately following the protagonist's marriage into the family. Sarasa looked at the servant woman; her expression was pure, showing only untainted belief in her having achieved a dream marriage.

"Say, do you think I can become a lady worthy of this place?"

"Whether you're worthy or not, there's only one person who should be called the lady of this manor."

The actress playing the servant answered blankly, and for a moment, Sarasa seemed timid. Then she smoothed her face back over with a smile that showed just the slightest tinge of anxiety.

"I'm sorry. I asked something strange."

As he watched, Naoya thought, *Ah, so this is acting.* Sarasa was good. Everything, from the way she spoke to her facial expressions, was different than how she had been while speaking with Takatsuki before. Naoya had only seen a few of her movies and TV shows before, but by no means could Sarasa Fujitani be called a bad actress. Even though Miyahara had said she was only just reaching the critical moment in her career.

Then—

Suddenly, as Sarasa was delivering a line to the other woman in the scene, she gasped.

"Hey! Cut! What happened?!"

The director stopped the shoot immediately.

Her big eyes brimming with fear, Sarasa pointed one slender finger toward the second floor of the set.

Everyone turned to look where she was pointing.

The second floor of the set was a corridor that surrounded the entrance hall and was lined with doors. One of the doors was ajar. Someone was standing, totally still, in the darkness of the open door, staring down from above. The figure wasn't easy to see, but—Naoya could make out a white dress, and black hair hanging in front of a face.

The crew started to panic. Jun screamed. The director shot up from his chair.

But it was Takatsuki who reacted faster than anyone else. Without hesitating, he burst onto the set, practically flying up the stairs on his long legs. Naoya rushed after him. He thought he heard the director yell, "Hey, who the hell is that?!" after them, but he ignored it for the time being.

Takatsuki pushed open the door in question.

There was no one behind it.

The other side of the door was nothing more than an offstage area made of bare boards and pillars, completely unlike the wallpapered set. It wasn't even a proper room, just an empty area the same width as the corridor. The door Takatsuki had opened seemed to be the only one that properly worked, as looking to the left and right revealed nothing but featureless planks of wood. Cardboard boxes stuffed full of paint cans and packing tape and the like were piled up on the floor, as if the space was being used as a storeroom. There was nothing that could be mistaken for a long-haired woman wearing a white dress.

At the back of the space was a small, sliding window that opened up to the outside of the studio. Takatsuki walked over to the window, opened it, and looked down. Naoya joined him, but all he could see was a row of trash cans lined up along the building. He couldn't see any people.

Then the set door opened, and the director and some crew came in.

"Hey, you there! What are you doing? Outsiders shouldn't be back here!"

"Ah, please excuse us, we just came to observe, but then a ghost appeared, so I wanted to investigate a little. We'll be leaving shortly."

At Takatsuki's reply, the director whipped his own hat off his head.

"...Enough! All anyone can talk about is ghosts! I've had it! Just because we're filming a horror movie doesn't mean the real thing is gonna appear, you idiots! Let's shoot that scene again, now! Get back to your positions! And you, get out!"

Some of the surrounding crew attempted to calm the furious director, while others forcibly escorted Takatsuki and Naoya off the set.

The studio was in an uproar. The sound mixer, Hamamura, was fiddling with the microphones, his face sullen. Sarasa sat on the sofa in the living room set, having her hair fixed by the person in charge of hair and makeup. Miyahara stood next to her, handing her a bottle of water. Sarasa seemed to still be in shock, trembling as she accepted the bottle from her manager. At that moment, the door that led out of the studio building opened and several crew members came inside—Wada, the prop master, among them. He looked around in surprise at the chaos, then grabbed Jun as she went running by and asked her, "Hey, did something happen?"

A bunch of people were speaking at once: "Did you see that just now?" "I saw it." "I did, too." "It was a ghost." "This movie is cursed. I knew it." "This happened at my last job, too." Naoya touched a hand to his ear. All of the voices sounded muffled, but he didn't get the feeling that any of them were distorted. All those mouths moving and voices coming out of them—some of them could be spewing utter lies, but...

Naoya couldn't stand it any longer.

"...Professor."

"Hm? What's wrong, Fukamachi?"

He could tell Takatsuki was looking at him.

"Um... I'm sorry, but...I'm going home. I don't think...I can be of any help to you here..."

Unable to return Takatsuki's gaze, Naoya managed to get those words out at least, then turned away from the other man. He made a break for the studio door, like he was trying to escape.

He knew Takatsuki was chasing him. He could hear the yells of "Fukamachi, wait!" Naoya pushed the heavy outer door open without looking back.

But as soon as he made it outside, Takatsuki caught up to him.

"Just wait, Fukamachi. Listen—"

At that moment, the studio door opened again, and Sarasa came flying out.

"Professor Takatsuki! Professor Takatsuki, please wait! Are you leaving already? Please don't go yet, you still—"

As she pleaded with him, Sarasa clung to Takatsuki's arm as if to keep him from going anywhere.

Naoya saw his chance to get away from Takatsuki—but suddenly, he found a thin man in a black down jacket standing in front of him.

The man was holding up a camera with a big lens.

"Hey, you're in the way. Come on now, move it."

The man pushed Naoya aside with one hand, repeatedly pressing the shutter button on his camera with the other. A sneer broke out over his unshaven face.

Startled, Sarasa looked at the man.

"Wait a minute, what news agency are you with?! How did you get in here?!"

"Oh, don't you worry! I got a nice shot, dear Miss Sarasa Fujitani! The headline will say 'Lovers' Tryst with a Handsome Model Type at the Film Studio'!"

The man laughed as he turned on his heel. Ostentatious camera held high, he took off in a different direction than the front gate.

Not understanding what just happened, Naoya unintentionally let the man get past him. A short while later, he realized the man might have been a paparazzo or something like that.

Sarasa, who had been standing up straight while holding onto Takatsuki's arm, gradually sank down into a crouch on the spot. Unmindful of their styling, she ran her fingers through her bangs in agitation and groaned.

"...That's enough, no more... Forgive me, please..."

Naoya and Takatsuki ended up leaving the studio soon after that. Filming was going to continue, apparently, but as the director had screamed at them to get out, Takatsuki seemed to have decided it would be best for them to go.

At the same time, Sarasa was dragged back inside the studio by Miyahara.

On the train home, Naoya finally opened up about his ears to Takatsuki. Takatsuki didn't get upset with him or ask for any further details. He just spoke in his usual soft voice.

"I see. Take care of yourself."

And that was all.

They parted ways when one of them had to transfer to another train. Naoya had the vague thought that he might never go to Takatsuki's office again.

Life returned to normal the following week. All that remained of the campus-wide excitement that had been SeiwaFest was a pile of signs in front of the club assembly hall and posters that had yet to be torn down. Classes were held as usual, with listless-looking students dozing off and playing with their smartphones during lectures. Wednesday's third period Folklore Studies II was as popular as ever, and Takatsuki talked joyfully about urban legends the whole time.

Naoya's everyday routine didn't change.

Even though his ears had become normal, the way he spent his time at school was the same. He was still alone more often than not, and he tried to be as uninvolved with his surroundings as possible.

Rather, Naoya was, quite possibly, avoiding others more than ever.

He had no idea if anyone was lying to him. He hadn't realized how uneasy that would make him. The feeling that everyone around him was a liar only grew, and he became afraid to spend time with anyone at all.

And then, on Thursday—the man showed up.

All of Naoya's classes were done for the day, and he was on his way out of campus, walking through the school gate.

Suddenly, a hand shot out from the side and grabbed his arm, hard.

Whipping around in shock, Naoya saw a bearded man who was

wearing sunglasses, even though it was evening. He was grinning, his grip tight around Naoya's arm.

"Hey, what are you doing?! Who the hell are you?!"

"Calm down, we can discuss details in a bit, okay? For now, why don't we go have some tea together?"

"What are you talking about?! Please let go of me!"

Just as Naoya was about to yell for help, the man leaned in close to his ear.

"Now, now, don't be so scared. I just wanna talk about that professor, Akira Takatsuki, okay?"

"Huh…"

The man's gravelly voice muttered that into Naoya's ear, and he looked at the man in surprise.

Smirking, the man tugged on Naoya's arm, pulling him across the street to a building with a café on the second floor. He went straight for an empty window-side booth without waiting to be seated, shoved Naoya into the bench closest to the window, then took the one opposite for himself.

When an employee came to take their order, the man barked "Two house blends" without bothering to check what Naoya wanted, then took out a cigarette.

The man put the cigarette in his mouth, but just as he was about to light it, he looked at Naoya as if something had occurred to him.

"Ah, yeah, that's right. Hey, do you remember me?"

"Why would I? I don't know you."

At Naoya's response, the man took off his sunglasses with a disappointed look.

"That's rude, y'know. We just met the other day. You could at least remember my face."

The man suddenly jutted his pointed chin toward Naoya. His face was thin. He had disheveled, unruly hair and stubble growing around his mouth. The corners of his eyes drooped slightly, and his smile was overly friendly, giving him an overall air of what could only be called untrustworthiness. He looked to be in his late thirties.

Frowning, Naoya scanned the man's face, wondering where he could have met him before—then he realized.

He was the man outside the studio on Sunday, with the camera. Naoya remembered his black down jacket and his stubble.

"How do you do? I'm Iinuma, a freelance journalist."

The man—Iinuma—who must have seen the recognition on Naoya's face, threw his business card down on the table. Above the name 'Takashi Iinuma' was the logo of a gossip magazine Naoya had often heard the name of. Since he said he was freelance, it probably just meant that was one of the publications he wrote for.

"You see, the thing is, I'm in a bit of a bind. The powers that be rejected the picture I took the other day of Miss Sarasa. I mean, it's not like it would have been a big story or anything, but it was pretty annoying, since I went to the trouble of getting the photo. There hasn't been a whole lotta gossip about Miss Sarasa before, so I thought it would be nice and novel, plus I took such a pretty picture. It really ticked me off, y'know? I ended up doing all that work for nothing. Can you believe it?"

Elbows propped up on the table, Iinuma spoke in a peculiar, fast-paced tone while he puffed his cigarette. Naoya drew back from the smoke and scowled at Iinuma.

"Why did you bring me here? I have nothing to talk about with you."

"Come on, now, kiddo. If you jump to conclusions like that, you'll miss the whole point. I was just getting to it. You were with that guy—the one Sarasa was clinging to. The model-looking one. I mean, I already looked him up, so I know his name. Associate Professor Akira Takatsuki of Seiwa University."

Iinuma stuck his face out again, cupping a hand around his mouth like he was sharing a secret.

"Truth is, just between you and me, it seems the order to nix that photo didn't come from Sarasa Fujitani's office."

"What?"

"The editor-in-chief was being all evasive, so he didn't tell me straight out. But it looks like it came from the top of the company. I thought it was weird, like, 'who the hell is this good-looking guy?' I couldn't help but be interested. I tried my best to look him up. I mean, I bribed the crew at the studio just a little and they gave me his name right away. Then I did some research from there—and I found something interesting."

Iinuma's eyes drooped a little further as he gave a satisfied smile. He tilted his face upward and deftly blew a smoke ring into the air.

The fluffy white ring floated up while Iinuma followed it contentedly with his eyes and spoke again.

"That professor, he's the son of the president of the Takasaki Corporation."

"The Takasaki Corporation?"

"Even students who aren't on the job hunt yet know the name, right? One of Japan's largest general trading companies and a leading conglomerate in Asia! It's a huge company, so putting pressure on a puny editorial department was child's play. I thought they must have quite a lot of nerve to take things that far, though. And by the way, his mother is Sayaka Takatsuki, former world-famous prima ballerina who even won an award at the Prix de Lausanne. No wonder his face is so damn pretty; his mom is a knockout."

Iinuma brought the cigarette to his mouth and inhaled.

Naoya was hearing all of this for the first time. He remembered Sasakura telling him before that Takatsuki was the son of a wealthy family, but he hadn't learned anything specific about his parents.

"But seriously, randomly blocking my photograph just because the son of Takasaki Corp.'s president was caught with an actress? Ain't that a little odd? I was curious, and I wondered if there was more to it, so I did a bit more digging. I just had a feeling something was up—call it my reporter's intuition. Anyway, all I found was that the professor was kidnapped when he was a kid. It was a big story at the time, all the weekly publications calling it the 'Kamikakushi Incident' and such. Plus, the perpetrator was never caught. His grandfather was the company president at the time. His old man, the current president, took Sayaka's name and married into the Takatsuki family."

Iinuma was still grinning.

"In cases like that, even if it's an open criminal investigation, if the missing kid is found alive, they clamp down on sharing information right away. I couldn't find a lotta details about it, even when I dug up articles from the time. Plus, that professor, he went abroad for high school, and when he moved back to Japan for college, he lived alone the whole time, like he was kicked outta his home. Seems like the family fell apart after the *kamikakushi* incident. What a shame!"

As he spoke, Iinuma spread both his hands out in an 'oh well' gesture. His tone didn't sound at all like he felt bad for Takatsuki, despite what he said.

Looking at the other man, Naoya felt disgust rising steadily in his chest.

"...And so? How is any of that your business?"

"It isn't, yet. I'm going to make it my business, starting now."

Iinuma gave another sneering grin.

He snuffed his cigarette out in the ashtray and looked at Naoya.

"Y'know what? I think there's something fishy about that professor. Something that would be perfect for an article. Plus, don't you think he would look good printed in a magazine? I got rejected last time, but if I take the story to another company, they might pick it up. I'd love to have material that interesting be published. Something like, 'The Real Truth Behind that Kamikakushi Incident.' Don't you think that would be good?"

"Are you saying you know the real truth?"

"I'm saying I'm shoring up my evidence. I've taken as many photos of that guy as I can get. And I noticed, y'know—sometimes, his eyes turn blue."

Seeing Naoya's shoulders twitch, Iinuma narrowed his gaze.

"Well, I'll be. You've noticed it too, haven't you, sonny? It's weird, isn't it, since both of his parents are supposed to be Japanese. No matter how bright the light is, Japanese people's eyes don't look blue."

"So what are you saying?"

"Here's my theory—you listening? I think that professor's mom had an affair with some foreigner somewhere, and he's the result of that."

"...Huh?!"

Flabbergasted, Naoya stared at Iinuma. Where did this guy get off, spouting ridiculous nonsense out of nowhere like that?

Iinuma lit a second cigarette and splayed himself along the back of the bench.

"That's why his eyes look blue. Because he's only half-Japanese. His former ballerina mother lived overseas for quite a while before she got married. It wouldn't be weird for her to have a lover or two during that time. I bet you when he disappeared, it's because his real father kidnapped him for a month. Then somehow or another they got their kid back, but the husband recognized his wife's infidelity and the family collapsed, and the son was sent to live abroad with his real dad for a while. When you look at it like this, it makes a lot of sense, right? Sayaka Takatsuki completely withdrew from the ballet world after getting married, but she's still fairly well known. Something like 'The Real Truth Behind that Kamikakushi Incident, a Former Prima Ballerina's Tainted Relationship!!' would be pretty great material for a magazine article, don't you think?"

Iinuma's tone as he explained his reasoning was smug.

But Naoya knew his logic was flawed. Sasakura had told him Takatsuki's eyes turning blue had started after the incident. If his eye color was due to him being biracial, it should have been that way when he was born.

Listening to any more was a waste of time, so Naoya made to stand up.

"It seems like the kind of preposterous, insensitive story a gossip reporter would write... I'm going home. This has nothing to do with me."

"Now hold on! I was just getting to that!"

Sticking a leg out to block the way, Iinuma stopped Naoya from leaving.

"Actually, I've got a job for you, kid. I'll pay you a part-time rate, so it's a pretty good deal, don'cha think?"

"What?"

"I want to find out more about that professor. It could end up being valuable."

The strangely gritty timbre of Iinuma's voice—whether caused by drinking or tobacco, Naoya didn't know—was further polluted by his crude laughter. Naoya hated the way it sounded.

"Are you close with him, kid? I want you to hang around him for me and pass along anything you learn. Even the smallest detail would be fine."

"Why would I... Please move. If you don't, I'll call the police."

Naoya knocked Iinuma's leg out of the way. He nodded at the barista who was just coming to deliver their coffee and headed for the exit.

Iinuma called out at his retreating back.

"Oh-ho, leaving so soon? Well, fine! Even if you don't help me, **I've got plenty of dirt on that professor already!**"

Startled, Naoya turned to look back at the other man.

Thinking he had gotten Naoya's attention, Iinuma laughed and kept talking.

"Not like I care, I just want to write an interesting article, that's all. I just need solid proof for it. **I already have what I need in general**, but it would be nice to have info that's a bit more current, too! I thought you might be able to help me, but I guess not! Good thing **I've got other sources!**"

Iinuma's voice sounded distorted. Here and there, his rough voice swung chaotically between outrageous lows and metallic highs.

Naoya covered his ears with his hands.

"...Liar."

The words slipped from Naoya's mouth along with a sigh.

"The things you're saying—they're lies."

Iinuma had been rattling on arrogantly, but he stopped short with a "huh?"

Naoya took his hands away from his ears and leveled his gaze directly at Iinuma.

"You don't really have any information about Professor Takatsuki.

All you've got is speculation. That's why you asked me to help you, even just a little. I can tell, you know."

"Wha…? What're you…"

Iinuma looked like he was preparing to fire back in a loud voice. But the moment he made eye contact with Naoya, something made him freeze and snap his mouth shut.

The look on Iinuma's face was one Naoya was quite familiar with—the look that said, "this kid is freaking me out." He had been on the receiving end of that look countless times. He could feel the corners of his lips curving up in a bitter smile.

But for some reason, somehow, he felt relieved.

For the first time, he saw his ears as a weapon rather than a liability.

"Gossip articles may be about writing baseless lies, but I have no intention of lending a hand with that. If I talk to you any more than this, I'm gonna be sick."

Iinuma scowled.

Naoya barked out his next words before the other man could say anything.

"Now, if you'll excuse me. Please don't approach me again."

Even though he had walked out of the café seeming all composed, Naoya worried what he would do if Iinuma followed him, so he decided to return to campus.

He didn't see any signs of the journalist chasing him when he looked over his shoulder. He kept walking anyway, not wanting to run into the man ever again.

What should I do? Naoya wondered. There was no doubt that a real nuisance of a person had set his sights on Takatsuki.

After worrying about it for a short while, Naoya took out his phone. He only had one person he could call.

He had added the number to his contacts after having received it in case of emergencies. He tried calling to no avail, but soon after the call failed to connect, Naoya's phone started ringing.

A steady, straightforward voice—Naoya couldn't help but think of wooden practice swords—came through the speaker.

"Fukamachi? What is it?"

"U-um—Mr. Sasakura. Are you busy right now? There's something I wanted to talk to you about."

Sasakura was Takatsuki's longtime friend and a police officer to boot. Naoya couldn't ask for a more suitable person to discuss the matter with.

As Naoya relayed what had just happened, Sasakura listened in complete silence, not even chiming in now and then to show he was following along.

When the story was done, Naoya heard him sigh on the other end of the phone.

"...Dammit. More trouble to take care of."

"I'm s-sorry."

"It's not your fault. Akira's too careless. All right—to start, don't go anywhere near that reporter anymore. Got it? Just let him be."

"Huh? But he might keep tailing Professor Takatsuki."

"He isn't gonna find anything no matter how much he snoops around. When the *kamikakushi* incident happened, the police turned over every stone they could... I read the case reports from that incident once," Sasakura said.

"I didn't learn a single thing from them. Where he was during that month, who could have taken him—it's all a mystery. Nothing new is gonna come to light, even if that journalist goes searching for it. If he comes up with some fake story, it'll get crushed just like the photo with that actress did. That's the kind of guy Akira's dad is."

"...What do you mean?"

"He's done stuff like this before. He's almost entirely estranged from his kid, but he'll still destroy any and all unflattering news about him. I heard a rumor that when Akira was on TV and caused a bit of a stir, every single source that was going to put out a story that connected him to his dad was forced to shut down... I don't know if he did that to protect Akira, or himself."

Naoya really didn't know much about Takatsuki's parents.

His mother's mental state was apparently thrown off balance by the *kamikakushi* incident, and when it became difficult for Takatsuki to keep living at home, he was sent overseas for a while to live with a relative. Even after his return to Japan, it seemed Takatsuki hadn't really interacted with his family. That was all Naoya knew.

What did Takatsuki's father, the president of a large company, think about his son now? The article about him and Sarasa was suppressed shockingly quickly. Was his father really keeping an eye out for even the most trifling bits of news?

It was like Takatsuki was under surveillance.

"Anyway, you don't have to worry about it. I'll talk to Akira later... Oh, but if that guy approaches you again, contact me right away. I mean it."

"...Yes. Understood. Thank you."

After ending the call with Sasakura, Naoya put away his phone and looked around.

Even though the last classes of the day were already over, there were still lots of students on campus. A group of about ten of them were walking in the opposite direction, probably talking about whether to go out drinking.

As he passed them, Naoya could hear some of the voices among the group as they warped and distorted.

"Sorry! **I have stuff to do tomorrow!**"

"Oh, that movie! **I saw it too! It was great, it made me so emotional!**"

They were just petty lies. But Naoya could hear the distortion clearly.

Naoya reflexively stared at one of the people who had lied, and they looked back at him, perplexed. But in the next moment, their eyes moved on and they returned to the conversation they were having.

Naoya stopped walking.

Without realizing it, he had arrived in front of the faculty building. He looked up at the section of windows where he knew Takatsuki's office was. The lights were on—maybe Takatsuki was still inside.

He worried that it would seem too self-serving to bother the professor just because he had regained his ability.

But still, Naoya wanted to tell him.

He went inside the building and up to the third floor. Standing at Takatsuki's office door, he knocked. When a familiar voice called "come in," he felt his heart skip a beat. Taking a deep breath, Naoya opened the door.

"—Ah, Fukamachi. Perfect timing."

Takatsuki greeted him with his usual smile.

As Naoya made to enter the room, he stopped short, realizing there was already a visitor inside.

Sarasa Fujitani was standing in the office. She was wearing a black coat with fur trim this time. Miyahara, her manager, was nowhere to be found—apparently, Sarasa had come alone. She was glaring at Naoya as if he was nothing more than a nuisance.

Naoya hesitated in the doorway, but Takatsuki put a hand on his shoulder and led him into the room.

"Ms. Fujitani came to ask us to investigate the studio one more time. But I'm not sure. The director yelled at us for being there, after all."

"I'll talk to the director! Please, Professor Takatsuki. **Strange things kept happening after that day, and I've seen the ghost so many times!**"

Sarasa's pleading voice warped so clearly.

Naoya automatically covered his ears and looked up at Takatsuki.

Takatsuki, glancing down at Naoya, nodded once.

"—Why don't we put an end to this, Ms. Fujitani?" he said, his tone firm.

Sarasa stared, taken aback. Takatsuki faced her and continued talking.

"I've thought from the beginning that your story sounded like a lie. Even what you said about having extrasensory perception. But even the boy who cried wolf met with the real thing in the end. I couldn't be positive that the ghost at the studio in this case wasn't real. So, just in case,

I agreed to go investigate. But now I have conclusive proof that you're lying. So that's enough. Let's call it, Ms. Fujitani."

"Wh... Lying, how could you... You think I'm lying?! You saw it yourself, didn't you? You saw the ghost!"

"Ghost? No, what I saw was Mr. Wada, the prop master."

"...Huh?"

Sarasa froze.

Takatsuki, his handsome mouth spread in a wide smile, went on.

"He was in disguise, right? Before filming, Mr. Wada went up to the second floor of the set. There are two staircases at either end of the back of the set, and the large staircase on the front. At the time, the cast and crew were all gathered around the entrance hall set. When you pointed up at the second-floor door, acting like you'd seen a ghost, I went up the front-facing stairs. If someone was backstage on the second floor and came down using one of the rear staircases, someone would have noticed. But that didn't happen."

"...Y-you see! No one came down the stairs, but there was no one up there, either, right? So it must have been a ghost!"

"No. If that were the case, Mr. Wada should have been on the second floor. His not being there would be strange in and of itself."

"Huh...?"

"I didn't see Mr. Wada come down from the second floor before filming began. And yet, after all the commotion, Mr. Wada came back into the studio through the outside door. It's strange, isn't it? When and how did he go outside? The answer is probably that sliding window at the back of the set. There are large trash cans lined up beneath the window, so he probably climbed down onto them. And when I looked out from the window, he was probably hiding inside one."

"Well... You probably just didn't notice him when he came down the stairs! The studio is so big, and there were tons of people. It's only natural that you'd miss something, isn't it? What are you even saying?"

"—Unfortunately," Takatsuki replied, still smiling, "as far as my eyes are concerned, it's impossible that I would have missed something."

Takatsuki traced his long fingers over his own eyes.

"There were areas I couldn't see because my view was obstructed, but I could see the exit door the entire time. As long as something is in my field of vision, I'll see everything that's going on and remember it clearly. I've always had better eyesight than other people, and my memory is quite good."

"Wh-what baseless accusations!" Sarasa cried. "This is all nonsense!"

Unconcerned, Takatsuki barreled on.

"Besides, Mr. Wada lied, too. He said an actress committed suicide at that studio once. He didn't say he heard about it; he told me plainly: 'A failing actress committed suicide in this studio before.' So later on, I got a detective friend of mine to look into it. I asked him if that suicide really happened—the answer was 'no.'"

"Wh…"

At a loss for words, Sarasa's mouth opened and closed several times. She probably hadn't expected Takatsuki to investigate so thoroughly.

"And then there was Mr. Hamamura's lie as well. When I asked him about the audio problems at the studio, he seemed oddly uncomfortable. The way he spoke was evasive, too, and it made me think, 'Ah, he doesn't want to talk about this.' But as a test, I asked him to tell me about a strange incident he experienced at a different location, and he was totally forthcoming, his demeanor totally changed. I think Mr. Hamamura is probably quite a good person. Honest, the type who's bad at lying. That comes out in his face and his demeanor. Ms. Fujitani, if you're going to ask people to lie for you, you have to be careful in your choices. Mr. Wada aside, picking Mr. Hamamura was a total miss."

Sarasa's expression twitched, and she grit her teeth.

Naoya also stared up at Takatsuki in surprise.

Even without relying on Naoya's ability or anything like that at the time, Takatsuki had already seen through the lies.

"If Mr. Wada's and Mr. Hamamura's stories are both false, that means the story of the ghost appearing in the studio loses its credibility as well.

That means the music box you said you heard at the beginning of all this was your own doing. Yours, or the work of someone fulfilling your request. It's easy to make sounds happen with a smartphone. Ah, Ms. Miyahara could have done it. When you told us about the music box, she was acting a little odd, too."

Sarasa's gaze flickered for a moment. Takatsuki had probably hit the bull's-eye.

If Naoya remembered correctly, when Sarasa had told them about the strange occurrences at the studio, the only time Miyahara had interjected was in reference to the music box. That might have been because she felt uneasy, in her own way.

"...𝔜ou're wrong. I'm not...lying..."

And yet, those words were squeezed out from between Sarasa's clenched teeth.

She stuttered and shook, her voice creaking harshly.

"I saw, a ghost...at that studio... I saw it, I really did!"

"The ghost of the 'long-haired woman in white'? The second you said that, you know, I thought your story sounded made-up."

Sarasa was struggling in vain to put up a fight, but Takatsuki took her down with a smile on his face.

"Sure enough, the 'ghost' story you came up with was a bit clichéd. Though I suppose you wanted to model it in such a way that everyone would think it was a ghost."

"...What do you mean, 'model' it...? Clichéd? What is?"

"I'm talking about what ghosts look like," Takatsuki said.

He turned toward one of the bookshelves and ran a finger along a row of spines.

"Ghosts have long been a favorite subject in the worlds of literature and art. Following the definition of ghosts being the souls of dead people, they must have had names while they were alive. Even now, there are some lasting stories with ghosts known by their personal names, like Oiwa and Okiku. But there are also many ghost stories where someone just happens to come across the spirit of a stranger somewhere.

In the past, it was common for the ghosts in stories to reveal their own names and positions in life, but as ghost stories proliferated, information such as who they were while alive became unimportant. They were all just lumped together under the label of 'ghost.' In the early modern period, works depicting ghosts flourished, but nearly all of them described, simply, a 'ghost'—not 'the ghost of so-and-so.'"

Speaking like he was delivering a lecture, Takatsuki pulled a book down from the shelf called *Japanese Ghost Paintings: The Sanyūtei Enchō Collection at Zenshō-an*. It appeared to be a catalog from the ghost scroll exhibition they had gone to see in the summer.

"A resulting phenomenon from the generalization of the word 'ghost' is the typification of ghostly appearances. A fixed notion of what ghosts generally look like was born. In the past, a white kimono and untied hair made up the common burial attire. Many of the ghosts depicted in the early modern period were shown like that. Due to the influence of ghost paintings made during that era, for a long time, Japanese ghosts didn't have legs."

Takatsuki opened up the book and showed Sarasa one of the pages inside. Printed on it was Maruyama Ōkyo's *Ghost* painting, of a woman with long hair, wearing a white kimono, with no legs.

"However, in contemporary ghost stories, especially on-screen horror, the dominant ghost image is a woman in white clothes with her long hair hanging down over her face. They broadcast a lot of horror specials in the summer, and most of the ghosts introduced in those specials look that way. I like those kinds of programs, and I watch them often. So I have a good idea of what modern people picture when they think of a ghost."

Takatsuki was still beaming. He seemed to be having a lot of fun. Any time he talked about his interests he looked like a giddy child.

"Regarding the differences between that and ghosts of the past, you may think the shift from a white kimono to other white clothes was a natural progression, but the Japanese horror movie industry—known as J-Horror—has played a role in spreading and solidifying the 'long-haired woman in white clothes' image. Ghosts in those movies often have legs, so there aren't many modern legless ghosts."

Next, Takatsuki picked up a plastic sheet protector and withdrew one of the materials he had distributed during a class. Pictures on the paper depicted the vengeful spirits that appeared in both *Ring* and *Ju-On: The Grudge*. Sadako and Kayako definitely had legs.

Takatsuki held the paper out to Sarasa as he continued.

"The ghost you said appeared in the studio looked just like these, see? That's why I said it was clichéd. If you were going to go so far as to make up a story about an actress dying at the studio, you shouldn't have given it such a stereotypical appearance. If we assume that ghosts are the souls of the deceased who appear in the form they took while alive, their appearance should vary. At the very least, it would have been nice to see something more realistic than a Sadako-style ghost."

"D-don't patronize me!"

Sarasa threw the printout Takatsuki had handed to her.

The violently flung paper soared up toward the ceiling, then came fluttering down. Surprised, Takatsuki reached out and deftly plucked the sheet from the air.

Sarasa glared at him, breathing hard.

"**I can see ghosts.** Why are you insisting that I'm lying? You don't have psychic powers, right? So you can't prove that I don't, either! **I can see them! That's right, there are even ghosts in this very room! There, there's one! Behind that bookshelf, too! Even though you guys can't see them, they're here!**"

Sarasa's shouts warped intensely as she pointed wildly around the office. Frowning hard, Naoya covered his ears with both hands. Her voice was so loud, the distortion was painful to listen to.

"Ah, please stop yelling, Ms. Fujitani. My assistant will collapse."

Takatsuki put a hand on Naoya's shoulder.

"It's true; we don't have the ability to see ghosts. However—what we do have is the ability to tell that you're lying."

"What do you mean by that?!"

"I'll leave that up to your interpretation."

Once again, Takatsuki smiled.

Then he made Naoya sit in a chair close to the door and urged Sarasa toward a different one.

"Please have a seat, Ms. Fujitani. Why don't we calm down and talk a bit more? I'll make us something to drink."

Without waiting for Sarasa's reply, Takatsuki walked over to the table by the window. Sarasa glared, irritated, at his back, then pulled out a chair for herself and sat down with a *thump*.

A short while later, Takatsuki returned carrying a tray with three mugs on it: his own blue one, Naoya's dog mug, and the one reserved for guests.

Staring down at the bright, multicolored Great Buddha on the cup placed in front of her, Sarasa's face twitched.

"...What the hell is this?"

"Cocoa. Sweet things settle the mind," Takatsuki explained, pointedly avoiding mentioning the cup's design.

He sat down across from Sarasa and pulled his own mug—which naturally also contained cocoa—toward himself, taking a sip. He smiled, satisfied, and looked back at Sarasa.

"Now then, Ms. Fujitani. I'm already bored with your talk of ESP and such, but I am interested in why you did all this. I'm not great at putting myself in others' shoes, so I don't really get it. Why would you do something that would delay the progress of your own movie?"

Her gaze steady on the cup in front of her, Sarasa didn't answer.

Takatsuki carried on anyway.

"Why did you want to cause an uproar over a ghost? Do you not want to be in that movie? Do you hate B-tier horror films? You said you were betting on this film, and that didn't sound like a lie to me. Ms. Miyahara and members of the crew all said you were taking the movie seriously. So why?"

Sarasa clenched her teeth again against the barrage of questions. A maelstrom roiled in the depths of her cat-like eyes.

The fury in her gaze made Naoya worry that she would take a flying leap at any moment, but then Sarasa took a single, deep breath, and the fire was extinguished.

Her expression changed completely. In a moment, she was calm, hiding her naked emotions behind a placid façade.

"...I didn't want to become irrelevant. That's all."

Sarasa's voice was subdued, calm.

She crossed her slender legs, rested one elbow on the table at a perfectly calculated angle, and propped her chin up on her hand. Sitting in a pose that could have come straight out of a glamour photobook, Sarasa looked at Takatsuki, her face utterly composed.

"Actresses, you see, are precious while they're young. If they appear in something popular and make a name for themselves while they're young and beautiful, they're fawned over for a while. They do a string of TV dramas and movies and commercials, their names become more well-known, and thanks to that, more roles will come their way. Their agency will even work hard to promote them. But you know what? That only lasts through their early twenties. Unless they're lucky enough for the next big thing to come their way, the work will gradually decrease. Even when it comes, it's nothing major—no starring roles. Supporting cast, maybe bit parts. They slowly get pushed out by the younger, prettier girls who come after them. And before they know it, they're on the brink of obscurity. There's a marked drop in support and publicity from their agencies. The companies won't promote them, even though they know the actresses' popularity will suffer if they don't have the chance to appear in TV or magazines."

Sarasa's tone was matter-of-fact.

Miyahara had said before: This was a critical time for Sarasa Fujitani. If she didn't survive it, work would gradually dry up. Sarasa knew it, too.

"Everyone says 'Sarasa Fujitani's best work was and still is her debut, *What Sleeps in the Forest*. Nothing else compares.' And I was getting fewer and fewer TV roles... But then, I said 'I've seen a ghost before' on a variety show I happened to be on, and the next day it was picked up and spread around by online news sites. It started trending."

A solitary giggle bubbled up from Sarasa's throat.

"And what do you think happened next? I started landing more appearances on variety shows. They called me the 'Psychic Actress,' and they were all programs where I had to sit there and get made fun of by rows of comedians, but they were chances to be on TV. Taking them meant increasing my public stature, which meant I could get more drama roles."

"Ah, you know," Takatsuki said. "I think I've heard it said that what the television industry sells is image. 'This actress is pure and innocent, this actor is a stylish, urban type of guy, this pop star is cutesy.' Those personas tend to sell, don't they? Both commercials and dramas, too; they're easier to produce and better received by viewers if they're given a preconceived format. You were labeled as the 'Psychic Actress,' and society accepted that image."

And so Sarasa was given no choice but to play the part.

The role she herself had spawned of the actress who could see ghosts. That would be her image, forever.

"But it turns out," Sarasa murmured, "the roles I get because of it aren't the same kind I got when I was younger."

Her laugh was quiet and bitter.

With one hand, she brushed her long hair out of her face, then looked at Takatsuki.

"My long-awaited leading film role is in a horror movie, a genre that hardly ever turns out big hits. What's more, the director is practically a complete unknown. The screenplay isn't even based on a best-selling novel or anything. But that doesn't mean the end result can't be good. The director has a unique film sense. The story may seem B-tier if you just look at the synopsis, but there's a lot of ingenuity in the script. The art director is really incredible, too. But still—it's all going to waste."

Waving her hand around idly, Sarasa giggled again.

"I mean, there's been no publicity at all. It's gone largely unmentioned by the media. No interviews. It doesn't matter how good the movie is if the audience doesn't know it exists. If things go on like this, I thought, it'll go mostly unnoticed, and they'll pull it out of theaters after a short run."

"In short, you thought this ghost incident would serve as advertising."

Takatsuki nodded, as if he finally understood.

Sarasa made a show of shrugging her shoulders dramatically, nodding along with him.

"That's right. I mean, a real supernatural incident happening at the filming of a horror movie? That's bound to make the news a little. After all, I got the role because of my 'I have ESP' act. The film is scheduled to premiere next summer—the season when ghost stories are all over TV. I figured there's no way they wouldn't run a story about an actress having a ghost encounter on set. You've also been on one of those programs before, right, Professor? If we promoted it by saying you came to the studio to investigate, the odds of it being talked about would go up. There was a lot of buzz about the 'sexy associate professor' when you were on TV."

"Sorry to disappoint you, but I have no intention of appearing on a program like that again."

"Is that so? That's too bad. You're not like I expected you to be."

"Ms. Miyahara knew all about this plan—correct?" Takatsuki asked.

Sarasa nodded.

"She knew. She hated it. She called me a foolish child... But when I asked if the agency would spend more advertising money on me, she had nothing to say. Yep... That's how it is. That's the way things are. So...what choice did I have?!"

Out of nowhere, the intensity returned to Sarasa's voice.

Raw emotion surged over her face, her blank mask melting away. She glared at Takatsuki with tears glistening in her eyes.

"Yeah, that's right! I did it all because I want to be popular! What's the big deal if filming gets delayed a little? What difference does it make? If no one knows about the movie, it'll just get buried! It will never be a success! No matter how good the takes are, no matter how skilled the acting, no matter how hard the crew worked... That all means nothing if no one goes to see it! That's why... That's why I..."

Sarasa's words melted into tears.

Looking down, she pulled a handkerchief from her expensive-looking purse. She dabbed gently at her eyes with it, careful not to ruin her makeup.

Then she took another deep breath. She brought her emotions back under control and reverted quickly to her composed actress face.

Sarasa had probably been living her life that way for quite some time. An actress shouldn't cry unless it was written in the script. She forced her tears and her anger down, down into her chest with a single breath, keeping up her beautiful guise for the cameras.

"...That's it. I've told you everything. Are you satisfied, Professor?"

Staring fixedly at Takatsuki, she turned up the corners of her mouth.

"I'm sorry for causing you trouble. You must have thought I was a disgrace of an actress."

"No... In a sense, I thought you were a very sincere person," Takatsuki replied, shaking his head.

Sarasa barked out a laugh.

"I'd rather you didn't console me. Go ahead and mock me if you want. That would make me feel better."

"I'm not going to mock you. Just like the crew at the studio didn't."

Sarasa's mouth snapped shut.

His gaze steady, Takatsuki spoke in a gentle voice.

"You must have asked Mr. Wada and Mr. Hamamura to help you with the ghost story, right? They could have refused, but they didn't. They played along. I don't think they did that just to give the leading actress what she wanted... I think you probably spoke to them honestly, told them what you just told me. Is that right?"

For a moment, Sarasa's strong, shining gaze was wet with tears.

What Sarasa Fujitani had done was by no means the right thing to do. To the contrary, from an outsider's point of view, her actions would probably seem shameful and unbecoming of an actress. And to the studio crew besides, the delay in filming was likely bothersome. The average person would say it was ridiculous to attempt something like a fake haunting. And yet, both Wada and Hamamura had followed Sarasa's lead.

They'd done it because Sarasa had been that desperate.

And—because they themselves didn't want the film to fail, either.

"That being said, I think it would be best to call off the whole charade. Regardless of the circumstances, it's not fair to the director."

"…Yeah. I know."

Sarasa nodded meekly in response to Takatsuki's words.

Then she picked up the mug in front of her and took a sip, murmuring at the sweetness of the drink.

"It's been a while since I've had cocoa. You like sweet things, Professor Takatsuki?"

"It's best to eat sweets regularly, you know. Sugar is an important nutrient for your brain, and there's research showing that ingesting sweet foods can make you feel euphoric."

"You really shouldn't say that to an actress who has to worry about her figure."

"I'm not cut out for acting after all, if I can't eat sweets as I like."

Takatsuki smiled happily as he brought his own mug to his mouth.

After gently setting his cocoa back down on the table, Takatsuki looked at Sarasa once more.

"—I really liked your debut performance. In *What Sleeps in the Forest.*"

Sarasa wrapped both hands around her cup and glanced down.

"…Thank you. Everyone tells me that. But, you know, a role like that won't come around again."

"You're still an excellent actress. I look forward to seeing the movie."

Ever so slightly, Sarasa's shoulders trembled.

She might have been laughing, or perhaps crying. With her long hair falling into her face, blocking her expression from view, Naoya couldn't tell.

"Thank you. I intend to stick it out in the entertainment industry until I'm an old woman, so I hope you continue to support me."

Raising her head, Sarasa spoke in a strong voice, without even a hint of distortion.

Then she brought her mug to her mouth with both hands and knocked the entire contents back in a single gulp.

The drink went down easily, but sure enough, when she was done drinking, Sarasa's face twisted into a dramatic grimace.

"Blech, it's so *sweet*! Honestly, Professor, how can you drink this stuff?!"

"It's my favorite. If you'd like, I could get you a glass of water."

"No, thanks. I'm going home."

Sarasa stood up.

"Would you like me to see you out?" Takatsuki asked.

"No need. I can manage on my own. Thank you for the cocoa."

She started toward the exit, her high heels clacking against the floor. Just as she was reaching for the door—

"—Oh, Ms. Fujitani. There's one thing I forgot to ask you."

Takatsuki called after her.

Sarasa stopped.

Directing his question to her back, Takatsuki asked, "Why did you lie about having ESP in the first place?"

For a few seconds, Sarasa said nothing.

Then, still facing the door, she answered.

"I really could see them. When I was little."

"Pardon?"

"Ghosts. I saw them all the time until elementary school. I talked about it during our panel, remember? About seeing my grandmother's ghost. I didn't make that up."

Eyes wide, Takatsuki's head turned round toward Naoya. In a similar state of surprise, Naoya met his gaze and shook his head. Sarasa's voice hadn't warped at all.

That meant the story Sarasa told at the festival—the one that first caused Naoya to suspect he had lost his ability—hadn't been a lie from the start.

"No one would believe me about it, so I started pretending I couldn't see them. And then eventually, I really couldn't see them anymore... You don't have to believe me. I don't mind if you think I'm lying about this, too."

"No, I believe you!"

Takatsuki had shot up from his chair.

"Would you mind telling me a little more about that, Ms. Fujitani—"

"Sorry, that'll have to wait."

Sarasa opened the door, looking back over her shoulder at Takatsuki as she stepped out of the office. She gave him a brilliant smile, one that would have looked perfect in a commercial.

"I have to prepare for tomorrow's shoot. Like I said earlier, I'm focusing seriously on my acting career from now on. Good-bye, Professor Takatsuki."

Takatsuki dashed toward the door, but Sarasa closed it abruptly in his face.

The rhythmic clattering of her footsteps, receding as she walked down the corridor, suggested she had no plans to stop.

"...*Aaauuugh*, no way..."

Hands pressed against the closed door, Takatsuki sunk down to the ground. Naoya looked at him piteously.

"Give it up, Professor. If you chased after her now it would be a bit much."

"Yeah. I agree... But I never imagined there was some truth to her story!"

"I'm sorry, my ears were pretty useless until just a little while ago."

"No, it's not like that's your fault..."

Still crouching, Takatsuki turned to face Naoya. He hung his head in despair again, evidently not having regained the will to stand.

Naoya stared down at the soft-looking brown whorls of his hair and murmured, "Speaking of..."

"Huh?"

Takatsuki lifted his head and cocked it slightly to the side. The way he looked up at Naoya was so dog-like, it filled Naoya with an inde-scribable emotion. He thought about his old golden retriever.

"Speaking of, Professor... You could have figured out who was lying entirely on your own, even without me here."

"Yeah, well, more or less. If it's the kind of lie I can reason out."

He answered without hesitation. Looking down at him, Naoya was torn between feeling like he shouldn't be surprised and like he had been cheated.

"Then why didn't you just expose everything right then and there at the studio? You could have been done with this case a lot sooner."

"You're asking why...? At the time, the director was furious, and everyone was in an uproar. I thought that a complete outsider like me acting all self-important right then would have just been begging for more trouble. Besides—there was something I didn't understand."

"What was it?"

Naoya wondered what on earth could possibly have stumped Takatsuki.

"The whole time, I asked myself," Takatsuki replied, "'Why won't Fukamachi tell me about the problem with his ears?'"

"Huh..."

Naoya stared at him.

"Professor, did you... Did you know from the beginning? About my ears?"

"Yeah. Sorry, Fukamachi. I couldn't tell what you were thinking, so I didn't say anything about it, either. I've just been watching your behav-ior... I'm sorry, okay?"

He tilted his head again and kept looking up at Naoya from the floor.

Right, Naoya thought, covering his face with one hand.

Of course Takatsuki would have noticed. As smart as he was, always observing others, there was no way he wouldn't have caught on to Naoya's strange behavior immediately.

Takatsuki was really cunning. He certainly didn't tell lies, but that didn't mean he always told the full truth, either.

"Fukamachi? Are you mad?"

"N-no, I'm not mad! But, Professor, if you can detect lies yourself, you don't need to keep bringing me along on investigations! I mean, anyone could help you with directions and common sense, right? It doesn't have to be me!"

"What? No. I told you before: I want *you*."

"...Why?"

"More importantly, why didn't you tell me about your ears?"

Takatsuki stood up.

He bent forward, looming over and peering down at Naoya, who was still in his chair.

Naoya looked away instinctively. It felt dangerous to meet Takatsuki's gaze from up close at the moment. If he looked into the professor's eyes, he would say things he wanted to keep to himself.

But one way or another, Naoya thought, he was going to have to tell him.

If he didn't, he probably wouldn't be able to set foot in this office ever again.

"...Because..."

Still avoiding Takatsuki's eyes, Naoya spoke.

"Because, if my ears became normal... If they were like everyone else's... I thought you wouldn't need someone like me anymore. And when I had that thought, I just, for some reason...couldn't tell you."

His reply was mumbled, inarticulate. It was difficult to get the words out. He felt like his actions had been beyond childish, and he was extremely embarrassed.

Suddenly, Takatsuki's head drooped.

He turned it to one side, pressing a hand over his mouth.

Even so, he couldn't stop his laughter from leaking out, and ultimately Takatsuki let his hand drop.

"—Pfft, hah, ah-hah-hah, what, what're you, *that's* why... Ah-hah-hah-hah!"

"P-Professor. Is this funny to you?"

Seeing Takatsuki burst into sudden, raucous laughter made Naoya turn bright red.

Bent over double, Takatsuki kept laughing as he replied.

"Of course it's funny! Hah-hah, how dumb! I can't believe that's what you were thinking!"

"D-dumb?! You think it's dumb?!"

"Yeah, because it is. Listen, Fukamachi, just so you know, it's not just your abilities that I hold in high esteem. It's who you are as a person, too."

"You say that, but... Professor, you regularly lose interest in things the second you find out they aren't actually supernatural... So, if I..."

"Ah, that's the dumb part right there. Fukamachi, there's no way I'm going to let you go."

Takatsuki peered into Naoya's face again.

"Because you and I both—even if we were to lose our powers, it wouldn't change our pasts."

Startled by that statement, Naoya looked up at Takatsuki without thinking.

The night sky was looking back at him.

What Iinuma had said earlier was complete nonsense, after all. Those eyes weren't just the result of something simple, like having a Westerner for a parent. Naoya had never seen anyone with eyes that color, like an infinite darkness with countless twinkling stars strewn across it. Those eyes—they were the same color as the sky Naoya saw when he walked into that midnight festival.

"Even if I blinded my eyes and burned the scars off my back, it wouldn't change the fact that there's a month-long void in my past. I am who I am today because of that past. The same goes for you, Fuka-machi. Your past experiences made you who you are now. Fukamachi, we're the same. Both of us, from specific points in our pasts, ended up walking a different path than we had been on until then. A path that isn't quite the same as those that normal people walk on. One that straddles the boundary between reality and the next world."

There was no going back to the road they had walked before. Takatsuki understood that.

Naoya knew it, too. It was just as Takatsuki said—Naoya hadn't been able to live more freely while his power was gone. Not in the slightest.

The border between reality and the next world—the view was a little different than the one regular people had. Naoya and Takatsuki had both been walking that line for such a long time already. That was probably why Naoya felt out of place even when he was with someone else.

Oh, Naoya thought. That was why Takatsuki had said to him, over and over—

I want you to stay by my side. I would be happy if you were here. That was how he truly felt.

Takatsuki chose Naoya to be his companion through the endlessly dark borderlands.

"You see? So your worries were completely unfounded."

He grinned.

His night-sky eyes shifted back into a friendly, sparkling dark brown, and Naoya breathed a small sigh.

"...By the way, Professor."

"Hm? What?"

"You're too close. Back up!"

Naoya shoved Takatsuki away with both hands.

"Seriously, you need to take lessons in typical Japanese personal space. It's not so bad if you do that to me, but if you keep getting that close to women, you're really going to get sued someday!"

"I know perfectly well that Japanese people prefer more personal space, you know. But don't you feel like you can read people's emotions better when you get closer? Like you can see the truth in their eyes, or something."

"I wouldn't know."

Driven off by Naoya, Takatsuki started tidying up the office with a wry smile. He returned the book and sheet protector he had taken out earlier to their places on the shelf, but when he picked up the mug

Sarasa had used, he suddenly stopped short, realization dawning on his face.

Takatsuki looked like something extremely important had only just occurred to him. Naoya wondered what on earth it could be.

"Oh no... Crap! I forgot to get Sarasa Fujitani's autograph...!"

Naoya nearly burst into laughter at the other man's dramatic lamentation.

"Don't tell me you're a big fan of hers, Professor?"

"No, not me. KenKen is."

"...Huh?"

Come to think of it, Sasakura had come all the way to the school festival to watch her panel.

He had denied it at the time, but he was a fan, after all. It was pretty unexpected, nevertheless.

"What should I do? I won't catch up in time even if I chase after her now..."

"Yeah, probably not. Did he ask you to get the autograph for him?"

"He didn't, but...KenKen is always looking after me, so..."

Takatsuki looked totally dejected.

Traces of Sarasa's red lipstick were left on the mug in his hand. Naoya realized the faint smell of her perfume was still lingering in the office air as well.

Sarasa Fujitani really had been able to see ghosts, once.

What kind of influence did her past have on who she was now? Maybe her history of pretending she couldn't see ghosts had something to do with her current career as an actress.

When she said she was done with the farce and was going to work hard from now on, Sarasa's voice had been undistorted, beautiful, and clear.

I hope the path she's on now takes her to where she wants to be, Naoya thought, turning to look back at the door through which Sarasa Fujitani had left.

Chapter 3:
Miracle Child

As November was coming to an end, winter was rapidly approaching.

Christmas music filled the city streets, the greenery lining the roads was decked out in twinkling lights, and no matter where one looked, a Christmas tree was in sight. The university co-op was no exception; students were welcomed at the entrance by artificial fir trees draped with gold tinsel and cotton snow. Despite the cold, winter was an idyllic, splendid time of year.

Nevertheless, in Folklore Studies II, Takatsuki was once again telling a decidedly non-idyllic ghost story. The day's theme was "human-faced dogs."

"Human-faced dogs became a hot topic all over Japan starting in 1989 and lasting into the early nineties. Mass media played a big role in the spread. Various media outlets enthusiastically ran with stories about human-faced dogs at the time. The rumors and urban legends that had once been disseminated through word of mouth saw explosive rises in popularity through television and magazines and the like. Then, as soon as the media stopped reporting on a story, those legends and rumors would quietly die out. It's quite a sad consequence of no longer being talked about—that those stories gradually fade from people's memories and ultimately disappear."

Even if the topic wasn't idyllic, to Takatsuki at least, stories like this were a thing of beauty. His childlike eyes shone as he spoke, undoubtedly having a wonderful time.

"However, what's interesting about the human-faced dogs legend is that immediately following its heyday, there was a wave of 'human-faced' stories. This is because the media was looking for other things with human-like faces to report on following the popularity of the dogs. The most famous among these was the 'human-faced fish,' which was a koi fish living in a pond at Zenpoji Temple in Yamagata prefecture. The entertainment magazine *Friday* ran a story about the fish in 1990 which garnered a bunch of attention right away, causing the fish to overtake human-faced dogs as the trendy topic at the time. There's a picture of it on Handout 5."

An image of the human-faced fish was printed on the handout Takatsuki had indicated. It was probably just a koi fish, but it certainly did seem to have human facial features. The slightly protruding forehead above the fish's eyes truly resembled a man's chiseled face.

"Unlike human-faced dogs, who were said to have dog bodies with human faces attached, this fish simply has markings which bring to mind human features. Human beings are naturally inclined to recognize things that look like faces, and we can even recognize something inherently faceless as having a face if its features are arranged in a certain way. If you draw three circles in an inverted triangle formation, it looks like a human face. We call this the simulacra phenomenon in Japan. A related, more general term is 'pareidolia,' our tendency to convert information we see and hear into patterns that are familiar to us and recognize those patterns in places we know they don't exist. For example, seeing a human face in a stain on a wall, or the shape of a rabbit making mochi on the surface of the moon. They're optical illusions, not real. And yet—the human-faced fish caused a huge craze. People came from all over the country to see it, and they even sold buns that looked like the fish. The pond the fish lives in is also home to a legend about a dragon king and his queen, so there were also those who prayed to the human-faced fish as if it were the dragon god's blessing."

It was an odd story to think about. The koi fish must have been in the pond long before the media picked up its story. But as soon as the media brought attention to it, people traveled from all over Japan and went home satisfied with having simply prayed to a fish.

"By the time the human-faced fish craze died down, there was a human-faced tree from Chiba prefecture in the news. A newspaper reported that the cut end of a zelkova tree growing in a park resembled a human face, and the story was then picked up by TV stations. Of course, as soon as that happened, many people came to see the tree for themselves. It started being said that you would be blessed if you touched the tree, and people even left offerings around it. They treated it the same way they would a divine spirit, even though it was just a simple tree. You may think that's strange, but this is actually an extremely Japanese phenomenon. After all, deities suddenly coming into vogue— what we call *hayarigami*—is a long-standing tradition in our country."

Takatsuki wrote '*hayarigami*' on the chalkboard.

"*Hayarigami* are folk deities that appear suddenly at some point, enjoy a brief period of wild popularity, and ultimately fade rapidly into oblivion. Unlike the 'God' talked about in major religions, these deities can be 'created' by anyone, and they don't have to be Shinto gods or Buddhas. For example, in the seventh century, some people worshipped a 'Tokoyo no Kami' which was actually just a caterpillar. On Handout 6 you'll see an excerpt from the twenty-fourth volume of the *Nihon shoki* that reads: 'A man from the area around the Fuji River in the eastern country, Ohofube no Oho, suggested that the villagers worship a worm, telling them, *This is the Tokoyo no Kami. Those who pray to it shall receive wealth and longevity.*' Perhaps due to the cooperation of the local shrine servants, many people believed him and even laid down their fortunes to worship the caterpillar. It became a big enough social phenomenon that it was consequently recorded in the *Nihon shoki.*"

Facing the blackboard, Takatsuki scrawled "Tokoyo no Kami" and then, underneath that, an undefinable shape that was probably supposed to be a caterpillar. Though if someone told Naoya it was a drawing of a lump of fried dough, he would have believed them. Takatsuki had been blessed with several gifts, but artistic talent was absolutely not one of them.

"*Hayarigami* were all the rage in the Edo period. A large number of them were created and abandoned in that time. An unremarkable Buddha statue at a secondhand store would be worshipped as a magical object, the ornamental tops of bridge handrails would be prayed to as a cure for headaches and tooth pain. The reason anyone can make up deities as they like in this way is probably because Japan is a polytheistic country. It wouldn't be possible in a monotheistic culture. It's part of our national character that we believe gods dwell in all sorts of things, and so new gods can also pop up and disappear here and there. The manner in which their stories spread is very similar to how urban legends become popular today."

In other words, Naoya thought, *people believe what they want to believe.*

And to Japanese people, who weren't overly tied to a specific religion, the range of things that could be worshipped was quite vast. They held Halloween parties in the fall, decorated Christmas trees in winter, prayed at Shinto shrines in the New Year, and visited Buddhist temples and graves during the Festival of the Dead. Certainly, if it was said they could receive a blessing, they might even pray to an insect or a bridge railing.

The bell signaled the end of class. Standing up, Naoya put his arms through the coat he had set aside with his bag during the lecture.

Before class that day, he had received a message from Takatsuki that said, "Come to my office after the lecture. It's about work." In a country where caterpillars could become gods, there may also be mysteries born here and there that called for the help of a university professor.

As soon as Naoya arrived at Takatsuki's office, he was shown an email from a client. Looking at the request for help on the laptop display, he cocked his head to the side.

"What is the 'Miracle Girl of Okutama'?"

"I don't know much about it, either," Takatsuki replied. "It seems the story is only just starting to spread."

The request came from a male office worker living in Tokyo. He wrote that his parents had recently gotten caught up in something like a religious cult and wondered if Takatsuki would investigate it.

The cult-like group was centered around someone called the "Miracle Girl of Okutama."

"Is this 'Miracle Girl' like that fortune teller, Sumiko Kurihara? That sort of thing?"

"That doesn't seem to be the case. I did a little research and got quite a few results online."

Takatsuki navigated to a search results page on the laptop, showing it to Naoya. A list of hits matching his search terms was pulled up.

Clicking on one of the results, Takatsuki brought up what appeared to be someone's personal blog.

```
Here's a story I heard today. Do you know about
the 'Miracle Girl of Okutama'?
   They say she's the only survivor of a fatal
bus crash.
   Even though there should have been no way for
anyone to survive the accident, she somehow
made it out unharmed.
   It's truly a miracle. She must have been pro-
tected by the gods!
   Lately, there's been a surge of people visit-
ing the girl to share in her blessing.
   An acquaintance of mine went and received a
protection charm to put on his clothes.
   Later, he said he fell down the stairs at the
train station, all the way from the top to the
bottom, and didn't get hurt.
   Could the girl's blessing be real?
   Maybe I'll go visit the Miracle Girl next!
```

There were other articles and Twitter posts with largely similar contents. There were even websites that listed the Miracle Girl's address and showed a map of how to get there.

However, the Miracle Girl didn't seem to have a website or account of her own—all Naoya could see were accounts from people who had heard about her and those who had actually gone to visit.

There also didn't appear to be any sites that had posted the girl's name or pictures of her face, as one would expect, but there were pages that referenced the bus crash she was said to be involved in.

According to the articles, the crash had taken place in May. A bus carrying elementary schoolers on a field trip to Okutama had overturned and plunged into Lake Okutama.

A group of fourth graders, their homeroom teacher, and the bus driver had been on board. There had been three buses in total, each one carrying a single class. Only one of the buses overturned. The cause was determined to be the driver having a sudden heart attack. Everyone on the bus, other than the girl, had died. Due to the sheer tragedy of it, the accident had been all over the media, and even Naoya remembered hearing about it.

"Huh? It says the elementary school was in Suginami ward. But the Miracle Girl's address is in Okutama? I wonder why."

"If you look at older articles you see an address in Suginami, so I think she must have moved recently," Takatsuki said, fiddling with his laptop.

Naoya felt the case was of a slightly different kind than the usual requests.

A girl being the lone, unharmed survivor of what should have been a decidedly fatal bus crash certainly was mysterious. But it couldn't be called a paranormal phenomenon, exactly. He didn't expect Takatsuki would have much interest in it.

Seemingly as evidence of that, rather than diving right into the story with his eyes agleam, the way he would have with something that excited him, Takatsuki was strangely calm. On the other hand, as he scanned the article about the girl, his gaze was dreadfully serious, like something was concerning to him.

Something's up, Naoya thought, turning to Takatsuki.

"So, Professor, are you going to take the case?"

"Yeah, I think I'll at least go and hear his story. What's your schedule like, Fukamachi?"

"I'm pretty open. As long as it's not during my compulsory courses."

"Right. Then I'll contact the client," Takatsuki said, smiling. "Once we've settled on a date, time, and place, I'll let you know."

Takatsuki's smile looked as cheerful as ever, but for some reason Naoya couldn't quite put his finger on, he felt weirdly uneasy from that point onward.

One evening several days later, they met with the client at a family restaurant in the neighborhood of Ogikubo.

He was a short man who appeared to be in his forties named Yukiya Kawakami. He was dressed like a typical office worker headed home from the job, and the business card he handed over had the name of a well-known food company on it.

When Kawakami arrived, slightly late, he greeted Takatsuki with a look of apology that showed keenly on his pleasant, bespectacled face.

"Ah, um, I'm so sorry to keep you waiting. Work has been so busy... Also, it wasn't on your website, so how much is the consultation fee...?"

"There isn't one."

He looked confused by Takatsuki's reply.

"B-but I'm taking up some of your precious time... For instance, consulting with a lawyer costs quite a lot..."

"This is simply one of the necessary parts of doing fieldwork for my research, so please don't worry about it. Instead, I may use the contents of your consultation as an example in a research paper or something along those lines. Of course, if I do, you can be assured that all identifying information will be kept confidential."

Takatsuki's gentle statement made Kawakami look even more apologetic.

He ordered nothing but a soft drink from the self-service bar, then started telling his story in earnest.

"Um, as I wrote in my email, my parents, they got roped into something that's sort of like a religion... Except it also doesn't quite seem like a religion, so I'm a little worried. That's why I contacted you..."

According to Kawakami, his parents had always liked making offerings to deities.

Whenever they came across a temple or a shrine along the road, they would pay a visit. They were always eager to buy spiritual charms. They didn't care about who the deity was or what sect it belonged to. It seemed like they just wanted to feel as though they were benefiting in some way from things that might offer some form of divine protection.

Around the beginning of September, his parents heard about the Miracle Girl from someone in their neighborhood.

At the time, the girl was still living in Suginami ward, and the parents' neighbor had invited them along to go see her, saying, "It's nearby, so why don't you join me."

"My parents had heard about the bus accident, since it was all over the news. And for that girl to be uninjured, like she really was protected by the gods—they thought it was a tremendous miracle. They wanted to receive some of her blessing, so they went to visit her like the neighbor had said."

The girl had lived in a small, first-floor apartment at that time. But when Kawakami's parents visited, there was a surprisingly long line to get in.

Most of the people in the queue were carrying fruits or alcohol or some such thing. His parents asked why that was, and their neighbor told them, "I think they're gifts for the little girl." The neighbor herself was holding a box of traditional Japanese sweets, and Kawakami's parents were apparently annoyed that they weren't told in advance to bring something. They rushed to a nearby store to buy a box of baked goods and made themselves look presentable.

After a long wait in line, it was finally their turn to meet the girl.

The apartment was extremely ordinary, even a bit lacking. The rooms were old and cramped and overflowing with a sense of being lived in. And yet, sitting quietly in the midst of it all was a little girl wearing a knowing expression not at all befitting a child her age. Kawakami's parents said that when her lightly wandering gaze fell on them, it felt in some way divine, and they couldn't help but put their hands together in prayer.

"Then, a few days later, my father had to take the train for an errand. The bus he always took to the station tended to run late, but for some reason the route went smoothly that day, and he was able to catch an earlier train than planned. Then it seems the train he was originally meant to be on was involved in a fatal accident. When my father heard about it later, he was totally convinced the Miracle Girl had protected him... I'm really at a loss here."

"It's common for people to look to gods and Buddhas and curses as the cause of the blessings or misfortunes that happen around them. Like if someone were to blame losing their wallet on a black cat crossing their path, even though there might not be a direct link between what happened and what caused it, we tend to automatically connect them in our minds. Your parents' way of thinking is not especially strange."

Takatsuki smiled as he spoke.

But Kawakami shook his head, looking troubled.

"I mean, I understand that everyone thinks that way to a certain extent. But my parents' level of conviction is too much. Ever since then, they go to visit that girl and bring her a present about once every two weeks. Apparently, they're even giving her money. 'If we're able to support her livelihood,' they said. Isn't that basically just almsgiving? They still visit her, even after she moved to Okutama... These days every other thing they say is about 'Mana-sama.' I'm worried they've been brainwashed somehow."

"Mana-sama? Is that the girl's name?"

"Ah, yes. Her real name is Mana Kariya. And the protection charm she gave them, it's—how do I put this? It's deeply unsettling."

Kawakami took out his phone as he spoke. He tapped the screen a few times, then held it out for Takatsuki and Naoya to see. They both leaned forward to peer at the photo on the display.

"This picture is currently hanging in my parents' household altar. They got it from Mana-sama after asking her for a charm... They would have gotten upset with me if I took it out of the house, so I took a picture."

The photo showed what looked like a drawing made on drafting paper. The colors weren't very saturated, as if it was drawn with colored pencils or something similar. Although, there were signs of overlapping lines in some areas, like those spots had been vigorously traced over again and again.

At first, Naoya wasn't sure what the picture was supposed to be. After a little while, though, he realized it was a drawing of an overturned bus. There were people inside it. They were all upside down, with their hair standing on end, and their round, open eyes and mouths all turned toward the viewer.

Next to the overturned bus was a girl in a yellow hat, a white blouse, and a red skirt. Her shoes, for some reason, were different colors: The right was white and the left, red. Standing alongside the bus, the girl also stared out at the viewer with big, round eyes.

It was most likely a drawing of the accident. Naoya thought it was pretty ominous, and it was hard to believe Kawakami's parents had it adorning their altar.

"Um, even if they're just a weird religious group, would you please look into it? I mean, that happens all the time, right? You hear about people signing up for a yoga class or something, but it turns out it's actually a religious gathering. Even if that's all it is, I just need to know. Please!"

Kawakami bowed his head to Takatsuki.

The story Kawakami had just told had been entirely truthful. Naoya didn't hear even a single distortion in his voice. It was clear from his expression that he was quite troubled about the matter.

Naoya glanced at Takatsuki. This truly wasn't the kind of story that would have had him jumping for joy. What the professor was searching for wasn't miracles; it was monsters.

But Takatsuki was once again smiling in Kawakami's direction.

"I understand," he said. "I'll find out as much as I can."

And with that, he accepted the job.

That weekend, Takatsuki and Naoya decided to make inquires in the area around the Miracle Girl's former apartment in Suginami ward.

They started by going to the apartment building itself, but just as Kawakami had said, it was quite small, old, and run-down. It really didn't look like somewhere a religious group's guru would live. Apparently, the unit where the girl had lived was currently unoccupied.

Next, as usual, Takatsuki walked around the neighborhood to talk to people.

As always, all the stay-at-home moms in the area were happy to stop and speak to Takatsuki, with his refined and handsome features and gentlemanly demeanor. Every time Naoya got to witness the professor's aptitude at gathering information, he thought the man would be an excellent private investigator or commercial researcher. His university title might lend him a certain amount of trustworthiness, but even so, it was incredible how much he managed to avoid arousing any suspicion in the people he approached.

"Oh, that accident… It was dreadful, wasn't it? An entire class. I was so shocked."

A woman who said she lived nearby shook her head sadly as she spoke to them.

Another woman with her also shook her said, saying, "My child goes to that school, too… They held a big farewell ceremony for the children who passed away, but I couldn't bear to watch it. Those poor families. I can't imagine losing my child that way. It's so awful…"

The area they were in was the school district of the elementary school affected by the accident. The local residents were quite concerned with the incident, along with being particularly interested in the girl.

"Did the girl who survived participate in the farewell ceremony?" Takatsuki asked.

"No, I don't think so. If I recall correctly, she was in the hospital for a while after the accident due to shock. I mean, even without physical injuries, she must have needed mental and emotional care. I think that lasted for about two weeks, and then she went back home to that apartment with her mother."

"That's right. And then it was a little while after that, right? That mass of visitors."

The two women looked at one another, nodding.

According to them, when it started, there hadn't been enough people to form a line. There were just enough people going to and coming from the apartment that it was noticeable, and at first, they assumed the visitors were relatives and friends stopping in to check on the family.

But before long, the number of visitors increased to the point that they started to queue up, each one of them carrying some kind of souvenir, no less.

"At the busiest point the line even went all the way outside the apartment complex. We were a little nervous, thinking they had formed some kind of cult."

"So the two of you didn't pay her a visit?"

The women gave strained smiles at Takatsuki's question.

"No, well… We were already acquainted with her, you see. Suddenly treating her like some kind of living god would be…"

"I certainly do think it's a miracle that she survived, but going to pray to her or something is a bit much."

"Then were you well acquainted with that household before?" Takatsuki asked.

The women exchanged glances again.

"Not really. They didn't interact much with the neighborhood."

"It's true. The girl's mother is unmarried, and she was always busy with part-time work. I don't think they had very much money. Mana was always wearing the same clothes. And she was always by herself. I almost never saw her playing with kids her age… If anything, it seemed like she was being bullied, didn't it?"

"Yes, I even saw her coming home from school soaking wet and crying once! I asked her what happened and of course she just mumbled that she fell into a pond."

"Oh dear, doesn't that mean she was probably pushed in?"

Though their faces were frowning, the two women's eyes were practically glittering. The atmosphere around them was one of neighbors gleefully sharing gossip. Even though their children went to the same school, the accident had happened to children in a different grade, so despite their concern, they probably had a strong sense that, ultimately, this was someone else's problem.

Another housewife in the neighborhood told them that Mana didn't attend school much after the accident.

"My child is in the same grade as Mana. Because every other child in her class was gone, they moved Mana to the same class my child is in. But... How do I put it? It seems neither the teacher nor the students knew how to treat her. It's like they felt they were dealing with an abscess... Also, Mana seems to have stopped talking almost entirely since the accident. I think she went to school once, maybe twice, and then didn't show up again. And then she and her mother moved in around the middle of October."

They even managed to find several people who had actually gone to pay a visit to the girl.

One of them, a white-haired man who had retired the year before, said he lived in a different neighborhood than the girl's apartment. He liked to take walks and often ended up in the area. When he saw the lines forming at her building, his interest was piqued.

"Ah, yes, it seemed like it was all anyone was talking about, and since I was in the neighborhood, I thought I would go take a peek... Well, I thought it might be some strange form of solicitation, at first. But it wasn't like that at all. The girl was just sitting in a small, ordinary room, and her mother served tea and snacks, and we just talked a little. The girl didn't say a word, she just sort of stared blankly into the distance... Her mother very kindly asked me, 'What's troubling you?'

We made small talk for a while, and that was it. She didn't even ask me to buy a charm or anything, so it was a bit anticlimactic... A blessing? No, I didn't get anything like that. I mean, I showed up empty-handed, after all."

Once they were finished gathering information, they returned to the girl's former apartment complex and stood outside.

"Hmmm, it doesn't feel like a religious group, in any case. They aren't recruiting people, they don't ask for donations, they don't record their visitors' names and addresses."

"If anything, it seems like people started gathering on their own through word of mouth."

Everyone they spoke to who had actually visited the girl said something like, "A line was forming for some reason, so I got in it just to see," or, "I went because everyone was talking about it." There were even people among her visitors who only learned that she was the survivor of the bus crash after the fact.

"Well, it's part of the human psyche to want to line up when we see one forming."

"It's kind of like when some store's pastries or fish cakes go viral on social media and orders start flooding in, isn't it? People see it trending and think, I want to try it, too. Oh—"

Realization hitting him, Naoya looked up at Takatsuki.

"It's really similar to what you talked about in class, right, Professor? *Hayarigami?*"

One day, something is suddenly deified, the story spreads through word of mouth, and it becomes a massive craze. That was *hayarigami*, and it was also exactly like the Miracle Girl's story. Naoya got the feeling that the people who had lined up to see the girl were no different than the ones who had rushed from all over the country to worship the human-faced fish.

Takatsuki nodded.

"Indeed. I think so, too. She's a modern *hayarigami*."

"But those kinds of trends die out soon after the hype ends. Does that mean the Miracle Girl story will also disappear soon?"

"It might… But I'm still a bit concerned that the object of worship in this case is a living child."

Naoya watched Takatsuki as the other man murmured and ran a finger along the apartment complex fence, a strange feeling in his chest. What was it that had Takatsuki so worried?

Noticing Naoya's gaze, Takatsuki looked down at him and grinned.

"Hey, Fukamachi, how do you feel about an overnight trip?"

"What?"

"I was just thinking it might be difficult to make a day visit to Okutama."

"Huh…? Are you going to Okutama?"

"Well, I came this far, so of course I want to meet the Miracle Girl herself, you know? Okutama is a lovely place. The autumn leaves will be gone already, but there's plenty of nature, and a hot spring. Don't you want to go?"

Takatsuki sounded excited as he peered into Naoya's face.

Even if it was for an investigation, considering how long it had been since Naoya had traveled or been to a hot spring, he couldn't help but find the idea appealing. However, as a broke college student, he had a slight issue.

"Um, I can't really afford it."

"Don't worry about that. I'll take care of the travel expenses as your employer."

"What? Is that okay?"

"Since I'll be taking you away for more than an entire day, sure. You could think of it as your earnings in the form of a vacation? Oh, right—Fukamachi, do you get carsick? And are you someone who needs your own room to sleep in at night, or anything like that?"

"No, nothing like that…"

"Oh? Good. Then it sounds like a three-person room would be fine!"

Takatsuki's eyes were sparkling, and he had his golden retriever expression in place. Naoya looked up in amazement at that face, which was just as excited as a dog about to go on a walk. He wondered if the three-person room was so that the client, Kawakami, could also go.

The idea of sharing a room with a relative stranger wasn't very appealing, after all, but he felt awkward about voicing that thought, since he had just said it was fine.

"I'll contact you again once I've coordinated the schedule, okay? I'll make the arrangements for a place to stay, Fukamachi, so you just have to bring your overnight bag."

With Takatsuki practically wagging his tail, Naoya felt even more like it would be rude to complain, so he simply replied, "Got it."

A few days later, Takatsuki called to ask if Naoya was okay with going to Okutama in December during the week. On a Thursday and Friday, to be specific.

He didn't have any compulsory classes that day, so he gave the go-ahead.

"But you do have general classes those days, right…? I'd feel bad for making you skip them…"

Takatsuki's voice sounded extremely apologetic.

But it seemed the schedule couldn't be changed, apparently because those were the only days Kawakami was available. As he replied, Naoya thought it was odd, since office workers usually had Saturdays and Sundays off.

"It's okay. It's not like I haven't missed those classes before, and I have someone I can borrow the notes from."

"Oh, I'm glad you at least have a friend you can count on to that extent!"

You don't have to sound that happy about it, Naoya thought. Exactly how much time did this man spend worrying about Naoya's lack of friends?

"…There's someone in my language class that I talk to regularly. We're at least acquaintances. So it'll be fine."

"It's so like you to call him an 'acquaintance' instead of a 'friend,' Fukamachi, really... Oh well, in that case, I really am sorry, but let's go with those days. On the morning of...could you be waiting in front of the National Garden in Shinjuku by ten o'clock? I'll come pick you up by car. I'll send you the exact location later. Make sure you dress warmly!"

At that point, Naoya really couldn't say that he didn't want to share a room with a stranger.

Well, it was only for two days. Naoya didn't know how likely Kawakami was to tell lies on a daily basis, but if it became a problem, all Naoya had to do was distance himself a little. He expected Takatsuki would understand.

Mind made up, Naoya waited for the day of the trip to arrive.

On the morning of their departure to Okutama, as Naoya was waiting at the designated pick-up spot, a silver sedan pulled up. The passenger side window opened, and Takatsuki's face peeked out.

"Good morning, Fukamachi! Sorry to keep you waiting in the cold. Get in, quick!"

Wondering why Takatsuki was sitting in the passenger seat, Naoya noticed a fierce face and eyes like a rabid dog at the steering wheel on the professor's other side.

"Oi, Akira, don't open the window. It's cold. Fukamachi, hurry up."

"M-Mr. Sasakura?!"

Despite being startled, Naoya rushed to open the back door and climb into the car.

Sasakura started the car while he waited for Naoya to fasten his seatbelt.

"Huh? Wait, why is Mr. Sasakura here? I mean, don't you have work today?"

"I'm off duty. Just finished up a case," Sasakura replied.

Of course, Naoya realized. They were going on a weekday because it suited Sasakura's schedule.

"Okutama is more convenient to get to by car," Takatsuki said. "If

KenKen was busy, I figured we could take the train or the bus, but it worked out somehow."

"...Come to think of it, Professor, you don't have a car, do you? I've only ever seen you travel by train or bus."

"Yep. I don't own one."

"Ah, I thought so. Well, if you live in the city, you don't need one at all."

"I do have my license, though. I passed the test on the first try, and I think I'm quite good at driving, but...KenKen told me, 'You are absolutely not allowed to drive!'"

"Why's that?"

Sasakura glanced at Naoya through the rearview mirror.

"What do you think would happen if a bird hit the windshield while this guy was driving?"

"...He would faint on the spot, and possibly cause a major accident, depending on the circumstances."

"Right?"

Naoya and Sasakura nodded at each other through the mirror. That would be a bad situation, for sure.

"But even so, going out of your way to accompany Professor Takatsuki to Okutama on your day off... Don't you have anything else to do? I mean, Mr. Sasakura, it's like you're his guardian."

"That's rich coming from a student hitching a ride in someone else's car. I'm just going to soak in the hot springs and drink in the evening. You need to have a little more respect for the hard work I do every day. You should be thanking me."

"All right, all right, enough bickering, you two. Fukamachi, did you eat a proper breakfast? I have some snacks. Do you want one?"

"No, thank you. Besides, this isn't a field trip! Why did you buy so many snacks from the convenience store?"

"Come on, what's wrong with that? Let's enjoy ourselves while we have the chance. It's important to have fun, you know!"

Takatsuki was wearing the same coat as he usually did, although he wasn't in a suit, for once. Because they were headed to Okutama, there was some talk of possibly hiking in the mountains. Wearing an indigo sweater over a white shirt, Takatsuki looked more relaxed than usual, and somehow even younger.

Meanwhile, next to him, wearing black from head to toe, Sasakura looked a bit intimidating. Naoya wondered if there was anything to be done about the way he looked like he was scowling even though he wasn't angry.

"I made sure to book us a place to stay that has a hot spring! And the rooms are big, so we could have a pillow fight!"

"You serious? Can you imagine having a pillow fight with *our* strength? One wrong move and we're gonna make a hole in the wall."

"...Uh, Mr. Sasakura, just how seriously do you take pillow fights? Anyway, we aren't going to fool around, we're going to investigate!"

"Fukamachi is so serious. It's rare to see that among today's youth, isn't it?

"No kidding. Take life that seriously and you'll start aging prematurely. You're gonna get all bald and wrinkly."

"...Oh, I see. Now I understand why you look so young, Professor."

"Huh? What do you mean?"

Don't look back at me all wide-eyed, Naoya thought, as Takatsuki did just that.

The drive to Okutama took about two hours. They had lunch in front of Okutama Station, then headed in the direction of the Miracle Girl's address.

Her house was near the lake where the accident had happened. There weren't many private residences in the vicinity, and the house was hidden by the mountains, but even from a distance, they could tell they had found the right place. There were cars parked nearby and several people outside the home. Even though she had relocated to Okutama, it seemed the Miracle Girl was as sought-after as ever.

"It's a weekday, isn't it...? What do all these guys do for work?"

"Who knows? They might be self-employed, retired, or even just taking a personal day. In any case, it seems we'll have to get in line."

Sasakura parked along the road as the other drivers had done, and the three of them walked toward the girl's house. There was no nameplate on it.

There were five people waiting in line, though it seemed that the first four of them were paired in groups of two. The first pair was holding a package that looked like sake, and the second pair had brought a massive teddy bear. The man in line by himself was carrying something very carefully wrapped in cloth, though Naoya couldn't tell what it was. There were two portable heaters placed nearby so the visitors could keep warm while they waited.

Takatsuki queued up casually at the back of the line and spoke to the man holding the cloth-wrapped package.

"Hello. Is this, by chance, the Miracle Girl's residence?"

"...Yes. Is this your first time coming?"

The man turned around to speak to them. He looked like he was in his fifties, with neat salt-and-pepper hair, nice clothes, and a calm demeanor.

Takatsuki held his hands over one of the heaters and smiled at him.

"Yes, I've heard talk of her here and there, so I wanted to come meet her myself at least once. But everyone seems to have brought a gift. Darn, is it a problem if I didn't bring anything?"

"No, I don't believe so. Neither Mana-sama nor her mother asks for anything for themselves. This is really just a matter of mindset, I think."

"Mindset? Is that so?"

"Yes," the man said, nodding.

"I operate a restaurant chain. I'm about to open a new location, so I came here to pray for its success. Bringing something like this is like proof to myself that I made my prayer in earnest. Also...it's a symbol of my genuine gratitude toward the two of them."

"So you've come to see them before?"

"Yes, a few times before they moved to Okutama. I also heard about them from other people. I heard they're good protection against misfortune... I was skeptical during my first visit, but soon afterward, my business started to thrive. I have nothing but appreciation for Mana-sama."

The man's face was very serious. He wasn't lying at all. He really believed in "Mana-sama."

The other people in line were probably the same. They each went in carrying gifts, not because they were coerced, but out of genuine goodwill.

That was why they would link any good fortune they experienced to their visits to the Miracle Girl.

They paid their respects to her and brought presents as proof of their faith. They would surely receive blessings in proportion to their gifts. That was what they believed.

What on earth was this "Mana-sama" like, who attracted so much adoration? Did she appear to be that divine?

They waited in line for approximately one hour. More people lined up behind Naoya's group in that time, a testament to the Miracle Girl's popularity.

"I apologize for keeping you waiting. Right this way, please."

The woman who welcomed them inside was probably Mana's mother. In a red tunic sweater and skinny jeans, she gave the impression of being quite an ordinary woman. She appeared to be in her late thirties. She didn't wear much makeup, and her hair was tied back simply.

They were led to a small, subdued living room. The floor was covered in beige carpet. A glass patio door overlooked the yard, and in front of it sat an upholstered sofa set and a low table. Next to an average-sized television was a magazine rack stuffed with newspapers, periodicals, and a collection of fairy tales that were all upside down. The laundry hanging on the clothesline in the garden fluttered in the wind.

The house seemed exceptionally normal and filled with the trappings of everyday life. There were no religious symbols, nor even the slightest trace of what one would picture a living god's residence containing.

The living god in question, Mana-sama, was sitting not on the sofa, but neatly on the floor, doodling with colored pencils on a drawing pad she had spread over the table.

She was a petite girl. Her hair went just past her shoulders, and she was dressed in a black cardigan and red checkered skirt. She had adorable round eyes and a button nose, but her mouth was pursed tightly. She colored with single-minded intention, as if she didn't even notice Naoya, Takatsuki, and Sasakura entering the room.

"Please have a seat. I'll serve some tea."

The woman headed for the kitchen that was attached to the living room.

As they lowered themselves onto the sofa across from where Mana was sitting, it happened.

They heard the small fluttering of wings.

Takatsuki jolted in surprise. Naoya's head whipped around toward the direction the sound had come from.

In front of the glass door, hidden behind the sofa, was a birdcage. A gray Java sparrow perched inside it.

"Professor, are you all right?"

Naoya turned to Takatsuki, whose face had gone stiff and slightly pale.

"Ah, yep, I'm okay… If there's just one bird of that size."

The professor pressed a hand to his face and let out a small breath. He didn't look like he was going to faint, but his hands trembled somewhat.

Sasakura called out to the woman in the kitchen.

"Sorry, but could you move that birdcage to a different room for now? This guy really can't handle birds."

"Hm? Oh…I see. I'm sorry, I'll move it right away."

She took the cage into the next room. Lifting her head, Mana silently watched it go.

The next room seemed to be something of a storage space for visitors' gifts. Naoya could see the stuffed animal that the couple from earlier had been carrying. The room was also filled with alcohol, fruits, toys, and boxes of candy. The majority of the people who came here likely brought presents with them.

"That sparrow was given to us by a previous customer. I was told it would do good for Mana's emotional wellbeing to have an animal close to her... She doesn't seem very interested, though."

The woman smiled as she returned to the living room and set a tray carrying teacups and a small kettle on the table. Mana returned to her picture. She was drawing what looked like a forest in green colored pencil. Sitting on the couch directly behind Mana, the woman put her hands on her knees and bowed slightly at them.

"Thank you for coming despite the cold. You're all first-time customers, yes? I'm Mana's mother, Makiko. It's a pleasure to meet you. I'm very sorry, but as there are a lot of customers today, our conversation will last for only twenty minutes. I hope you understand. Now then— what is troubling you today?"

"Not that we don't have our troubles, but that isn't why we came today. The truth is we're here for a slightly different reason than the other customers."

Takatsuki gave his business card to a puzzled Makiko.

"My name is Takatsuki. I'm an associate professor at Seiwa University in Tokyo. These two are my friend and my assistant."

Makiko studied Takatsuki's card for a moment, then raised her eyes.

"I see. A university professor... Then what is your business here today?"

"There's no point in lying, so I'll be frank. I've come to find out what the 'Miracle Girl of Okutama' is all about. Is it actually a religion, or perhaps something relating to folk belief? It seems there are people who are concerned."

"Goodness... That was quite frank."

Looking uncomfortable, Makiko picked up the teapot. She poured green tea into the cups, setting one each in front of Takatsuki, Naoya, and Sasakura, along with small plates of jellied snacks. Neither the tea nor the treats looked cheap. More than likely, they had also been gifts from customers.

"We aren't a religion. We don't follow any particular dogma, and I don't force anyone to donate. People may bring something out of the kindness of their hearts, but..."

"Yes, that's what I had heard. And looking around this room now, it doesn't have the feel of someplace religious. But you do seem to get quite a lot of visitors. You mentioned a twenty-minute conversation—what happens during that period?"

"I just hear people out. Many of them are struggling in some way. I'm not in a position to give advice, so most of the time I only listen, but even that alone seems to provide some relief."

"There are also people who have received a picture that 'Mana-sama' drew, I believe?"

"Ah, that. Some customers say they want proof that they came, anything will do. But I don't have anything to give, and when I ask what they would like, they say they would be happy with one of her pictures... She's often drawing while customers visit, you see."

Makiko stroked Mana's head as she spoke. Mana continued coloring her forest drawing, not particularly responding to the touch. She filled in a tree trunk that stretched toward the sky with a brown pencil.

Takatsuki glanced at the picture, suddenly frowning.

He looked back up at Makiko.

"Today's a weekday. Is Mana not going to school?"

"Ever since the accident, she's withdrawn into herself... She's been in no condition to go to school since before we moved here. She's enrolled in a distance learning program."

"Do you deal with visitors all day long? It must be difficult to manage that number of people. Do you have any time to deal with household matters?"

"Everyone spends their precious time coming to visit us, so it's no trouble. Besides, we take short breaks for meals, and I don't allow late-night visits. And I don't let Mana stay inside all day, because it's better for her to play outside sometimes. When she's outside, I handle customers by myself, or ask them to return at another time."

"Please excuse me for asking, but what do you do for work at the moment?"

"...I quit since the number of visitors increased. I can't leave my daughter alone all day, after all."

"But then, do you have trouble with living expenses?"

"That's… Everyone is very generous, so we manage somehow…"

Makiko's answer was slightly vague. There probably were a lot of visitors who brought money instead of gifts, after all. Considerable amounts of money, no less.

But even though Makiko had hesitated slightly to answer, her voice hadn't distorted at all. It was true that they weren't a religion and that they weren't coercing people into making donations.

Still, Naoya thought, glancing at Takatsuki, who sat beside him.

For a while now, Naoya had been more concerned about Takatsuki's demeanor than Makiko's.

The professor, who was always grinning while he spoke with others, hadn't cracked even the slightest smile. His face had remained stiff and anxious, and it was so unlike him that Naoya grew worried. Was it because of the bird in the house?

Sasakura chimed in.

"What about this house? Considering your previous situation, it doesn't seem like you'd be able to move to a new place very easily."

"One of the people who visited us had a vacant property and very kindly bequeathed it to us. Our last apartment was small, and it was difficult to see customers, plus we had the attention of the neighbors… Besides, living close to the site of the accident like this, it also becomes a place to mourn for those lost."

The sudden warping of Makiko's voice made Naoya press his hands to his ears with a start.

Living here to grieve for the people who had died—that was a lie.

But why, out of everything she said, was that the one thing that was distorted?

Noticing Naoya's reaction, Takatsuki frowned again.

Stroking Mana's head again, Makiko continued.

"Well… Truly, we aren't a religious group or anything like that. But this child really is a 'miracle.' What else would you call her being spared in that accident, if not a miracle? It's only natural that there are those who want to share in her good fortune, and it would be wrong to refuse them. So as long as people want them, we will be sharing our blessings."

Makiko's gaze was affectionate as she looked at Mana. Immersed in her own world, however, Mana just kept moving her colored pencils around and around the page.

"May I ask about the circumstances of the accident?" Takatsuki asked. "How on earth did Mana survive?"

"The police believe that she was thrown from an open window the moment the bus started to roll, because she wasn't wearing her seatbelt. Her backpack was found inside the bus. With no bag weighing her down, being as light as she is, she simply got extremely lucky and was thrown out—that's what they told me. It was truly miraculous. She only had scrapes on her arms and legs. Other than one of her shoes flying off in the impact, she lost nothing, not even the hat on her head. I was told that was a stroke of good luck, too. That it must have protected her head when she hit the ground."

There had been three buses on the field trip, and the one that turned over was the last one.

When it rolled, the other buses ahead of it and the cars driving behind all came to a stop. Tons of people gathered around. In all the commotion, someone suddenly said, "Hey, what's up with that girl over there?"

Crouched alone on the side of the road, crying, was Mana.

"Strangely enough, no one noticed she was there at first. No one thought there was any chance a child had survived the crash."

Makiko chuckled.

"But when I talk about that, some people say Mana might have teleported from the overturned bus and materialized outside of it. They wonder if she's psychic, or if a deity or something carried her to safety. Everyone has their own interpretation, but I don't care what the truth is. Whether she was thrown out a window like the police said, or she teleported, or she was saved by God… All that matters is that she survived."

Makiko hugged Mana, telling them she was just grateful that her daughter was spared, regardless of the circumstances.

She rested her cheek lovingly against Mana's head.

"I brought this child into the world as a single mother. She's all I have. Without her, I probably wouldn't be here. I am truly thankful—to fate, to the gods, to the world—for not taking her away from me... She stopped talking after the accident, but really, I love her so much I can't help it. That's what I say to the people who come to visit her, too. I tell them that it's a loving, grateful, accepting heart that invites miracles to happen. You might say that kind of thing makes me sound like a religious leader again, but it's what I truly believe."

Voice trembling, Makiko stroked Mana's head over and over.

Mana, who was simply allowing it to happen, suddenly lifted her head from within her mother's arms.

Blinking slowly, Mana stared at Takatsuki. Beneath her long eyelashes, the girl's dark eyes gave away nothing. Takatsuki stared back at her silently.

At that moment, Sasakura looked down at Mana's drawing.

He muttered, "...Hey. Isn't there something off about this picture?"

Naoya took another look at the paper.

It was an extremely childlike depiction of a forest. The grassy ground was represented with green lines, from which a number of trees grew up toward the blue sky. Something that looked like a fence spanned the bottom of the drawing, so it might have been a picture of a park somewhere. The leaves on the trees were drawn as masses of fluffy greenery, rather than being shown individually. Naoya recalled drawing quite a few pictures like this when he was a child.

Then, suddenly, an intense discomfort washed over Naoya.

The picture in front of him was very ordinary. A simple drawing of a forest done in colored pencil. It was made well enough that anyone could tell what it was at a glance.

But that wasn't why it was so easy for them to recognize the picture.

It was the orientation. It was wrong.

The paper on the table was placed so that the ground side was facing Naoya's group, and the sky was facing Mana.

As if the world had been flipped on its head—Mana had drawn it upside-down.

Mana's eyes moved.

She stared at Sasakura, Takatsuki, and Naoya in turn. The eyes she turned upon them were dark, cold, and hard, without emotion or passion, just like the glass balls used as the eyes of stuffed animals. At the same time, her gaze radiated an air of intimidation that made it hard to believe it belonged to a child.

Mana's eyes shifted again.

Staring directly at the door to the room, it was as if she was saying—

—Hurry up and leave.

As they got into Sasakura's car after leaving Mana's house, Takatsuki let out a breath from deep in his chest.

"Akira, you okay?"

"Ah, yeah, I'm fine... As expected, I don't do well when I know there's a bird nearby. I was nervous. Maybe I should eat something sweet."

As he answered Sasakura's question, Takatsuki took a box of chocolates out of the convenience store bag.

Sasakura stared hard at Takatsuki, who seemed to be pushing himself to smile.

"Don't get too caught up in this case."

About to peel the transparent plastic away from the box of chocolates, Takatsuki paused for a moment.

Then he tore the plastic away in one go, opened the box, and smiled as he popped a piece of chocolate into his mouth.

"Why? I'm fine."

"Because—"

"You're a worrywart, KenKen. Here, you have a chocolate, too."

Takatsuki thrust the box out toward Sasakura, cutting him off.

Sasakura stared at Takatsuki for a while, then accepted the box without a word. He took one chocolate for himself, then handed the box back.

Somewhat suspicious of their exchange, Naoya leaned forward from the back seat.

"So what are we going to do now?"

"Good question. Just in case, let's go to the accident site. I guess we'll go to the inn afterward."

"Okay... Um."

"Hm? What is it, Fukamachi?"

Takatsuki turned to look back at him, but Naoya wasn't quite sure how to say it.

"Earlier...when Ms. Makiko talked about her reasons for moving here, she was lying. She didn't come here intending to mourn the people who died."

"...I see."

"So then why on earth would she live here? I mean, Mana became mute because of the accident. Living near where it happened... I don't think that's a good idea. Why would she do that?"

"Isn't it just because the house she was given just happened to be in Okutama?" Sasakura said.

"To her—I guess I shouldn't say 'devotees'—to her customers, that Mana girl has a strong connection to Okutama. They probably thought it was an appropriate gift. A secondhand house of their own is better than their old, run-down apartment, even for those two. They don't have to worry about nosy neighbors, and they can get a fresh start."

"That's true. I think KenKen has a point," Takatsuki said, nodding.

He took another chocolate from the box and, holding it between his fingers, stared at it.

"Although—I don't think living here will be any kind of fresh start for that family. If that's what they really wanted, they should have gone somewhere far away from here."

Takatsuki put the chocolate between his lips and ate it.

The accident site was on a road alongside Lake Okutama.

The road hugged the lake's winding edge, resulting in countless large curves. A mountain rose up on the opposing shore. The guardrail that must have been destroyed by the rolling bus had already been replaced, and there were no traces of the accident left on the precipice beyond.

Nevertheless, it was still as plain as day that an accident had occurred on the spot.

Dozens of flowers had been left there.

More than half a year had passed already since the crash. And yet, among the offered flowers were ones that looked like they hadn't been there for very long. The parents of the children who were lost still came to leave flowers at the site.

"Seriously… How could anyone survive this…?"

Sasakura peered down into the lake at the spot the bus had rolled off the cliff. The car was parked on the side of the road. Standing next to him, Naoya looked down as well. Perhaps because it was a cloudy day, the water looked more gray than blue. From their vantage point all the way up on the cliff, the surface of the lake was so placid that it was hard to believe it had once swallowed up the lives of an entire bus full of children. The longer Naoya looked at it, the more he felt like it would swallow him up as well.

"Did you know that Lake Okutama is often cited as a hotspot for ghosts?" Takatsuki said from behind them. "They say you'll be dragged in by the spirit of a woman who committed suicide here, so be careful."

Without thinking, Naoya took a step away from the guardrail. He turned to glare at Takatsuki.

"…Why would you say something like that right now?"

"If not now, when would I say it?"

"It's in poor taste."

"Ah, you're right. I'm sorry."

Naoya nodded in acknowledgment of Takatsuki's earnest apology.

It seemed that there was no information to be gained from the site of the accident. All they had been able to confirm was that Mana's survival truly had been miraculous.

"Akira. What now?" Sasakura asked.

"Well, for now—I think we've done enough. We got what we came here for, more or less."

"What are you gonna tell the client?"

"I'll tell him they aren't a religious group. At the very least, there's no present need to worry about them recruiting members or anything. And even if Mr. Kawakami's parents continue to visit Mana, if they bring her money, that's their choice to make. I can't be the one to intervene. They'll have to discuss it as a family, or he'll have to wait until his parents lose interest."

"They might not be one now, but do you think there's any possibility this will grow into a religious group in the future?"

Takatsuki tilted his head to the side slightly at Naoya's anxious question.

"As long as some new-age cult doesn't set its sights on Mana, I think it'll be fine. Ms. Makiko didn't seem inclined in that direction."

Makiko's repeated insistence that they weren't a religious group hadn't been a lie. They weren't the kind of organization Kawakami was worried about, there was no disputing that.

The joy Makiko felt over Mana being spared in the crash was genuine, and it was also true that she listened to other people's troubles because she wanted to share in the miracle. As for the gifts from visitors—the feeling that they ought to take what they could get was probably at play.

In any case, what they had learned should be enough to satisfy Kawakami's request.

"So what do you wanna do now? It's still a bit early to go to the inn. Should we do a little sightseeing or something?"

"Good idea... Ah, then there's someplace I want to go!"

Takatsuki's eyes suddenly lit up.

Sasakura scowled at him.

"...Don't tell me it's somewhere haunted."

"How did you guess? You know, the abandoned Lake Okutama Ropeway is an extremely famous ghost hotspot, and I've never been before."

"Nope, no way in hell! Pick somewhere more normal!"

"Wha-a-at? Even though we're all the way in Okutama?"

"Enough out of you. Hey—Fukamachi. Isn't there someplace you wanna go? Hurry up and find somewhere."

"Uh, um, please give me a minute."

Naoya hurriedly pulled out his phone while Sasakura glared at him. He typed in a search for "sightseeing in Okutama."

"Ah, it looks like there's a limestone cave nearby. It says you can explore inside it."

"How late is it open?"

"Umm… In December, until four thirty PM."

"We can still make it. Okay, let's go."

"Are you talking about Nippara cave? If I remember correctly, that place is also famous for being the site of a lot of spirit photography! Also for a man going missing there and only his right arm being recovered!"

"Akira! Don't open your mouth again!"

Takatsuki stopped talking after Sasakura smacked him on the head. Naoya returned to the car, wondering if maybe Sasakura, who was also climbing quickly into the driver's seat, was afraid of ghosts.

Just as he was about to get in the car as well, Takatsuki turned his gaze to the other side of the lake. He stared hard at the top of the mountain.

"Professor? Is something wrong?"

"…Ah, sorry. I'm coming."

Takatsuki smiled brightly at Naoya, then slid into the passenger seat.

They ended up going to Nippara cave. Most of the other tourist areas nearby were hiking trails, and considering the time required and the cold, those seemed best saved for another day.

It was warmer inside the cave, which was said to be the largest in the Kanto region, than it was outside of it, apparently because it maintained a fairly constant temperature throughout the year. There weren't many other people there, perhaps because it was a weekday. Between the rather steep staircases and the narrow paths, descending into the cave felt like traversing the underground labyrinths and dungeons seen in movies and video games, which was a little exciting.

But parts of the cave had been named things like "Infernal Ravine" and "River of the Dead," and since Takatsuki had mentioned beforehand that the cave was haunted, there was also a strong feeling of foreboding. A massive stalagmite which had been dubbed "White-Robed Kannon" looked frighteningly like it could come to life at any moment.

"What's up with all these ominous names…"

"It's all very Buddhist, isn't it?"

"Probably because this was a site for mountain worship. The Shugendo ascetics considered it a holy place. They regarded the entire cave as a temple, named the stalactites and stalagmites that look like that one after Bodhisattvas, made pilgrimages here, and trained here. Though—this lighting makes it look like we're in an amusement park, doesn't it? It's pretty, but it has no relation to religious faith. It's very modern."

The ceiling was illuminated in seven colors by some lights that had been set up in some large hollows. Looking up at them, Takatsuki narrowed his eyes a little.

When he had looked up Nippara cave online, all the pictures Naoya found showcased this section of the cave. It was the only one where the craggy rock faces were wondrously bathed in blue and green and red lights. Compared to the dim passages that were centrally lit with nothing but white lights, this one seemed like another world.

"This place looks like it would definitely be popular with people who use Instagram. It has the feel of somewhere that would get more customers because it's popular with young people."

"That's true. I mean, everyone likes beautiful things."

As he spoke, Takatsuki took out his phone and snapped a photo.

A little surprised, Naoya asked, "Huh, Professor, are you on Instagram?"

"I'm not. But I was hoping I would get a picture of a ghost."

"…Makes sense."

That was the type of person Akira Takatsuki was.

Suddenly, Takatsuki pointed his phone in Naoya's direction.

"Okay, Fukamachi, KenKen! Look over here!"

"What?"

"Huh?"

Caught off guard by the shutter noise, Naoya and Sasakura both inadvertently froze.

Takatsuki was already reviewing the photo he had just taken.

"Pr-Professor, don't tell me you tried to take a picture of our spirits or something?"

"What on earth are you talking about? It's a commemorative photograph of our trip."

"Huh..."

Takatsuki's retort, delivered as if the thought of a commemorative photo should have been obvious, made Naoya falter.

Sasakura was peering at Takatsuki's phone from the side.

"Then you should be in it, too. You're the one who brought us here."

"Hmm, but there's no one else around, and I've never taken a selfie before. Anyway, KenKen, your outfit is so dark it blends into the background. This looks like a picture of a ghost."

"...So why not just take the picture outside. Here, give that to me. I'll take one of you two," Sasakura said, snatching Takatsuki's phone away.

Takatsuki stood next to Naoya, looking happy.

"Huh, no, I don't really want to be in any pictures—"

"Just smile, Fukamachi. You're supposed to smile for photos."

But Naoya was so unused to both smiling and pictures that he couldn't simply pull a smile out of nowhere just because someone told him to.

While he wondered what kind of expression he was supposed to make, Sasakura went ahead and pushed the shutter button. The resulting photo wasn't great, with Naoya looking a bit strained and Takatsuki grinning.

"I'll send you the picture, Fukamachi."

"What? No, I don't want it. It's not a good one anyway."

"Too bad, it's a souvenir!" Takatsuki replied, sending the photo anyway.

I'll just delete it later, Naoya thought, stowing away his phone, which was laden with one more image.

Then, all at once, he realized this was the first trip he had ever taken that wasn't with his family or for school.

Naoya had never dared to imagine he would travel with someone, staying overnight somewhere and going sightseeing.

Finding himself strangely embarrassed over how much fun he was having despite himself, Naoya slowed his pace a little, a few steps from where Takatsuki and Sasakura had started walking again. But Sasakura scolded him—"Hurry up."—the second he noticed. Reluctantly, Naoya caught up with the other two men, wondering what their group of three must look like from the outside. There was no way to mistake them for blood relatives, so it was possible they just appeared to be some kind of mysterious gang.

Now, that's enough to make me smile, thought Naoya, casually touching the pocket his phone was in. As far as deleting that photo went… He decided to give it a little more thought.

After leaving the limestone cave, they headed for the inn where Takatsuki had made the reservations.

The inn, situated near Hatonosu Gorge, looked more like a modern hotel from the outside, and their room was a mix of traditional Japanese and Western elements. There were beds for two people, and it seemed the third person would have to sleep in a futon on the tatami-matted section of the room.

They decided to play a brutal round of rock-paper-scissors for the beds, and Naoya lost handily… From the start, he had suspected that was how things would turn out.

"I'm sorry, Fukamachi. I'd be happy to trade if you need to be in a bed to sleep, though."

"No… It's fine. I'll be okay. Please don't worry about it."

There was still time before dinner. Naoya thought it might be a good idea to go to the hot springs before they ate. According to the hotel information guide, he had the choice between an open-air bath and a large indoor facility.

Putting his bag down on the tatami mats, Naoya looked over at Takatsuki, who was sitting on his bed reading something. It looked like the local tourism brochure he had received at the front desk.

"Um, is it all right if I go to the hot spring?"

"Oh, yes, please do. Why don't you go, too, KenKen?"

"Yeah, I'll go."

Sasakura nodded.

Takatsuki, however, made no move to get up. He was staring intently at the brochure—what inside of it could possibly have grabbed his attention that much?

Naoya cocked his head to the side.

"You're not going, Professor?"

"Nope, I'm good. The room has a bath, after all."

"What? But the hot springs…"

As Naoya started to reply, Sasakura grabbed him around the nape of his neck.

"Let's just go."

"Wh—? Wait, Mr. S-Sasakura, neck, my *neck*, hold on, you're going to choke me…!"

Unconcerned with Naoya's fussing, Sasakura grabbed towels and robes for the both of them in one hand and steered Naoya out of the room in a hurry with the other.

He let go after they had been walking down the corridor for a little while, and Naoya gave the other man a piece of his mind.

"Who do you think you are, Mr. Bad Cop? You can't just hold onto people the way you would hold a kitten!"

"Shut up… Akira can't go into public baths. So don't ask him to."

Sasakura spoke in a low voice, and Naoya instinctively went quiet. He had to hurry to catch back up to Sasakura, who had kept walking while Naoya paused.

"He can't? Why not— Oh."

As soon as the question started to leave his mouth, Naoya realized the answer.

It was the scars on Takatsuki's back.

Naoya had never seen them, but he had heard they were still quite large and distinct. Takatsuki probably didn't want anyone to see them.

"That's why he picked a hotel that has baths for each room," Sasakura said. "Besides—he must be exhausted from today. Leave him alone."

Embarrassed, Naoya walked along in Sasakura's long-legged wake.

The bathhouse was almost empty, probably because it was a weekday in the winter. Naoya took off his glasses and got undressed in the changing room alongside Sasakura. The other man, whose toned physique was apparent even when he was wearing clothes, became even more impressive to look at when he was out of them. For reasons he didn't quite understand, Naoya was overcome with a sense of defeat.

"…What are you moping for? Don't be weird."

"No, it's just, I was wondering what I would have to do to get muscles like that… I mean, your abs are really defined…"

His own reedy build was pitiful. Naoya still hadn't regained much of the weight he had lost when he was ill the month before. Thanks to that period, he felt like he had lost his already meager amount of muscle tone.

"What, you wanna work out? Well, it couldn't hurt, that's for sure."

"It's not that I want to work out… That time when Professor Takatsuki collapsed, I couldn't carry him by myself."

Sasakura had thrown Takatsuki over his shoulder with ease, but it wasn't like Naoya could call Sasakura every time there was trouble. At the very least, Naoya wanted to be able to move an unconscious Takatsuki on his own. Though he was hoping he wouldn't be in a situation like that ever again.

"I dunno if you could carry him on your back, considering your height."

"How tall are you, Mr. Sasakura?"

"About six foot, two inches."

"And Professor Takatsuki?"

"Just under six feet, I'm pretty sure. You?"

"…Five foot eight."

"Yeah, not happening. Don't even try."

"Come on!"

"Fine, then start drinking milk every day, from today. And if you wanna work out, then as soon as you get back to the room, do some sit-ups, back extensions, push-ups, and squats."

"Huh?"

"You wanna get stronger, right? Akira does his own training, too. Muscle is heavier than it looks. If you don't start working out, you'll never be able to carry him."

Naoya felt like maybe he had gotten a little ahead of himself. He wasn't going to set himself up for being sore the day following their hot springs trip.

However, it had been Sasakura who had taught self-defense techniques to Takatsuki. Perhaps it would be a good idea for Naoya to learn self-defense, too, just in case. Accompanying Takatsuki sometimes meant getting into dangerous situations.

There was a big window in the large, stone-built bath facility, which was probably perfect for viewing the gorge scenery during the daytime. Getting clean in the washing area then submerging oneself in the hot spring felt somehow revitalizing. It was wonderful to feel all the blood vessels in one's body, all the way down to the fingertips, expand in the heat.

The guests who had already been in the bath left as Naoya and Sasakura got in. Looking around at what had become their own private hot spring, Naoya let out a little sigh.

Takatsuki could have come, too, he thought, since there was no one else around.

But even so, Naoya had the feeling the professor wouldn't have joined them. He wouldn't have been able to relax if he was worried over someone else walking in—and anyway, Takatsuki might not want Naoya to see his scars, either.

"...Um."

Naoya opened his mouth, and Sasakura looked at him.

"The scars on Professor Takatsuki's back... Are they that bad?"

Sasakura was quiet for a moment, then he sighed.

"...Let's just say they stand out."

"Have you seen them?"

"Yeah," Sasakura replied, reticent as usual.

Deciding not to push it, Naoya sank up to his chin in the water, his gaze cast downward.

Takatsuki's obsession with the supernatural came solely from his desire to find out what had happened to him in the past. He might have been kidnapped by *tengu*, or perhaps he hadn't. Naoya couldn't help but feel anxious about it, because he didn't know one way or the other.

Someone had abducted him, peeled the skin from his back, and thrown him away. It had already been more than twenty years since then—too long ago to investigate for himself. And so, Takatsuki collected ghost stories and urban legends from the public, hoping he could find a case like his own. If he could investigate a case like that, it could lead him to his own past.

Despite his typically sunny disposition, there was a deep, murky darkness dwelling at Takatsuki's core.

"Oh yeah," Sasakura piped up. "That journalist. He didn't try getting close to you again after that incident, right?"

He had to be referring to Iinuma. Naoya shook his head.

"No, I didn't see him... But is it really okay not to do anything about him?"

"Probably. I warned Akira about him, just in case...and I told you before, right? Even if some sketchy article gets written about him, his dad will take care of it."

"About that... What is his father like? His family?"

"—Don't."

Sasakura cut him off.

Naoya looked at him in surprise.

Brushing his wet bangs back, Sasakura fixed his razor-sharp gaze on Naoya.

"It's not a fun thing to talk about. Unless he tells you about it himself, you don't need to know."

"...Got it."

Naoya sank back into the water gloomily.

He got the sense that he was being kept out of the loop after all.

He knew almost nothing about what Takatsuki was dealing with. The professor barely talked about himself. Everything he did know about Takatsuki's past was something Sasakura had told him before.

It wasn't as though Naoya thought he would be able to help, somehow—nevertheless, he would have liked to learn a bit more, at least as much as was relevant to his own involvement with Takatsuki.

Still, Naoya couldn't force the information out of him. Takatsuki didn't want to talk about it because discussing his own emotional trauma was just that painful. Naoya couldn't help but feel depressed over it anyway.

Takatsuki had built a wall around himself to ward off other people, just like Naoya had done. And Naoya hadn't been allowed beyond that wall...even though he thought they were supposed to be fellow travelers on a dark, mysterious path.

"Hey. Get up before you make yourself lightheaded," Sasakura said toward Naoya's mostly submerged form.

Naoya turned his head toward the other man.

"...Mr. Sasakura, can I ask one more thing?"

"What is it?"

"Are you, possibly, afraid of ghosts?"

Sasakura's left cheek twitched just for a moment.

"I was just thinking, because of the way you reacted earlier today, that could be the case... Wh—*pbbft!*"

All of a sudden, one of Sasakura's huge hands clamped onto the back of Naoya's head and shoved him underwater.

Bull's-eye, apparently.

The next day, once they were done packing up and preparing to check out of the inn, Takatsuki spoke up.

"Before we go home, there's someplace I wanted to stop by. Is that okay?"

He opened the tourist brochure he had been reading the night before and showed it to them.

He was pointing to a place called Miharashi Hill. It was a spot overlooking Lake Okutama, and the brochure said there was a trail that took between one and two hours to complete.

"The weather is nice today, and we might as well see it while we're nearby, right?"

All they had planned for the day was the drive home. There was nothing wrong with talking a little stroll before that. Naoya and Sasakura both agreed, and just as Takatsuki wished, they went to Miharashi Hill.

Only—as soon as they got there, Naoya realized he had been misinformed of the situation.

The trail wasn't suitable for a "little stroll"—rather, they were in for a bit of light hiking. The moderately steep path was riddled with stones and curved at several points throughout the ascent. If it had been the season for cherry blossoms or autumn leaves, they could have at least enjoyed the surrounding scenery, but it was winter. All the trees were barren, and there was nothing nice to look at except Lake Okutama below.

Viewed from a high vantage point on a sunny day, the lake certainly was beautiful. The surface had looked gray the day before, but now it was an amazing hue that could be called neither blue nor green and sparkled faintly under the deluge of sunlight. Compared to the two older men walking ahead of him, however, Naoya's legs were quite short. It was pretty difficult just to keep up with their pace. Eventually, Naoya realized he was watching his own feet move instead of taking in the scenery. People tended to look down when they were tired.

But suddenly, a question popped into Naoya's head: Why had Takatsuki wanted to come here? Could it be that, like the limestone cave, this hill was also rumored to be a hotspot for ghosts? It didn't really have that kind of sinister aura, though. The reason it was relatively deserted was probably simply because it was the offseason, not because it was haunted. The occasional person they passed on their way up was inevitably someone walking their dog, rather than a sightseer.

Then—

"—Oh!"

Takatsuki let out a small sound and stopped walking.

Naoya followed his line of sight and found his own eyes widening in surprise.

There was a child on the viewing platform just ahead. It was Mana. She was dressed in a navy-blue coat and a green skirt, with a small red purse slung diagonally across her body from shoulder to hip.

He started to wonder why she was in a place like this, but then Naoya remembered that Makiko had said something like, "If Mana wants to go outside, I let her." They probably weren't very far from her house. She might have come here to play.

Looking closer, Naoya could see Mana was holding something that looked like a pamphlet in her hands. She stared at the open pamphlet with a serious expression, then looked around as if to confirm something. She stepped unsteadily up to the fence surrounding the platform and looked down.

As Mana stood there unmoving, Takatsuki slowly approached her.

"Mana, what are you doing?"

Startled by his voice, Mana looked back at them, hurrying to shove the pamphlet into her bag. That reaction alone made her seem far more human than she had at her house the day before.

The pamphlet, upside down and unceremoniously stowed away, was bigger than the purse itself. More than half of it was sticking out. It looked like it was made from sheets of photocopy paper bundled together, and the words "Field Trip Guide" were written across the cover.

"Mana, was that given to you on the day of your school trip?" Takatsuki asked.

The girl hesitated, letting her gaze wander, then gave a tiny nod.

"May I see it?"

Her eyes remained restless, but ultimately, she held it out to Takatsuki without a fuss.

He opened the crinkled, curling pages carefully. Inside, there was information about the time and location of the field trip, a map of the destination, and a list of important notes about the excursion.

Takatsuki closed the pamphlet and handed it back to Mana.

"As I thought, Mana and the other kids came here—Miharashi Hill—for their trip. There are other trails, but when you consider where the accident happened and what kind of terrain the children's legs could handle, this is the only one that makes sense. Plus, I wondered if the picture you drew yesterday was of this place. The shape of the fence is very similar."

Naoya's eyes widened again. Was that why Takatsuki had wanted to come here?

Takatsuki squatted down in front of Mana, speaking to her at her eye level.

"What were you looking at just now, Mana?"

Mana averted her gaze as if she didn't want to answer. Her small hands clutched tightly at the strap of her bag.

"Hey, Mana, were you actually—"

It happened as Takatsuki started to speak again.

Out of nowhere, Mana shoved Takatsuki away as hard as she could, then took off running.

The professor, who had landed on his rear end, was helped to his feet by Sasakura.

"You okay?"

"Yeah. She's gone, isn't she? I hope she doesn't trip and fall."

They could see her tiny form already racing down the hill.

Takatsuki didn't try to follow Mana. Once he was done brushing the dirt from his clothes, he turned to look over the viewing platform fence where the little girl had been. Naoya and Sasakura followed suit.

Beyond the fence, there was a long, steep drop. The trees growing on the slope obscured the view somewhat, but they could see the lake below, and the road that encircled it. Naoya wondered if maybe the site of the accident was visible from the platform, but that didn't seem to be the case.

In one swift movement, Takatsuki put his hands on the fence and leaned his upper body out over it.

"Akira? What are you doing? That's dangerous."

"Kenji."

Gaze scouring over the slope, Takatsuki said Sasakura's name.

"Do you have a rope in your car?"

"A rope? I think there's one in the trunk."

"Would you go get it for me?"

"Why?"

"Sorry, but—I really, really want to go down this hill right now. So I need a rope."

Takatsuki's voice was stubborn. He wasn't going to be dissuaded.

Naoya looked in the direction the professor's gaze was fixed on, but he couldn't see anything that stood out. It was all scattered trees and withered grass.

Sasakura looked at Takatsuki from the side and scowled.

"Akira, what are you thinking?"

"I just want to uncover the truth, obviously."

"You already did what the client asked… You're getting too involved in this case."

"Just get me the rope. Quickly," Takatsuki implored, staring intently over the fence.

Sighing, Sasakura shook his head.

"…Fine. I'll be right back, so don't move. Also, if someone is gonna climb down there, it'll be me."

The second time they visited Mana's house, there were, as expected, several people lined up outside.

Unlike their first visit, however, Takatsuki did not wait obediently at the end of the line. He slipped past the queue without a word and walked right into the house without knocking. Naoya and Sasakura followed in his wake, shocked to see him casting off his usual gentlemanly behavior.

A short while before, Sasakura had tied the rope from his car to the fence on Miharashi Hill, using it to climb down to a tree that was halfway down the slope from the viewing platform, per Takatsuki's instructions. He grabbed *something* that had been caught in the tree, then climbed back up.

As soon as he laid eyes on the object, Takatsuki's complexion had changed.

Face hardened dramatically, he had declared, "I'm going back to Mana's house."

When he strode into the living room, the customer who was already there speaking with Makiko looked around in alarm. Mana was already home, once again sitting on the carpet and drawing a picture.

"E-excuse me! You have to wait your turn!"

"I'm very sorry, but consultations are over for today. Please leave, and please convey the message to the people outside as well."

Takatsuki responded bluntly to the affronted customer.

As the man looked like he was on the verge of starting a fight, Makiko moved to calm him.

"I am so sorry, but that will be all for today... I apologize for the inconvenience."

"I'll go if you tell me to, Ms. Makiko, but who the hell is this guy? You're not in some kind of trouble with him, are you?"

Makiko gave the scowling customer a mild-mannered smile.

"No, it's nothing like that. However, it seems his business is quite urgent... If there's an argument, it will drive off the blessings and good fortune. So, if you don't mind."

Makiko bowed her head to the man, who stood up reluctantly. He cursed at Takatsuki, then looked frightened for a moment after noticing Sasakura's feral glare behind him. The customer left without even glancing in Naoya's direction.

Annoyed, Makiko turned to Takatsuki.

"Professor Takatsuki, what on earth are you doing? Forcing your way into the house like this... I expected a university professor to have better manners."

"I apologize for my rudeness, but this truly is an urgent matter... Also, I'm sorry, but if you could move that—"

Takatsuki pointed to the birdcage which was once more sitting in front of the glass door. Makiko's brow remained knit with consternation, but she carried the cage into the adjoining room as requested.

With the bird gone from the room, Takatsuki breathed a little sigh. He took a seat on the sofa, just as he had the day before, and Sasakura and Naoya joined him.

Once Makiko had returned to the living room and taken her usual seat behind Mana, Takatsuki spoke.

"I'll get straight to the point. You need to stop all this and take your daughter to a hospital as soon as possible."

"...Excuse me?"

Her mother's head was cocked to the side, but Mana just kept scribbling away with her colored pencils as if she hadn't heard a word Takatsuki just said.

"Your daughter..." Takatsuki went on "...is probably experiencing some kind of brain dysfunction... Now, when she reads something, she always turns it upside down, doesn't she?"

Makiko flinched.

"A little while ago, we ran into Mana at Miharashi Hill. She was reading her field trip guide. She had it turned upside down."

Takatsuki looked at the magazine rack in the corner of the room.

It was stuffed full of magazines and collections of fairy tales from around the world. At first glance, the rack just seemed to be in a state of disarray, its contents shoved in randomly. But on closer inspection, it became obvious that all the magazines were oriented properly, while every single fairy tale book was flipped on its head.

"I've heard there's a kind of functional neurologic disorder where up and down are reversed. I suspect that's what your daughter has. I mean, her drawings too, they're all upside down."

Takatsuki pointed at the picture Mana was in the middle of coloring. Mana's hands stopped moving.

She had drawn an upside-down house. It looked like it was supposed to be the one they were currently in.

"Ms. Makiko, there's no way you didn't notice this," Takatsuki said, his tone relentless. "You live with her. Why have you neglected to deal with this until now? Your daughter needs to receive appropriate treatment right away."

Suddenly, Makiko pulled Mana close to her with anxious hands. Perhaps she hadn't realized the seriousness of the situation.

"B-because…at the time, I didn't have that kind of money! And there didn't seem to be anything else wrong with her… That—if it's brain dysfunction—then it must be from getting thrown out of the bus and hitting her head in the accident! It's been months since then already! What good would treatment do now?!"

"No. I don't think this was caused by physical trauma. I believe it's psychogenic in nature. That means treatment could still be effective, even now."

The professor shifted his gaze to Mana.

Wrapped in her mother's arms, Mana stared back up at him, meeting his eyes directly.

"After all…you probably weren't on the bus when that happened, were you?"

That was the conclusion Takatsuki had come to—

Mana wasn't miraculously spared by being thrown from the bus when it rolled.

—She hadn't been on the bus at all.

Eyes wide, Makiko looked down at the girl in her arms. Mana simply continued to stare at Takatsuki, her gaze blank.

"This is all going to be conjecture on my part, but I hope you'll hear me out."

Takatsuki wasn't speaking to Makiko anymore—his words were directed at Mana.

"The day of the field trip, you and the other children were supposed to take the bus home after having some time to explore Miharashi Hill in groups. But you were late getting back to the bus. Because…you lost your shoe off the viewing platform."

As he said that, Takatsuki withdrew an object wrapped in a handkerchief from his coat pocket.

It was the thing Sasakura had grabbed out of a tree on the steep slope of Miharashi Hill.

Quite faded from an extended period of exposure to the elements—a child's small, red shoe.

When Mana was spotted after the accident, one of her shoes was missing.

"You gave someone one of your drawings before, right? I've seen that one. It's a picture of an overturned bus with a girl standing beside it. The girl in the picture has one red foot and one white one. It's white because the girl is missing a shoe… The girl in the picture is you, isn't it, Mana? The girl outside of the bus."

Takatsuki might have been entertaining that scenario in his head from the moment Kawakami had shown them that drawing. But he hadn't had proof of it, at the time.

When he found Mana's shoe on that hill—that's when he knew his theory was correct.

"It would likely be impossible for a child to climb down the slope from the viewing platform. Even so, you were probably trying to think of some way you could get your shoe back. But because of that, you lost track of time. The other children left you—just you—behind and returned to the bus. Then the bus left without you. Your teacher probably didn't check thoroughly to make sure everyone was present—but it's possible some of the other children had a hand in that, too."

Takatsuki's version of events was based on a guess. Nevertheless, it was probably the truth.

Mana, on the verge of tears, staring down the slope at her shoe, which was stuck in a tree far below the fence. Her classmates, looking on indifferently.

It was also possible that those classmates were the reason Mana's shoe was lost. Naoya remembered that when they had been gathering information before, the neighbors had said it seemed like Mana was being bullied.

No matter how far Mana leaned out over the fence, there was no way to retrieve her shoe. And yet, it was a shoe she couldn't afford to lose. At the time of that field trip, her family had been poor. The neighbors also talked about seeing her in the same outfits all the time. Who knew if her mother even had the money to buy her new shoes?

Before long, the call that it was time to go home came, but Mana couldn't just abandon her attachment to her shoe. Soon, she realized there was no one else around. She was alone. They had left her behind. She hurried down the path toward the parking lot. The bus was only just about to leave. Inside it, the teacher was calling out, "Is everyone here? Make sure everybody in your group is present!" A mean-spirited classmate answered: "We're all here!" Mana's bullies had taken her backpack as well. The only thing that didn't make it onto the bus was Mana herself.

The bus drove away.

Mana, only just making it to the lot from the hill, ran after it, waving her arms to be noticed. But no one saw her. Even when she tripped and fell, skinning her knees, the bus kept going.

Crying, she got to her feet, forcing her stinging legs to follow the bus. She raced after it desperately, losing sight of it countless times around the curves in the road.

"You chased the bus. If we looked for them, we might even be able to find people who saw you running along the guardrail on the side of the road. And you saw it, didn't you? While you were running? The bus crashing and rolling—upside down—off the cliff."

That sight must have been seared clearly into Mana's brain. Across several twists and turns in the road, the sight of the bus flipping over and falling. The sight of her classmates, inside of it, all turned on their heads.

And so, since then, Mana's world had been upside down.

As Takatsuki talked, Mana's typically emotionless eyes began to fill with tears. When the first one spilled over her cheek, it was like a dam breaking. Her doll-like face crumpled and contorted and turned bright red. Tears poured down her pale cheeks. Finally, her small voice welled up, and she began to softly sob.

Her reaction seemed to prove that Takatsuki was right.

"Mana…"

Makiko hugged her daughter close, rubbing her back. Mana clung to her mother, starting to wail in earnest.

Takatsuki continued, his voice cold.

"Ms. Makiko. I think you realized. I think you knew there was a chance that Mana wasn't really on that bus."

Once again, Makiko flinched.

"You said you didn't have the money to seek treatment at the time of the accident. That's probably true. But you're a mother. If your daughter had really hit her head and was experiencing some kind of brain injury, you would have done anything you could to get her cared for. The fact that you didn't—isn't that because you realized she hadn't hit her head?"

Makiko's expression changed. It wasn't like when Mana's condition was first pointed out, or when Mana cried and clutched at her. The look in her eyes was, in some way, cowardly.

"…Yes. I was vaguely aware of that possibility," she said, her voice quiet. "Just that it was a possibility, to be clear… A horrible possibility that I didn't even want to consider."

She went on.

"The hospital's examination revealed nothing abnormal in her brain. No physical trauma…but she was acting strange. She spoke for a little while, immediately after the accident. But as soon as I asked her about it, she stopped. Just once, I asked, 'Your shoe came off in the accident, right?' She... She looked down when I asked her that. Mana has a habit of looking down when she lies."

"Then why?"

"Then are you saying I should have just accepted the fact that my child was being bullied?!"

Suddenly, Makiko exploded into a furious shout.

She hugged Mana tighter, baring her teeth menacingly.

"I'm a single mother, and we didn't have a lot of money. I knew, in some way, that the other children were bullying her because of it. Of course I wanted to buy her new clothes! Cute notebooks and pens for school, just like the other kids had! But...we didn't have the money... Even when the kids scribbled on her school shoes, she just kept using them and didn't tell me... She told me she didn't really want to go on the field trip, either. But I made her go because I had to work that day... I felt more at ease sending Mana to school than having her at home!"

Makiko's voice was like a howl. In her arms, Mana stiffened.

"All the kids who bullied her dying, that's just them paying the price! They got what they deserved! She survived, isn't that what's important? It had to be divine intervention. Everyone else says so, too! Mana is a miracle child. She didn't just happen to survive because she was bullied—she was saved!"

"That's just what you want to believe!"

In a tone as fierce as Makiko's, Takatsuki shouted back.

Makiko's face was strained.

Takatsuki, his eyes fixed firmly on that face, kept yelling.

"You should have never turned your daughter into this 'Miracle Girl'! As her mother, you should have protected her, gotten her treatment, and helped her live a healthy life! So why... Why would you start something like this instead?!"

As the mother of the "Miracle Girl of Okutama," Makiko entertained visitors, she accepted countless gifts. She made her daughter an object of worship.

It wasn't the same as a religion, not really. It wasn't that organized. But there was no doubt that they had amassed a wildly devoted following—just like the *hayarigami* of old.

"...I didn't. It wasn't me who started it. It was someone else."

Those words tumbled out of Makiko's mouth.

At the same time, tears spilled over her face.

"An old woman we met in the hospital, she looked at Mana and said, 'You were the only one spared in the accident, right? You must have been protected by the gods. Please let me pray over you.' Other people saw her and came over to do the same thing. They kept saying, 'Bless you, bless you.' At first...I didn't really understand. But after that, more people came... They even started showing up at our house. They brought us food and money..."

Hayarigami were created out of the blue, at some random time, by some random person.

This is a god. Those who pray to it shall receive wealth and longevity.

It wasn't done with malice—just out of the desire for some kind of divine protection.

People were always longing for the divine.

For a convenient deity they could implore, pray to, and feel gratified by.

"I felt embarrassed by it at first, but then it made me happy. No one had ever paid any attention to our family before. But suddenly, we were adored. People gave us incredible sums of money with kind faces, telling us to use it for our living expenses... Seeing that made me think, Mana is a miracle child, after all. A child who brings blessings into our lives. Since I didn't have to leave the house to work anymore, I could stay by her side all the time. And before long, one of our customers came to us and said, 'I have a house in Okutama that's vacant. Why don't you move into it? This child has a deep connection with that place, so it might increase her spiritual power.' I would have been happy to move any-where... I hated that tiny, old apartment. But Okutama of all places? And just around the corner from the site of the accident, no less? But then I thought—maybe that would be even better. A place where we could look down on all the brats who bullied my daughter. Somewhere we could show off how we live now to the fools who looked down on us! Mana is touted as the 'Miracle Girl'! I wanted those dead kids to know! Look at her now, she's practically a god!"

Holding Mana in an iron grip, Makiko shrieked, her face twisted with tears and laughter at once.

Takatsuki shook his head.

"Doing that... Making her lies a reality... That's what made Mana lose her voice."

"What...?" Makiko said, expression hardening.

Takatsuki replied in a soft voice.

"You should have asked Mana for the truth. You should have made her tell you that she wasn't on that bus. I'm sure she really did want to say something. But you made her into the Miracle Girl, so Mana swallowed her words. Those words clogged up her throat—so she couldn't speak at all."

"What..."

Makiko looked down at the girl in her arms.

Bit by bit, her hardened expression crumbled.

"I...did this? I'm the reason you don't speak...? That can't be... It can't..."

Then Makiko completely broke down. Her mouth went slack, and a small cry escaped her lips. Looking exactly like her daughter, Makiko dissolved into tears.

She had probably been turning her eyes away from the truth the entire time.

The possibility that Mana hadn't been on the bus. When she thought about Mana's backpack and her shoes, she had probably realized what happened right away. But she hadn't wanted to believe it. Instead, Makiko put her faith in the words of the well-meaning people surrounding them. She dismissed the truth that had for a moment made itself known to her, not realizing that doing so would result in Mana withdrawing into herself.

Mana raised her head. She looked up at her sobbing mother, still battling tears of her own. Then she glared sharply at Takatsuki and shook free of her mother's arms. She ran into the next room.

She was barely gone for a second before she came back, holding the birdcage in her hands.

Takatsuki's whole body went rigid. Her face scarlet, Mana lifted the cage into the air. She shoved the bird in Takatsuki's direction as if she were trying to ward off a vampire with a cross.

"Shut up! Shut up, you idiot!"

Mana was shouting.

Inside the cage, the sparrow flapped its wings. Takatsuki let out a small gasp. He was shaking.

"Mama didn't do anything wrong! She didn't! **I was on the bus! I was on the bus then! I was on it, and I was saved!**"

Her voice was a high-pitched shriek. It warped and distorted horrifically.

She continued to thrust the birdcage out in front of herself. The sparrow kept flapping its wings; the fluttering resounded in the room. Takatsuki, his face contorted painfully at the sound, staggered to his feet. Sasakura put out a hand to stop him, but he shook it off, falling to his knees in front of Mana.

Takatsuki looked at the girl through the birdcage and spoke.

"...Mana. That's a lie. Lies can't go on forever. Even the 'Miracle Girl' legend will eventually die out. You can't keep living this life."

"Shut up, shut up! Be quiet! You're the liar!"

"Mana, I... I know how you feel. I know why you went along with what your mother started. It's because...if you did, your mother would stay with you."

Mana bit her lip. Tears started to roll down her cheeks once more.

Breathing hard, Takatsuki kept talking, frantic.

"If you were the Miracle Girl, your mother wouldn't have to leave the house to work. She would be with you all the time. That must have made you happy... But, you know, Mana? You aren't a 'Miracle Girl.'"

"..."

Mana's shoulders shook violently. Inside the cage, the sparrow flapped its wings harder than ever.

With one hand, Takatsuki clutched at his own head in anguish. With the other, he reached out for Mana.

"You're human. A normal girl, no different from anyone else. You're not the Miracle Girl... You shouldn't ever try to become something like a god. Never."

"Shut up!" Mana screamed again. "Get out of here! Stop being mean to Mama, you dummy!"

Then, from behind, Makiko wrapped her daughter in a hug.

"Mana, that's enough!"

The little girl froze.

With Mana and the birdcage in her arms, Makiko pleaded.

"I'm sorry, Mana... That's enough. Let's stop this. No more... Let's stop lying. It's not a good thing to do. Mama was wrong. I was wrong, I'm sorry..."

Over and over, Makiko murmured apologies to Mana, who finally let out a tiny sob.

The next second, Mana dropped the birdcage to the floor, threw her arms around her mother, and started to wail. The two of them held each other fiercely, crying together, their faces alike.

On the floor, the caged sparrow thrashed about, screeching.

Slowly, Takatsuki stood up.

But his knees gave out almost immediately, and he started to collapse.

"Whoa, there!"

Sasakura shot to his feet and reached for the professor. Takatsuki fell into his arms like a puppet with its strings cut.

Naoya stared, dumbfounded, at the single tear running down Takatsuki's already unconscious face.

He had never seen Takatsuki shout like that before.

He had never seen him shed tears, either.

Several days later, Naoya was summoned to Takatsuki's office.

When he saw Naoya walk inside, Takatsuki's smile was thin.

"...I'm sorry you had to see me like that the other day."

That day—

Takatsuki hadn't regained consciousness at all on the drive back from Okutama. Naoya was let out in Shinjuku, and he watched Sasakura drive away with Takatsuki in the car.

The professor started to speak as he made coffee for Naoya, as he always did.

"I made the report to Mr. Kawakami yesterday. I told him it's not a religion. And he told me his parents started going to a new shrine, so everything is probably all right. A place in Kyoto, I think? Well, the shrines there have a history, at least, so that's not a problem."

"...It's like you said. *Hayarigami* go out of style quickly, don't they?"

"They do. If a more profitable god appears somewhere else, people jump on it. As long as they can get the benefits and good fortune of their choice, they don't care."

Naoya didn't know what became of Makiko and Mana after that day. Right after Takatsuki collapsed, their group left.

Maybe the two of them closed down the "Miracle Girl" attraction and started living their lives peacefully. That's what Naoya wanted to believe happened.

"...Even you are capable of criticizing someone that harshly, huh, Professor?" Naoya muttered.

The Takatsuki that Naoya had known until now was always gentle. He had never once seen the other man vehemently call someone out that way.

But then, ever since the beginning of this case, Takatsuki's behavior had been strange.

He had gotten weirdly fixated on a story that normally wouldn't have appealed to him. And yet, he didn't act at all like his interest was piqued.

Takatsuki had seemed tense the entire time they were at Mana's house, but Naoya had chalked that up to there being a bird in the home.

Perhaps that wasn't the only cause.

There had probably been other reasons as well.

There must have been an element to the story that ran Takatsuki's heart ragged. That's why he had fainted because of a single small sparrow, which he had said wouldn't be a problem.

Returning to the table with a tray in hand, Takatsuki set the dog mug down in front of Naoya.

He sat in the chair at Naoya's side, pulling his own blue mug toward himself.

Coffee and cocoa—the same drinks they always shared in this room.

But Takatsuki didn't take a sip of his cocoa before he started talking.

"My mother was the same way. She was like Ms. Makiko."

Naoya's eyes widened.

Staring at the marshmallows slowly dissolving in his cup, Takatsuki continued.

"After I went missing, I was found in a place near Kurama, in Kyoto. Kurama is famous for *tengu*. I had two scars on my back that looked like someone had cut wings off me. *Tengu* are known for having wings. My mother's cousin was the first one to say it. 'Akira was kidnapped by *tengu*. They were going to turn him into one of them. But for some reason, they sent him back to our world...after they cut off his wings.' That's what she said. It sounds absurd, but my mother believed it."

At the time, Takatsuki's mother had been in a state of considerable distress.

Her precious son had disappeared for a month. There were no leads, and even though they searched for him frantically, he didn't turn up. When he was finally found, he had permanent scars carved into his back. What was more, his eye color and demeanor weren't what they had been before. He was afraid of birds, his memory was extraordinary, and sometimes, his eyes would turn deep blue.

When the police failed to turn up even a single clue about his missing month, they found themselves at an utter loss and decided to close the investigation. They hadn't provided Takatsuki's family with any information at all.

But his mother wanted to know—what had happened to her son in the time he was gone?

After all, people feared what they didn't understand. They couldn't help but be anxious about it.

She needed some kind of justification, some interpretation, to fill the void in her son's case—even if that interpretation was nothing more than fantasy.

And so she jumped at the story about *tengu* that was presented to her.

"It's not that I don't understand how my mother felt. I mean, if it wasn't *tengu*, that means I was kidnapped by a person. To think about what I would have been subjected to for a month by a criminal who ultimately peeled off my skin and threw me away... To a parent, that would be horrific."

Takatsuki spoke dispassionately, his lips slightly twisted.

"My mother turned me into a living god. The boy who returned from the world of the *tengu*. She called me the 'Tengu's Child.' She even tried to spread the idea to the people around her. Her father was the president of a large company, which he would eventually hand over to her husband. So she did a lot of socializing with the wives of company executives and business partners... They would spend the whole day at the salon drinking tea and chatting, and my mother would try to spread the word about the *Tengu's* Child."

Takatsuki's mother might have done that because she wanted other people to share in her delusion. Perhaps she thought that if more people believed in it, it would become the truth.

And in no time, faith in the *Tengu's* Child tore through the women's social circle.

Just like things had spread about the "Miracle Girl of Okutama." Just like a *hayarigami*.

"But that was my fault, too. At first, I cooperated with the whole thing. I listened to the people who came to me to talk, I settled their worries, I gave them advice, I helped them find what they were missing.

Even though all of it was just things I came up with in my own head. I deliberately acted as if I were some kind of sacred, divine being who had all the answers."

"…Why did you do that?"

"Because it made my mother happy."

Takatsuki wrapped both of his hands around his mug.

His expressionless face looked just a little like Mana's had.

"I just wanted her to tell me 'You're amazing, Akira.' That's all."

The smell of cocoa was wafting gently through the air. Takatsuki stared down at the drink, savoring nothing but its scent.

"This is why my father still squashes any articles that appear about me in the weekly news. Belief in the *Tengu's* Child was present only in a very small community that was centered around my father's company. If my father wanted something kept quiet, it probably wouldn't ever get out. But he's still afraid of it happening. Because to him, the whole thing is an embarrassment to the family."

And so Iinuma's article had gotten caught in Takatsuki's father's surveillance web and effortlessly crushed.

"…But, as my mother tried fanatically to spread the story, I became more and more afraid. I told her, 'I'm not a god. I'm done. I can't behave the way you want me to anymore.'"

But Takatsuki's mother couldn't accept that.

She had become such an anxious, sensitive person.

She took Takatsuki's words as a rejection.

Feeling spurned by her son, she rushed to turn the tables on him.

There was no way her own son would say something like that to her.

Her gentle boy would never reject her that way.

So—this child must be an impostor.

That's what she thought.

"My own biological mother asked me 'Who the hell are you?'"

Who are you?

Give me back my son.

You're an impostor. My son is actually somewhere else.

Half-crazed, she repeated those words over and over, until eventually, she started ignoring the boy who was right in front of her.

"...Maybe 'ignoring' isn't the right word. It's more like, she stopped seeing me."

"Stopped seeing...?"

"Yes. She stopped perceiving me. Even if I was standing right there, it was like I didn't exist. She didn't hear me when I spoke to her, she didn't react if I touched her—to my mother, I was invisible."

His father, unable to bear it, sent Takatsuki to live abroad with a relative. But his mother never returned to her right mind.

She believed her son was still missing.

The son who existed in this world was nothing but an impostor.

Takatsuki stared down quietly at his mug of cooling cocoa.

"But...I mean, what else could I have done? I was so scared. My mother treated me like a god, like a *tengu*. But *tengu* aren't gods, they're winged monsters. I became increasingly unsure of whether I was a human, or a god, or a monster... Every dream I had was a nightmare."

Naoya remembered the dream Takatsuki had told him about before—the one where his back split open and black wings grew out of it.

A nightmare where he was reduced to a grotesque, inhuman monster.

"I think my father made the right decision, sending me to live with a distant relative. I don't know how I would have ended up if I had remained in that house. My relative is a really good person. A bit strange, though."

"So...someone like you?"

"Ah-hah, perhaps."

Finally, a definite smile surfaced on Takatsuki's face.

He brought the mug he had been cradling in his hands to his mouth at last. He took a single sip of cocoa, breathing out a small sigh afterward as if soothed by the sweetness.

"Despite all that, I think I've been blessed. Even though I've been distanced from my parents, I have that relative, and KenKen—people who allowed me to be human. You know, Fukamachi, that's why you need to find someone like that for yourself."

"Huh?"

The topic of conversation suddenly shifted to Naoya, and he blinked at the professor in surprise.

Takatsuki looked at Naoya with his gentle, dark brown eyes.

"I worry, sometimes, when I look at you. Because it's like looking at a version of myself, in the past."

"...What are you talking about?"

Was he trying to say that at present Naoya was like Takatsuki used to be?

When Naoya was sick, Takatsuki had gone out of his way to take care of Naoya at his house. He had done that because he knew Naoya wouldn't voluntarily turn to anyone for help.

Takatsuki had probably been like that, too, once.

"I said before, didn't I? You and I are walking the line between reality and the next world. If we mess up, we might tumble down over that line. If that happens, I don't think we'll be human anymore. To prevent that, we need to tether ourselves to this world as much as possible."

"Tether... It's not like we're ghosts."

"It's the same principle. I mean, that's how the dead stay in this world," Takatsuki said.

"Ah, or maybe 'tethered' isn't the right way to put it. Right, okay, so basically, I'm saying you need to find lots of things you love. Something you like, something that's fun, something you can think of as precious— we have to have a lot of those things. They are what keeps us connected to this world... They let us know it's going to be okay, even when we have bad dreams."

"...Oh. Is that why you're always telling me to make friends and memories and stuff?"

Takatsuki smiled and nodded at Naoya's words.

"I mean, didn't you have a little fun at that barbecue we had in the summer? And when we went to Yanaka with Miss Ruiko and KenKen? Oh, and the limestone cave! That was fun, right? We even took a picture!"

"Yeah, that awkward one."

"Don't say that! It's a precious memory of our time!"

Even so, Naoya couldn't help but think it was a pretty bad photo.

Clearing his throat a little as if to bring the conversation back to heel, Takatsuki went on.

"You know, Fukamachi, I think your ability makes living in this world really difficult. Because it was a power given to you to make you lonely. But you can't let it do that. Don't turn your back on this world completely. You aren't alone."

"...Don't you think it's a bit late to be saying that?"

"Of course not. You have me, at least."

Takatsuki's smile was bright.

"I told you—there's no way I'm going to let you go. It's okay. I'm never going to let you be alone."

Naoya stared at Takatsuki's grin—and, without meaning to, let out a deep sigh.

"...*Why* would you say something like that when you can't guarantee it...?"

"Hey now! What's with that nasty expression?! I'm pretty sure I just said something really nice!"

Looking vexed, Takatsuki slapped his hand against the table.

Naoya brought his mostly room-temperature coffee to his mouth and gulped it down.

Even though he had said there were no guarantees, he knew what Takatsuki had just said wasn't a lie. Takatsuki really believed it.

Although, Naoya had recently come to realize that just because Takatsuki didn't tell lies didn't mean he was entirely trustworthy. This man was unexpectedly cunning. Instead of lying, he simply didn't say the whole truth. Naoya knew that, much like himself, even though Takatsuki made a show of being personable, he had drawn a line around his own heart and mind to keep other people from seeing it.

...And yet, Naoya got the sense that this man who didn't share anything important with others had divulged quite a bit of himself today.

Did that mean Takatsuki had welcomed Naoya inside his walls?

That thought made Naoya happy, somehow.

Of course, that was just Naoya's own interpretation of things.

But it meant that Naoya had let down his guard enough around Takatsuki that he could hope it was true.

The lines they had drawn around themselves to keep others out.

Even if those lines never disappeared, it might be all right to let them cross.

So that, while they walked side by side along the border between reality and the next world, they could at least keep each other facing toward the light.

Takatsuki, who had been pouting like a sad puppy in Naoya's direction for a while, got out of his seat and went over to the bookshelf.

He squatted down, rummaging through the space at the bottom where a cardboard box was kept as a sort of storage space.

"What are you doing, Professor?"

"I just realized I'm a little hungry. I'm pretty sure Miss Yui keeps her snack stash around here— Ah, found it! Look, there's chocolate rice crackers, and cheese ones, too. You can have the cheese ones, Fukamachi, since they're not sweet."

"...Is it okay to just eat them without asking?"

"It's fine, I'll make sure to buy her more later."

Takatsuki came back to the table with the bags of snacks in hand. The large bag full of individually wrapped square chocolate crackers had been opened and subsequently clipped shut, but the bag of cheese snacks was untouched. Naoya accepted it when it was handed to him, even though he wondered if it really was all right to eat them.

Blissfully stuffing his mouth with chocolate, Takatsuki seemed to already have returned to his usual state. Watching Takatsuki out of the corner of his eye, Naoya felt it was hard to believe that this man was ever like him.

The Takatsuki he knew was always cheerful and having fun—though that might be the result of Takatsuki actively searching for things that made him happy.

If that was true, did that mean Naoya could be like him someday?

He tried imagining it for a moment, then internally shook his head. He just couldn't picture himself with a big, friendly, puppy-dog smile.

But, Naoya thought, if he could end up with a lot of things to "tether" him to this world, as Takatsuki put it, that wouldn't be so bad.

The truth was…he still had that photo they took in the limestone cave on his phone.